Fleeing Beauty

A Jamie Richmond Mystery

Mark Love

Fleeing Beauty
Copyright © 2015 Mark Love
All rights reserved.

ISBN: (ebook) 978-1-939590-70-1
(Print) 978-1-939590-71-8

Inkspell Publishing
5764 Woodbine Ave.
Pinckney, MI 48169

Edited By Amanda Roberts
Cover art By Shades of Rose Media

DEDICATION

For Kim,
One more chapter in our story.

MARK LOVE

PROLOGUE

I don't want to die.

I'm not ready for it. There are too many things I haven't experienced yet. Places to go, people to meet, adventures waiting to be discovered. I want to gaze at the stars over the Mediterranean Sea while making love with Malone. I want to fly in a sailplane. I want to stand on a beach in Key West and dip my toes in the ocean and the gulf. I want to travel to exotic lands, dine on their cuisine and dance my little ass off to the local music. I want all of that and much more.

But I don't think any of that is going to happen.

We're all going to die.

Once this gang gets what they're after, there is no reason to leave us behind. They're not going to lock us in a closet and make a run for it. We've all seen their faces. We know their names. We can identify them. There is no way they will let us live. Their leader has a violent streak and it's only a matter of time before he lashes out again.

My mind is flashing through ways out of this. But nothing makes sense, nothing that will allow me to stop them, to guide us out of here safely.

I don't want to die.

But there is nothing I can do to prevent it.

CHAPTER ONE

I should have known better. Everything had been calm and quiet the last couple of months, which was very unusual for me. But I had been lulled into a false sense of security. The warmth of the late afternoon sunshine could have been to blame. That made perfect sense to me.

I was in the front yard, kneeling on a thick foam pad, my fingers caked with dirt. This was an unusual activity for me. But Malone had pointed out that it was the perfect spot for some flowers and at his urging I bought a flat of brightly colored flowers that would liven up the space. So on this sun-swept day in early June, I was discovering my abilities as a gardener. There was about an hour before Linda, my best friend, would arrive. I was enjoying the warmth of the sun on my back and shoulders. Days like this made me want to break out the tanning lotion and sprawl on a blanket in the yard. But no matter my efforts, I could never achieve the golden brown color that Linda was capable of. I just get pink.

As I was tamping the last bit of earth back in place, my cell phone started ringing. Wiping the excess dirt on my shorts, I pulled it from my back pocket. I answered without even looking at the screen.

"Jamie, this is Bert. Are you anywhere near a television?" My step-father's deep voice boomed in my ear. He didn't sound angry, nervous, or upset.

"I'm at home. Let me go turn it on. What's happening?"

"Look at Channel Four. This should be one of the lead stories."

I ran inside and fired up the television. A commercial was wrapping up and I watched the five o'clock anchor open the broadcast. As I watched, I lowered the phone from my ear. My eyes flicked to the ticker across the bottom of the screen. In bold letters ran the words "Treasure Trove Discovered". The anchor tossed the story to one of the onsite reporters.

"Thank you, Carmen, and good afternoon. I'm standing outside one of the many converted commercial buildings that serve as art studios populating the area around Wayne State University. It was here today that workmen found what appears to be a trove of previously undiscovered artworks created by local legend Peter Richmond in the months before his death more than twenty years ago. The workers were called in to repair a broken water pipe. During their efforts, they learned that water pressure had punched a hole through a wall. Further inspection revealed a hidden storeroom adjacent to the studio Richmond himself used for years. It is uncertain how many pieces have been discovered or what condition they may be in.

"Richmond is known for his dramatic works in a variety of mediums. Many of his larger pieces are prized possessions in museums, including our own Detroit Institute of Arts. Other examples of his work can be found at Meadowbrook Theater in Rochester and on the campus of Wayne State University. I was able to interview a representative from the DIA, who said that if it can be confirmed these pieces are indeed the work of Peter Richmond, the collection could be priceless. Attorneys for

Richmond's estate were unavailable for comment. Additional police units will be stationed around the site to ensure security is maintained. Reporting live from Detroit, I'm Lauren Podell, Local 4 News."

I was staring at the screen dumbfounded. In the distance I could hear someone calling my name. It took me a moment to realize Bert was still on the phone. I silenced the news and managed to get the phone back to my ear.

"Holy crap, Bert! Did you know about this?"

He snorted a laugh. "I got a call five minutes ago. The firm that handles your father's estate has been trying to reach Vera all day. Somewhere in their archives they found a copy of our marriage license and tracked me down. I'm surprised they hadn't gotten to you."

I don't own any property and don't even have a landline telephone in my name. While they may know I existed, there was no easy way to find me. I told Bert as much. He agreed.

"So what did the attorney want?"

"He's hoping we'll come down to their offices in the morning. There's a lot of paperwork to go over. We can also go to the studio and see what they found. They will need to do an inventory. I understand there were some files and papers found in this storage room as well." He hesitated before asking the inevitable. "Do you know where Vera is?"

I wracked my brain for a moment. "The last I heard from her, she was sailing with some friends up from Florida. That was a couple of weeks ago. I think they were bringing somebody's yacht up to Rhode Island or Maine for the summer."

"You should try to contact her. She may need to get back to town."

I could hear the reluctance in his voice. Bert was Vera's third husband. Even though they were divorced for more than ten years, she could still make him crazy. It was a feeling I knew well. She has that effect on a lot of people.

"Do you think I should meet with these attorneys?"

"I'll go with you, Jamie. And you may want to bring Malone along too. An extra set of eyes and ears from an objective party would be a good idea."

"Are you still at the office?" Bert is a captain with the Michigan State Police. He oversees one of the posts where troopers are stationed. Malone is a sergeant with the MSP. I met him while doing research for a novel. We started dating about nine months ago and have lived together since January.

"No, I'm at a meeting out in Novi. I was able to step out and take the call from the lawyer and then got to a screen and saw the newscast when you did. Jamie, this could be a fortune in artwork we're talking about."

It took me a minute to voice what was racing through my mind. "It's even more than that, Bert. It's a link to my past."

****

After ending the call with Bert, I proceeded to flip through the other local channels to see if there was any more information. The ones I caught were pretty much the same. I was about to check the website for the Detroit Free Press when a shadow appeared at my front door.

"Jay Kay, what in the world are you doing?"

Glancing up I saw my best friend, Linda Davis, on the small front stoop. Her sunglasses were pushed back into her thick curly hair. Linda looks like a fashion model. She could make a potato sack look sexy. Today she was wearing a pair of navy blue shorts with a red sleeveless blouse. Her shapely legs were bare and already starting to tan. Her hands were on her hips and she was trying her best to look stern. It didn't work. She started laughing as she opened the door. When it's just the two of us, we use the nicknames we've carried since childhood. I'm Jay Kay and she's Algae, a combination of her initials.

"You've got topsoil all over the porch. And it looks like you've got some on the couch too. What's going on?"

"It's a long story. You'd better come in."

"Why don't we put away your gardening tools first?"

Together we cleaned up the mess I'd made out front. Realizing I was covered with dirt and sweat, I took a quick cool shower and changed into khaki shorts and a white tank top. By the time I was dressed, Linda was putting the vacuum away. She had taken care of the dirt on the Jewish Aunt, my overstuffed sofa. Linda was sprawled at one end. Logan, her golden retriever who went practically everywhere with her, had his head in her lap, enjoying a vigorous massage. I flopped on the other end of the sofa and filled her in.

"Jay Kay, did you ever go to your father's studio?"

I nodded. "Vera used to take me there occasionally. But the last time must have been when I was five or six years old. All I remember was a huge room with big windows. And there were special lights, like spotlights."

"So you haven't been down there since he died?" Linda nudged Logan aside and sat up. This is no easy feat since the 'aunt' has a tendency to push two people together, usually in a horizontal position.

I shook my head, feeling a little spray from my damp red hair. "I had no idea the studio was still there. Vera has always dealt with the attorneys. This is a complete surprise."

"Do you have any idea what kinds of work might be there? Or how many?"

"Not a clue. Bert's going to pick me up in the morning. We have an appointment with the attorneys who handle the estate at ten."

"Do you still want to go out for dinner?"

As if on cue, my stomach growled. It was loud enough for Linda to hear it. "Sure, I could use a good meal. What did you have in mind?"

She mentioned a barbecue joint not far from the house.

We decided to grab some carryout chicken and ribs and have dinner on the picnic table in the backyard. It was too nice an evening to be sitting in a noisy restaurant. While we were eating, Linda told me about her day. She's a history teacher at the high school in Northville, one of the nearby suburbs. Classes were winding down. There were just two more days of grading exams and preparing her classroom for the summer. Because she missed a lot of time earlier in the year, Linda decided to teach summer school. It wouldn't be a full load like during the regular year, but it would keep her busy. We were wrapping up the extra food when my phone rang. It was Malone.

"Hey, Jamie, have you seen the news about your dad?"

"Yes, Bert called me just before five. I know how busy you can be, so I figured we'd talk when you got home. How did you hear?"

"One of the guys from the day shift saw it and recognized your name. I checked the website during a lull here." His deep voice calmed my nerves. "Are the reporters camping out on the lawn?"

"Not yet. But I have a feeling they will be soon."

"Remember, Jay, you can always say 'no comment' and refer them to the lawyers."

The comment about the attorneys reminded me of tomorrow's meeting. I explained it to Malone. He quickly agreed to accompany me. Somehow knowing both he and Bert would be with me gave me some immediate peace of mind.

"I've got to run, Jamie. I'll see you in a few hours."

"Bye, Malone."

Shortly after that Linda left. She was meeting Vince, her sweetheart, for a nightcap. On the Internet I did a Google search on my father. That sounds so weird. You'd think a kid would know everything there was about their own father. But Peter Richmond died when I was seven years old. He was in the midst of a big project, assembling a large outdoor sculpture at Cranbrook Museum out in

Oakland County, when he fell from a scaffold. He was pronounced dead at the scene. Other than a few old photographs that I've always kept in my room, he faded quickly from my life. Part of that may have been due to Vera's reactions. Within six months of his death, Vera remarried. Five years later she divorced that husband. A year later she married Bert. I was starting college when that marriage ended. Since then Vera has been like a gypsy, traveling the world, having affairs and marriages as she saw fit. She never talked much about my father. I suspected there was money when he died, but never really wondered how much.

Now on the Internet I looked at pictures of some of his work. I was surprised to find an official website. This included a biography, photos of Peter working, of him receiving awards and dedications of his sculptures. There were reviews from famous critics, calling him "masterful" and "inspired" and "gifted beyond comparison". I read them all. Then I read the biography.

Peter Mark Richmond was born in Detroit. From an early age, he showed a flair for art. But his talent wasn't restricted to any one medium. He used clay, bronze, paint and wood to create unique pieces. At sixteen not only was he accepted in the Center for Creative Studies, the art college in downtown Detroit, but he won a full scholarship. He completed the four-year program on schedule and started winning commissions for various projects. Just that quickly, his notoriety grew and with each project completed, recognition flourished.

Along the way he met and married Vera Ballard. Friends introduced them at a reception while he was still at CCS.

There was a photo of the two of them at an event shortly after they were married. Peter was lanky, probably a bit taller than me, maybe five-foot-nine with a trim athletic physique. His red hair was thick and worn in a ponytail, which looked out of character with the tuxedo he was wearing. I guessed the photo to be in the late seventies. It would have been stylish for the period.

It saddened me to realize that I'd learned more about my own father in the last couple of hours than I'd ever known. Vera wasn't exactly a fountain of information about the past. Considering her fleeting appearances after I finished high school, it's a wonder that I even know my own name.

****

There was a steady breeze keeping the mosquitos away. I was sitting at the picnic table, a glass of lemonade close by. The stars were shining brightly. It was almost midnight. I watched a couple of bats swoop across the sky. Maybe that's why the mosquitos weren't bothering me. Headlights flickered across the door of the detached garage. A moment later Malone walked around the corner of the house and headed toward me. As he approached in the starlight, my heart did a little dance step and I thought again how lucky I was.

In a different century, Malone could have been a cowboy. He's a little shy of six feet tall, with a wiry, muscular body. His dark hair is a perfect complement to the most incredible blue eyes I've ever stared into. I always think of the color cobalt when I see them. Malone's got this disarming, calm quality about him that will occasionally slip to reveal the mischief brewing inside. Tonight was a perfect example. He didn't say a word as he got to the picnic table. Malone just reached down and lifted me from the bench. Then his lips were on mine, surprising me with his intensity. What's a girl to do?

Malone wrapped me in his arms, pressing me tightly against his body. He was wearing jeans and a green T-shirt that fit him like a second skin. The feel of his muscular chest and arms was quickly getting me aroused. Still too busy kissing me to speak, Malone's hands found my waist.

Now he lifted me off my feet and placed me on top of the picnic table. But not before he managed to work the shorts off my hips. My legs were dangling off the end of the table. His lips moved to my neck and he began to nibble me.

"Damon, we have a very comfortable bed inside," I managed to say.

"I'm in the mood for a little moonlight madness."

The way he was kissing me was driving me mad. I reached for his belt, but he brushed my hands away. As Malone was sucking on my earlobe, I heard his zipper slide down. Malone leaned forward. He cupped my head with his left hand and eased me onto my back. I reached up to caress his face. Malone caught my wrist in his free hand and moved it above my head. Holding both of my arms above me, I felt him enter me. I was starting to cry out when he covered my mouth with his.

I knew I wouldn't last long. Malone has that impact on me. I peaked when he entered me and was soon rushing to another climax, urging him on with my legs when he peaked. He slowed his rhythmic thrusts, staying with me until I finished again. Only when he knew I wouldn't shout out his name did he pull his mouth from mine.

"We can go inside now, Jay."

"That's good, Damon. But I think you're going to have to check my buns for splinters."

Malone offered me one of those low voltage smiles of his that never fail to turn me on. "I'd be more than happy to take a closer look at your ass."

He pulled his jeans back on and picked up my shorts. Feeling extremely naughty, I walked bare-assed to the side door and into the house. I could only hope that my neighbors were fast asleep. In the bedroom, Malone pulled off my tank top and bra. Then he turned me around and ran his hands slowly over my ass. Satisfied that I was splinter free, he guided me to the bed. But sleep was the last thing on his mind. After another session of sex, I collapsed on top of his chest, gasping for breath.

"Are you sure you're not a hyperactive teenager, Damon?"

Malone chuckled. "Damon? Wrong again, Jay. Let's just say you awaken all my sexual urges every time I see you."

Mentally I crossed Damon off my list. Malone only uses his last name. Since we met, I've been determined to find out what his first name is. So each day I see him or talk to him, I give him a new first name. He's promised to tell me if I ever get it right.

Now that my heart was no longer racing, I raised my head to look at him. "Can you go with me to the lawyer's in the morning?"

"Sure. You said the meeting is at ten?"

"Yes. Bert is going to pick us up. We'll meet with the lawyer and go to the studio."

Malone was silent, running his fingers slowly through my hair. It was something I hoped he never tired of. I swear every nerve ending in my body tingled when he did it.

"This could be quite a discovery, Jamie."

"It's been so long since I was at his studio, I don't really remember it."

"I've seen some of his work, mostly in magazines and on the Internet."

I felt my eyes go wide. "Damon, I never knew you were interested in art!"

Malone lifted my hand and kissed it. "I'm interested in you, Jamie. And your father is definitely a part of you."

"When did you check this out?"

"Back when we first started dating. I thought it was a good idea to learn as much as I could about you."

I batted my lashes at him. "And did you find out everything you wanted to?"

"I'm still learning."

"That's a good answer, Damon. I want to always keep

you guessing. And I want to be able to keep you interested."

He drew me up so we were nose to nose. "Did you have any doubts about my interest in the backyard this evening?"

"No. You made your intentions quite evident. It's a good thing we have those tall hedges around the yard."

"What can I say, Jamie. You have that effect on me. The fact that you wait up for me to get home from work most nights is kind of nice."

I gave him a quick kiss. "I just try to stay awake so we can attack each other. Because when it's all said and done, I'm so exhausted I sleep through the night."

"Is that your motive?" He chuckled softly.

"That's the only answer you'll get tonight. Good night, Damon."

"Good night, Jay."

CHAPTER TWO

The law offices were in one of the high-rise buildings in downtown Detroit with a great view of the Detroit River. It was a clear day and from thirty stories up you could easily see Windsor, Canada on the other side. Pleasure craft were moving smoothly up and down the water. A couple of freighters were trundling by.

I stood at the window of the conference room admiring the view. I was too nervous to sit. Bert and Malone were talking quietly, sipping coffee from fine china cups. I don't have fine china cups. I have mismatched ceramic mugs. The conference room door opened. Two people walked in.

One was a guy close to sixty in a sharply tailored black pinstripe suit with a dark burgundy tie. He was shorter than me, maybe five-foot-six. He was solid, but not fat. Most of his hair was brown with streaks of gray at the temples. Although his hairline was starting to recede, I gave him credit for not attempting the dreaded comb-over.

"I'm Lincoln Banning. This is my associate, Helen Gaines."

I studied her for a moment. She looked barely old enough to drive. Helen was rail thin, with dark brown hair cut very short and close to her skull. I immediately pictured her as a tomboy, doing her best to prove herself in any competition. She was wearing a light green business suit with slacks and an ivory colored blouse buttoned to the throat. I wondered if the outfit was the standard uniform for the legal world.

Bert made the introductions. I moved to the table, shook their hands, and sat on the edge of the chair between Bert and Malone.

"Jamie, I don't know if you recall, but I was a friend of your father's. We met a couple of times at holiday parties, but you were very young," Banning said. His voice was smooth and clear, like an actor on stage.

"I'm sorry, but I don't remember you. How well did you know Peter?"

"We met when he was at the Center for Creative Studies. I was finishing up my undergraduate program and going to law school. By the time he graduated, I was already practicing estate law with a small firm."

"Is that your specialty, wills and estates?" I asked.

"Yes, it is. I didn't have the flair for criminal work. Helping people make plans for their families has always appealed to me."

"What about you?" I directed this question at Helen.

"Both my father and grandfather practiced law. Grandfather always said there was nothing finer than estate work. It's very rewarding to guide people and help them make the best decisions for their loved ones."

I turned my attention back to Banning. For a moment I felt out of place. I was wearing a navy blue dress that stopped a couple of inches above the knee. My legs were bare. As if sensing my discomfort, Malone lightly put a hand on my arm. He was wearing a black sports coat and slacks with a blue striped shirt. Bert was in one of his business suits.

"I have made several attempts to reach Vera Richmond. Unfortunately I have yet to receive a response," Banning said.

I nodded. "That's not unusual. Vera doesn't like to be easily accessible. I've left messages on her cell phone and her email account. But it could be a week before we hear anything. Is it necessary that she be here?"

Banning offered a thin smile. "Actually, there is a great deal we need to do. But whether Mrs. Richmond is present or not, I believe we can proceed."

Helen passed out copies of a list on the company's thick stationary. I rolled my thumb across the corporate logo at the top. This firm's reputation was well deserved. I'd checked them out last night while doing the research on my father.

"There may be other issues we need to address," Banning said, "but I believe we've outlined the most salient points. As the executors of Peter's estate, it is our responsibility to make certain the assets are secured. I've already taken the liberty of having the damaged wall repaired."

Bert clapped his hands together once and raised a meaty palm. "Let's get a little more background information on the table first."

"Of course. How foolish of me. I've been operating under the impression that you all knew about the estate. Where should I begin?"

"I've never seen my father's will. Vera never told me anything about it, just that he had left her enough money to support us."

Banning's expression seemed to soften. "Mrs. Richmond never cared for the details. I will make sure you have a copy of the will before you leave. Basically, Peter Richmond was very talented and whether he was very wise or he took the recommendations of a savvy mentor, I'll never know. But he put his assets into a trust. Vera was given a stipend for expenses, which was enough to maintain the lifestyle she'd enjoyed at the time of his death. There were provisions made for inflation as well. The trust was not to be touched until your thirty-fifth birthday, Jamie. At that time, the trust will be divided equally between you and Vera."

"How much are we talking?" Bert asked.

Banning shrugged. "It's difficult to put an exact figure on it. Peter invested cautiously in some stocks and bonds as well as real estate. There were several insurance policies. And of course, there's the building."

"What building?" I asked.

"Peter owned the building where his studio and the storage space are. I thought it would be a good idea to go there after our meeting, so you can get a better sense of it. That was a brilliant move on his part."

Malone had been calmly watching this exchange. "But hasn't this building been vacant for more than twenty years?"

"On the contrary, it's been utilized by artists since the late seventies. Peter bought it and kept one large studio for himself. The other spaces were divided up into galleries and studios. The rent payments were sufficient to cover the annual expenses for property taxes, utilities and insurance. The only stipulation was that his studio was never to be used by anyone outside of his immediate family. That would be either Vera or you, Jamie."

I shook my head. "I can't draw stick figures."

"Let's talk about this list," Bert said. "You understand Malone and I are here to support Jamie. Neither one of us has any claims beyond that."

"That is not a problem."

Banning gave us a moment to review the items. After securing the building and the studio, the list included creating an inventory, documenting the pieces, getting appraisals done, and determining the best course of action for the estate. There were other items, such as press releases and interviews. I stopped reading when I got that far.

"Did you know about this storeroom before?" I asked.

"No, I was as surprised as anyone. It's been years since I've been to the building. It's my understanding that Peter had a special wall constructed. I visited his studio a few times when he was working. He was secretive and clever."

"Why don't we go look at the building?" Bert suggested.

Banning rose smoothly to his feet. "That is a splendid idea."

****

Lincoln Banning and Helen Gaines were high priced tour guides, but they knew exactly where we were going. We'd taken separate cars. Bert parked in the lot beside the old industrial building and the three of us stood staring up at the structure. It was four stories tall, a converted factory of some sort with large windows high up on the walls of each floor. The parking lot was paved and the outside of the building was well kept. We followed the attorneys inside.

Banning used a set of keys to unlock the outer door. Past the entrance was a landing for the first floor and a flight of stairs. He unlocked another door and we turned left, going down a hallway. I was amazed to see solid hardwood floors that gleamed in the overhead lights. At the end of the corridor Banning stopped and flipped through his keys. As he unlocked this door, my eyes were drawn to a small brass plaque that bore the letters P.M.R. I dragged a finger across the initials. A childhood memory flashed through my mind. I must have done that during one of my rare visits here with Vera.

"Here we go," Banning said, swinging the door wide. He reached in and flicked on the lights with a flourish.

Inside the room was a giant square, probably sixty feet wide and sixty feet deep. The hardwood floor continued here, only it didn't gleam like the hallway. Dust thickly coated the floorboards. The space was empty except for four worktables and stools, a drafting table, several wooden file cabinets and an old rolltop desk. The others stood back while I slowly walked around. Near the door to the corridor was a section of wall that showed signs of recent repair. From here it looked like drywall.

"Where's the storage room?" Bert asked.

Helen Gaines walked to the far wall. This part was made of wood and looked similar to the moldings and rails I'd seen out in the hallway. Using the tip of one finger, she pressed what looked like a knot in one of the boards. There was a loud clicking noise. I watched in amazement as the section of the wall swung open.

"The foreman of the repair crew found this switch from the inside. Fortunately this area wasn't damaged by the water pressure," she said. Silently we all walked into the next room.

I don't know what anyone else was expecting, but I was stunned by what I saw. There was no haphazard jumble here. What welcomed me was row upon row of wooden crates. Some were so big I couldn't see over them and I was wearing two-inch heels. Others were small cubes, about two feet in every direction. Some were stacked on top of others, some were standing alone. There were five rows here. Each crate was identified with some kind of code. And each one was coated in a thick layer of dust that would have made an archeologist giddy with delight.

"Holy crap," I whispered. Malone was standing close by. I felt his hand squeeze mine. It took me a minute to realize I was shaking.

"Peter was always creating," Banning said quietly. "We spoke often about his work. He would have multiple projects going simultaneously. Some were pieces he'd designed and was commissioned to create. Others were something that struck his fancy. He suffered from insomnia, as so many creative types do. I think that just allowed him more time to work."

We walked around the rows of crates. Absently I trailed

a finger along the wood. I realized everyone else was quietly following my lead. Bert stopped beneath the windows, arms folded across his massive chest. I followed his gaze. The ceiling was probably twenty feet up. Across the beams were a row of lights, large bulbs inside metallic shades. They easily threw a large circle of light down on the crates. The back wall, which faced north, was solid cement for the first fifteen feet. The last section, five or six feet tall, were heavy windows reinforced with metal in the glass.

"This will be no easy task," Banning said as he moved back to the entrance in the wall.

"It's safe to assume these crates have been untouched for more than twenty years," Malone said, brushing the dust off his palms.

Gathering around one of the worktables, Helen brought out a copy of the list. "I've taken the liberty of making a few calls. There are not many firms that specialize in artwork. So far I've been unable to find one that would be willing to do the inventory. But I intend to keep trying."

"What about some college students? Maybe we could line some up while they are off during the summer," Bert suggested.

"This is going to be an interesting project," Banning said. "Perhaps we could find an art history professor who would oversee the efforts. The curator at the Detroit Institute of Arts may be able to recommend someone."

Somehow Malone was standing across the table from me. His eyes were on mine and I watched the beginnings of a low voltage smile touch the corners of his mouth. I was no longer listening to Bert and Lincoln Banning discussing options. Malone's eyes burned into mine. He nodded once. His lips silently formed two words.

"No," I said. "We're not doing it that way."

Banning seemed startled by my comment. "But, Jamie, we will need an expert's opinion on these works in order to determine their value."

"Yes, we will. But I'm not having a bunch of strangers going through this. These could be priceless works of art that no one has seen in twenty-five years."

"What do you propose?" Helen asked.

"I'm not proposing anything. I'm going to do it."

I glanced around the table. A wide smile split Bert's face. The two attorneys looked like I was suddenly speaking an alien language. Malone winked at me.

"Here's my plan. I will bring in the equipment to make a video of each crate as we open it. I'll take still photos as well, from every angle. Each one of those crates has a code or unique number on it. We'll document everything. I'll use the same codes and create a catalog with detailed descriptions. We can measure the pieces. Then when we have everything ready, you can arrange for an expert to come in and set the value."

Bert raised two fingers. "Two experts. Or maybe three would be better. That's a good plan, Jamie."

"There is ample money in the estate to pay someone to do this work," Banning said.

"That's good to know. I'll have to buy the video and camera equipment, along with some tools and other equipment for the project. I'll keep a register and all the receipts."

"Surely you're not planning on doing this alone," Helen Gaines said.

"No, I'm going to have some help."

Malone's smile grew. "I think I know who you have in mind."

****

Although Bert had taken the day off, Malone was still scheduled for duty at three. Bert took us for a late lunch at the Elwood Bar and Grille. Directly across the street is Comerica Park, where the Detroit Tigers play. When the new stadium was being constructed, the bar had been uprooted and moved to this new premiere spot. After ordering, Bert leaned back in his chair and looked at me for a moment without speaking.

"What?" I asked.

"Do you want to tell me your plan? Not that I have any doubt in my mind you can do it, but I am sort of curious."

"Peter Richmond has been a mystery to me for most of my life. Vera did very little to keep his memory alive. This is an opportunity for me to find out more about him. And I couldn't stand the idea of a bunch of strangers, who have no idea what they're looking at, tearing open those crates and drooling over his art."

The intensity of my response surprised all of us, including me. Bert folded his hands on the table. Malone chose that moment to take a sip of his coffee.

"Well, if it was up to me," Bert said, "I'd start with a whole bunch of dust mops."

"Shop vacuums will be one of my first purchases. I'm thinking two, along with some brooms and a few tools."

Malone nodded sagely. "I'll help you pick out some tools. A good heavy cleaning will be necessary before you do anything else. Are you thinking about putting Ian to work?"

"He is definitely on my short list of candidates."

Bert knew all about Ian MacKinnon. He was just finishing his freshman year of high school and as fate would have it, he went to the same Northville high school where Linda taught. His father, Asa, was an old friend of Malone's who was killed in a car accident last August. Malone was an unofficial big brother to the kid and he spent a few nights a week at our house. I knew that by the end of the week, Ian would be out of school for the summer.

"Do you think his mother would mind if I hired him?"

Malone shook his head. "She'll be happy to get him out of the house. But you'll need to work around his practice schedule. And they may have a couple of tournaments in early July. But I don't think that will be a problem."

Our food arrived, mushroom cheeseburgers for me and Malone, a bacon blue cheese burger for Bert. Conversation faded as we ate, but my mind kept spinning about the possibilities that I might find in those crates. I glanced down at my purse, where the keys to the building were buried under a copy of my father's will. Was all this really happening?

After lunch, Bert drove us home. Malone left to work his shift. As he drove away, I took Bert's arm and started walking down the block.

"This whole situation is surreal," I said.

He snorted a laugh. "Almost like discovering a treasure map in a box of cereal."

"Yes. In a way, I want to learn everything I can about him. But in another way, I'm scared and I don't want things to change."

He looked me in the eyes. "Change is inevitable. But it doesn't have to be a bad thing."

"I don't want things to change between you and me. We're finally at a place that feels so right to me. You are the father in my life, Bert."

He stopped walking and turned, putting both hands on my shoulders. "Jamie Rae that is the sweetest thing anyone has ever said to me. But you should know by now, you're stuck with me. Learning more about Peter, about whom he was and what drove him, may give you some inner peace. It might even help you understand more about yourself. But remember this. No matter what you learn, I'm not going anywhere. And if you want to share with me, I'll be here."

"I was kind of hoping you'd say that."

I felt his arms go around me for a paternal bear hug. Bert really was the father in my life. No matter what I discovered with this project, I made a vow not to let that change.

****

Linda stopped by after classes. Tomorrow would be the last day for regular students. Then she would have a couple of weeks free before the summer school programs began. I told her about the day's events. Despite my best efforts, I knew that I wasn't doing justice to the studio and the storeroom. Linda was anxious to see it for herself. She was already planning on joining me Monday.

"So what are you going to do now?" Linda asked.

"I need to get some equipment. Malone is going to take me to get vacuums and hardware in the morning, but tonight we can go shopping."

Linda fluffed back her curls and sat up straight. "Are we going for fashions appropriate for the art world? Something racy and revealing that screams artistic talents are present?"

"We're not shopping for clothes, Algae. We need electronics. I've got to get a video camera, a laptop computer, a camera and all the necessary attachments."

"I'm surprised you don't have a video camera, Jay Kay. You could hide it in the bedroom and capture some of those romantic evenings with Malone."

I felt a blush come to my cheeks. "I'm camera shy."

"Yes, and I'm checking into the convent," Linda said with a laugh.

We went to one of those big box electronic stores. We weren't inside two minutes before a young guy with a thick mane of dark brown hair and soulful brown eyes came over to assist us. If Linda hadn't been with me, I would have probably waited an hour to get some help. Ten minutes later we headed for the register.

"Jay Kay, you look like someone who just discovered a toy store," Linda said with a grin.

"It's going to take me a few hours just to get familiar with all of this stuff."

"Don't worry about it. I'm sure Ian can help you. These kids start using electronics when they are still in the womb."

CHAPTER THREE

Friday morning Malone and I headed out early. We stopped just long enough to pick up the supplies we would need for cleaning. I was anxious. My stomach was in knots and the thought of a big breakfast was out of the question. Malone sensed this. Just before entering the freeway, he stopped at a bakery and bought some muffins and coffee.

We lugged everything into the studio. To dissuade any unwanted visitors, I locked the door behind us. The media were still trying to get an update on the story. I hoped Lincoln Banning could continue to keep them at bay. This was going to be a private operation.

"Why don't we begin with the studio section, Jamie, and save the storeroom for later?"

"That's a wonderful idea, Leon." I batted my lashes at him.

"Wrong again, Jay."

"You can't blame a girl for trying."

With a grin he shook his head and started up his shop vacuum. Malone moved to the farthest corner where he set up a step ladder. In three quick strides he was at the top, working the extended wand of the vacuum up toward the ceiling. There was no sense cleaning the floors until we'd gotten the dust and dirt from above. I moved to the other corner and followed his example.

Two hours later we had cleaned everything in reach from the ceiling and walls. Several times we stopped to empty the drums of the vacuums. Malone was working on the floors while I moved to one of the sturdy worktables. I was leaning over the table, using the nozzle attachment to draw the dirt when two strong hands grasped my hips.

"Leon, what are you doing?" I looked over my shoulder at Malone.

"I'm giving in to my urges, Jamie. We didn't start our day in the usual way and I've been admiring your sweet ass for several hours now."

Knowing it was going to be hot and stuffy in the studio, I'd worn an old pair of denim shorts, tennis shoes, and a red tank top. I felt Malone's right hand move to the snap on my shorts and he smoothly undid them and ran the zipper down. The way he was holding me left me no room to turn. The vacuum was still on and the hose ran up between me and the table. I could feel a slight vibration coming from the machine. It was tickling my leg. Now he tugged my shorts off my hips, dragging my panties with them.

"Leon, you can't be serious!"

"Actually, I think it's more fun than serious," Malone said. At that moment his hand slipped between my legs, stroking me in a way that never failed to arouse me. Before I could respond, I felt him enter me.

He must have removed his jeans before he grabbed me. Now as he gained a rhythm, my body responded. Malone's hands were back on my hips, holding me tightly to the table. My body betrayed me, automatically matching his movements. The sensation was incredible. And I realized something was adding to it. With the vacuum still running, the hose was now pressed tightly in front of me, and the machine's vibrations were elevating my pleasure. I squeezed Malone as I peaked. Seconds later, I felt him explode inside of me. We stayed in that position until we could breathe.

"Who knew cleaning could be so much fun?" Malone asked as he stepped back and reclaimed his jeans.

"That wasn't cleaning, Leon." Reaching down to switch off the vacuum, I noticed my hands were trembling. My shorts and panties were bunched around my ankles. I glanced up at Malone. A wicked smile crossed his face.

"What are you grinning at, Malone?"

"A beautiful, bottomless woman. Maybe you should leave your clothes off while we finish this project."

He drew me close for a long kiss. I melted into him. Malone's kisses always make me feel like I'm no longer part of the planet. As we separated he caught me under the arms and boosted me up onto the table. Somehow I pulled my left foot free of my shorts. They dangled off my right foot. Without hesitation I wrapped my legs around his waist. Malone's eyes widened.

"Really, Jamie?"

"You started it, Leon. Let's try it without the machine running." My fingers were busy undoing his belt buckle.

"I thought that would help muffle any passionate cries."

"I'll bite my lip."

He eased me down onto my back then lowered his face to mine. "Let me do that."

I couldn't believe he was ready so quickly. Lost in his kisses, his eyes staring into mine, I pulled him to me with my legs. Together we started moving as one. My arms were around his neck, fingers twisting in his hair. His movements were steady. Slowly the tempo increased. I urged him faster. Faster. I hoped the table was as solid as it appeared. Simultaneously we shuddered to another climax. Malone held me close, kissing my face, my neck, and my ears.

"You're incredible, Jamie."

"You're pretty damn wild yourself, Leon."

After that, we focused on the cleaning. The rest of the morning and early afternoon flew by, but I was pleased with the progress we'd made. Malone was scheduled for work at three, so we grabbed some carryout pizza and headed for home. Maybe it was a combination of things, but my nervous state was gone. Working with Malone must have helped. Taking the first step to uncovering the past was probably part of it. Malone ducked into the bathroom for a shower before work while I wrapped up the leftover pizza. Reflecting on his actions earlier brought my own wicked smile into play.

Shedding my clothes, I stepped into the shower stall behind him. Malone was lathering up his chest and arms when he realized I was there.

"I don't have much time, Jay."

I pressed my body against his back. "Nonsense. There's always enough time."

Taking the soap from the rack, I worked up a thick lather with my hands. Before he could stop me, I reached around and took him in both hands. My guess was right. He was instantly hard. A groan escaped him.

"Jamie, you're incorrigible."

"I just want to make sure you're relaxed before you go to work, Leon." My hands were pumping steadily now. I pressed my body tightly against his back. The hot water sprayed from the shower head, beating down on me. I shook the water from my face.

Malone's breath was rasping. He pressed both palms against the shower wall and held himself still. My hands were moving faster. I ground my body against his, wiggling my hips.

He tipped his head back. Keeping his left hand braced on the wall, he reached his right hand around and clutched my ass. My hands churned faster. Malone let out another groan. I felt his body shudder as he peaked. My body trembled as my hands slowed their work.

"I've unleashed a monster," Malone said turning to

face me.

"Hey, that was going to be my line."

****

Saturday morning we gathered at the ballpark. Ian was playing two games. His mom, Terri, sat beside me on the bleachers. Malone was coaching third base. Terri listened intently while I described the project with the studio and the storeroom and the work that needed to be done.

"You don't have to pay him, Jamie. You and Malone do enough for Ian as it is."

"It's the estate that will be paying for him. And there is plenty of money. Malone seemed to think it would be good for Ian in several ways. He does some honest work, earns some good money and we'll work around his practice and game schedule. That's the beauty of this job. I'm very flexible with the time frame."

Terri hesitated a moment. "How much are you talking?"

I gave her a number well above minimum wage. Her eyes grew wide with delight. "Malone suggested that you might want to put some of it in a savings for Ian."

We watched as Ian came up to bat. There was one out and runners on first and third. He let the first two pitches go by, then connected with a smooth swing, sending the ball all the way to the fence in deep right field for a triple. The small crowd on this side of the bleachers jumped up and cheered. Terri was the loudest of the bunch. I watched fondly as Ian stood on third base, catching his breath and slapping hands with Malone. Then the kid looked over at his mom and beamed a wide smile.

"He's a good kid and he'll work hard for you, Jamie."

"There's no doubt in my mind. So you're okay with this?

Terri's eyes were glued to the field. "You bet I am. This gets him doing something productive during the summer and he'll be able to spend some extra time with Malone. Don't let Ian know I told you, but he really treasures the time they're together."

"I'll keep it our secret."

We watched the next batter hit a deep fly ball. Ian hesitated, taking only a couple of steps off base. When the fielder snagged the ball from the air at the last second, Ian tagged up and raced for home. He beat the throw easily. Terri was on her feet again, clapping loudly. His team now had a three-run lead. The pride in her son was easy to read. She glanced at me as she sat on the bleacher.

"By the way, Jamie, he also gets a kick out of spending time with you."

"That's good to know, because Malone will only be with us a few hours some days. Most of the work will be done by just Ian and me."

The game wound down quickly. Ian and his teammates had enough time to relax before their next competition. Malone waved us over. We chatted about the project. Malone flashed us one of those low voltage smiles and walked over to get Ian. Together we explained what we had in mind. Ian took a step back and looked at the three of us individually.

"Wait a minute. Did you guys just cook this up so I don't get a summer vacation?"

Malone calmly raised a hand. "Relax. You were grumbling last week that you wanted to find a part-time job. This one is perfect. Jamie and I will work around the baseball schedule. And you'll still have time to hang out with your friends in the evenings and on the weekends. With your mom working all day, this will keep you busy and out of the house."

"There will be some days that we don't go downtown," I said, "if there is other work I have to do or other appointments."

Ian scuffed his cleats in the dirt. "Yeah, but I want to have some fun this summer too."

"You will," Terri said, "and you'll earn real money in the process." She told him the hourly rate we'd agreed on. Ian's face brightened.

"So when do I start? Because Timmy is having a pool party tomorrow and the whole team is going to be there."

"You can stay at our place Sunday night and we'll head down there early Monday morning," Malone said.

Ian gave us all a grin. "Sign me up, coach."

****

It was late afternoon when I left the ball field. There was just enough time to run home, shower, and put on a sundress and sandals before going to a barbecue at Linda's. She and Vince put together a feast with grilled shrimp kabobs, homemade bread, tossed salad and fresh strawberries and blueberries. We relaxed on the deck behind her house, enjoying the sunshine and each other's company.

Linda reached across the patio table and rested a hand on my arm.

"Jay Kay, I have a huge favor to ask you."

"I'll do it."

"You don't even know what it is," she said with a laugh.

"Doesn't matter, you know I'll do anything for you."

Vince chuckled. "I can personally vouch for that."

We all knew what he was referring to. Linda had been kidnapped in early April. Being the stubborn redhead that I am, I was determined to find her. Eventually I did, but not before her kidnapper had severely beaten her. We'd managed to escape his clutches and the bad guy was still in jail, awaiting a trial. Now in the warm June sunshine, there was no visible trace of her injuries. But I still worried about the scars we could never see.

"We're being spontaneous," Vince said. "I've got us booked for a week's vacation in Montreal."

"That's great. When do you leave?"

Linda smiled widely, her eyes sparkling with delight. "Tomorrow afternoon. Vince surprised me with it just before you got here. The timing is perfect. But there's just one thing he didn't account for."

As if on cue, Logan came over and nudged my hand with his nose. "You don't have time to arrange for a kennel."

"You're right. I know it's a huge imposition, but could you take him for the week?" Linda asked. I noticed her sultry voice was soft and low. It was her sweet, innocent tone. One that I could never resist. I wondered if anyone else could.

"Of course I will. Malone and Ian will pamper him almost as much as you do."

"But I don't want it to interfere with your art project."

I considered it for a moment. "Chances are we won't be spending more than six or seven hours a day at the studio. With Malone working and Ian's baseball schedule, I'll be happy if we put in five hours at a time down there. So it won't be any different for Logan than the days you go to work. And I might take him with me once or twice anyway."

"He is good company," Vince said.

"And he's cute too."

"He's also very protective, Jay Kay." Linda reached over and tugged at his ears.

"So it's settled. Logan stays with me for the week."

"We'll drop him off tomorrow on the way to the airport," Vince said.

Now there would be one more visitor to my house. I wasn't complaining. I liked having the others around. While Linda cleared the dishes from dinner, I sat back and thought about her and Vince. They were an unlikely couple. Vince Schulte is my doctor and he's about twenty years older than Linda. They had known each other for years but only started dating recently. Malone liked to tease me about that. I was the one who set them up on New Year's Eve. The sparks were flying that night. From what I could tell, they still were.

****

There was no sense in putting it off any longer. The house was quiet. Malone was at work for at least another hour. So now, in the stillness of the night, I pulled Peter Richmond's will from my desk. The thick sheaf of documents felt heavy and serious in my hands. Slowly I began to make my way through the legalese.

Lincoln Banning was named the executor of the estate. The actual will had been drawn up by another attorney, so there was no possibility of a conflict of interest. Yet Banning did not have sole control over the finances. Each year he gave a report to three people, one of whom was Vera, my crazy mother. My eyes grew wide when I recognized one of the other names – a very well respected judge from Oakland County. The other was a name I didn't know. An attachment to the will included copies of the financial statements.

There was a list of assets. The converted factory that had become the art studio was at the top of the list. There were several other properties scattered around metropolitan Detroit. There were stocks in some technology firms, one of the automotive companies, a pharmaceutical giant, and a food conglomerate. Whoever was advising Peter from the beginning encouraged him to have a very diverse portfolio. There were also three life insurance policies that were worth significant money, all paid to the estate at the time of his death. One of the last pages indicated that any and all works of art created by Peter that were unsold would remain as assets until the estate was distributed on my thirty-fifth birthday. Only the executor, with agreement from all parties, could sell any assets.

I got up, went for a walk around the block in the dark, came back, and read it all over again. Without even considering the sculptures in the storeroom, the estate was worth millions. Vera was awarded a stipend each month. This was based on a budget from when they were married, adjusted to the current cost of living. Knowing her love of shopping, entertaining and travel, I doubted she saved any money at all.

Thoughts of my mother made me wonder again where she was. Somewhere along the line, Vera became a nomad. She was a constant fixture with a very wealthy crowd. Winters were usually spent in a warm climate, like Arizona, Florida, or maybe the Caribbean Islands. When the seasons changed, so did her mood. Vera loved being the social butterfly, jumping from one locale to another. After her sixth marriage a few years ago, she told me that it no longer made sense to marry. She was going to enjoy herself and if a relationship developed, so be it.

"Hey, Jamie."

I was sitting on the rocker in the living room, with just the kitchen light on low, so absorbed in my thoughts that I didn't even realize Malone was home. I jumped at the sound of his voice.

"Ezekiel, you scared the crap out of me."

He moved to me and pulled me up for an embrace. "What's got you so wound up?"

"I read the will. It's amazing how thorough Peter was. And it got me thinking about Vera. I wonder if her craziness impacted his actions."

"Do you realize you always use her first name when speaking about her?" His hands were making slow circles around my shoulders and back, lightly rubbing away the tension.

"When I was sixteen, she forbade me to call her Mom or Mother. She said people wouldn't believe she was old enough to have a daughter that age. She insisted I call her Vera. I was already referring to Bert by his first name, so it made sense."

Malone pulled me tighter. "That sounds kind of sad. Kids should always refer to the parents as Mom and Dad, or some variation of that."

"Ezekiel, I had no idea you were so sentimental."

"I have a few surprises."

His right hand came up and cupped my chin. As Malone eased in for a kiss, I felt his left hand slide behind my neck and undo the ties. This was a halter top sundress that fit me so well I didn't bother to wear a bra with it. Still kissing me, his right hand slid down my neck, across my collarbone, and flicked the ties forward. Malone eased back from his embrace and the top of the dress fell to my waist. Now his hands slid down my back. He bunched the material together from the skirt and gave the dress a quick tug. I felt the warm air caress my exposed skin as the dress fluttered to my feet.

"Malone," I whispered, "I'm standing here naked in front of the window."

"You're not naked, Jamie. You still have on panties and your sandals."

My arms were somehow around his neck again. He moved his lips across my throat and nuzzled my ear. Slowly, his fingers moved down my back until he touched the elastic at my waist. As I gasped a breath, Malone dipped a finger inside the waistband and wiggled the panties off my hips.

"Ezekiel, you're driving me crazy."

"That's been my goal all day."

Malone was taking charge. One hand slid over my buns, squeezing me then nudging my legs apart. My heart was racing as his fingers explored me, sliding down lower to confirm how aroused I was. I clung to him. I expected Malone to move me to the bedroom or maybe over to the Jewish Aunt, that thick plush oversized sofa that dominated the room. But he obviously had other ideas.

"You're shaking, Jay."

"It's the effect you're having on me, Malone." It was impossible to draw a deep breath. "I don't think I can stand much longer."

"Guess I'll have to hold you up."

His hands were now in front of me, clutching my hips. Somehow he took a step forward and nudged me past the rocker. I managed to step out of my sandals and kick one foot loose from the dress and panties gathered around my feet. As Malone's mouth found mine, I realized my ass was now pressed against the front window. Unable to do anything but groan I gave up as his fingers entered me. I was so close it only took me seconds to reach a peak. It was a minute before I could gather enough air to speak.

"Welcome home, Ezekiel."

"It's good to be home, Jamie. But I think it's time for bed."

"Yes, I'm much safer when I'm horizontal. I almost tripped trying to get out of my panties."

A wicked smile crossed his face and reached all the way up to his eyes. "Maybe you should stop wearing panties this time of year. I wouldn't want you to fall and get hurt."

"Malone! What kind of a girl do you think I am?"

He gathered me in his arms and lifted me off the floor. "You're my kind of girl."

CHAPTER FOUR

We took two cars Monday morning since Malone would have to leave to work his regular shift. I wanted to spend as much time downtown as possible. Ian slept in the car, but somehow was very alert when we got to the studio. He even helped lug in the video equipment and the laptop computer. The plan was to have Malone and Ian tackle the storeroom while I began looking through the file cabinet and the rolltop desk. I watched Ian's reaction to the studio.

"This is sweet. But I thought you said there was a lot of dirt to clean up and crates to open."

Malone nudged him and pointed at me. Like a magician's assistant, I touched the hidden switch in the wall. We all heard the click of the lock releasing. I pushed against the wall with just my forefinger. The door swung open.

Ian looked like a kid who'd found pirate treasure. He walked through the door and his head slowly swiveled back and forth, taking it all in. I imagined that was what I looked like less than a week ago.

"Holy cow, Malone, this place is a mess!"

"That's why we're here, kid. Let's get started."

I left them to it. Part of me was very anxious to open at least one box and see what was hiding inside. But there was a plan and I was determined to stick to it. From the ring of keys Lincoln Banning provided, I flipped through them until I found the one for the filing cabinets. They were wooden, maybe oak, with four solid drawers. The lock hesitated, but with a little coaxing it popped free. I rolled the top drawer open.

A neat row of folders hanging in sleeves greeted me. The tab on the first one had a mixture of letters, numbers, and symbols. I drew it out. It was thick with notes and neatly folded papers. I took it to the worktable and spread it out. Stapled to the inside flap was a three-by-five-inch card. This listed the title of the work, the date it was completed, and the components of it. The title was "Spring Dance" and it was done more than a year before Peter's death. The materials listed were bronze. Carefully I unfolded the papers.

On thick paper that reminded me of the kind you'd see in a butcher shop was a sketch done in pencil. It showed a thick circular base and what looked like the legs, torso, and arms of four dancers in a backbend. Their feet were all close together at the base and each figure was at a ninety-degree angle to the one next to it, as if they were stationed at the four points of a compass. There were different views of the piece.

I sat there staring at it for a while, just absorbed in the detail and the artistry. I wondered if the piece was in the storeroom. Other pages were of earlier drawings. Some features changed, like the angle of the figures, the length of the arms or torsos varied.

Wanting to document everything, I pulled the camera from the bag and spread the sketch across the table. I took a couple of pictures before curiosity got the better of me. Grabbing the file, I rushed into the storeroom. The guys were working away, vacuums roaring, drawing the dust down from the rafters and windows. I started on the row farthest from them and began searching.

One thing the file didn't indicate was how big the piece was. This could be something small and intricate that would fit easily on a bookshelf, or the dancers could be life size. Slowly I walked the aisle, trying to match the code to the crates.

"What's up, Jamie?"

Malone and Ian were standing at the end of the row. So absorbed was I in the search that I didn't notice the room had gone silent.

"I'm looking for this code number. It's from the first file I looked at."

The guys gathered around me. Carefully I opened the file on top of a dusty crate and showed them the drawing. A wide smile split Ian's face.

"Looks like treasure hunt time."

"Not so fast, kid." Malone's voice drew my eyes to his face. "I thought you wanted to wait until the dust was cleared before we started opening things up."

"I did, Eric, I really did. And I still do. But I just want to see this first one."

Ian was already moving down the aisle closest to the windows. I could hear his voice, but didn't understand what he was saying.

"He's chanting the code, Jay. Let's go find this one."

We moved in opposite directions, searching for the elusive box. I was about to give up, thinking this was something that had been sold or was commissioned long before Peter's death, when Ian let out a whoop.

"I think we have a winner!"

Malone and I went to look. The crate was about three foot square and at the end of the row by the far wall. It was under two other crates in a stack of five. I stood there staring at it while the guys watched me.

"I guess we should open it so you can see it," Ian said.

"No, I don't want it to get dirty."

"We could move it into the other room," Malone said.

I drew a deep breath. "What the hell! Let's rip this one open!"

The guys carefully moved the two crates on top of it onto the floor. Then they carried it toward the door. Malone insisted they set it down and vacuum the accumulated dust off before tracking it into the studio. I ran ahead to the toolbox. Inside there were two crowbars and a couple of hammers along with an assortment of screwdrivers and pliers and other tools. I grabbed the crowbars and a hammer.

"Let's set it on the floor by that bench," Malone said.

Ian's face was flushed with exertion. "Nobody ever told me art was this heavy."

"Don't be a wimp. Set your end down carefully."

They eased the crate to the ground. Malone took the hammer and a small crowbar. Carefully he inserted the edge of the bar along the lid. He smacked it a couple of times with the hammer. Nails groaned at his effort. I watched him circle the box, working the edge of the crowbar in and loosening the lid from the sides. Ian took the other bar from me and moved behind Malone, prying up the sections. In less than a minute the lid was free. They stepped back so we could all see it.

"Do you want to do the honors, Jamie?"

I shook my head. My nerves were so bad I'd probably drop the lid on my foot. "Let Ian do it. He found the crate."

The kid glowed with delight. He started to reach for the lid.

"Wait!"

Both guys looked stunned. "Change your mind?"

"No, Eric, but I want to capture this on video. We're going to record each crate being opened. I want to be consistent. I want to do it right."

With their help it only took a few minutes to set up the tripod and the video camera. Once we were filming, I read off the crate's code, indicated the date and time and who was present. Ian moved forward and lifted the lid carefully. Angling the camera, I could see that the contents were wrapped in burlap. Loose pieces of straw filled the gaps in the crate. Malone and Ian reached into the box and lifted out the sculpture. They set it in the center of the worktable. Malone pulled a knife from his pocket and gently cut through the coarse fabric. Once a rip was made, they pulled it apart. Malone tenderly lifted the sculpture off the table while Ian removed the burlap. I think my heart stopped. I know my breath did.

"It's amazing," Ian said. "This is so cool."

"It's just like the sketch in the file," Malone said.

I stopped the video. Unhooking the camera from the tripod, I passed it to Ian. "Do a slow pan, top to bottom, then move around and capture it from every side. I'm going to take some shots with the other camera."

Ian nodded and quickly accepted his new assignment. Malone was staring at the piece. Then he set the hammer on its head and leaned the handle against the sculpture.

"What are you doing, Eric?"

He shook his head. "Wrong again, Jamie. I'm just giving it a sense of scale. With the hammer in the picture, you can tell roughly how big it is."

"We should measure it," I said, stepping past him to take a couple of photos. "Do you have a tape in the toolbox?"

"No, but I've got a couple at home. We can bring one tomorrow and get the dimensions. Maybe we should weigh it too."

I glanced at him, eyebrows raised. Malone innocently raised his hands, but there was no hiding the smirk on his face. Like many women, I refuse to have a bathroom scale in the house. If I really want to know if I've gained any weight, there is a scale at the gym. Or I can use the one at Vince's office.

"I am *not* buying a scale."

"You don't have to. There's an industrial one back in

the corner of the storeroom, beneath the windows. Peter must have used it for the occasional shipment."

Ignoring the slight flush of heat on my face, I moved around the table and shot more pictures. Ian completed his circuit and returned the camera to the tripod.

"Let's get back to work," Malone said.

While the guys went back to attacking the dust, I booted up the laptop. I made a spreadsheet and started logging in the details. Once that was done, I returned to the file cabinet and opened the next folder. Somehow, having seen "Spring Dance" quelled my desire to rip open the crates at random. We were going to need a system. We might as well find them in the order of Peter's files. This would result in some shifting of crates, but it would work.

Time passed quickly. I noticed the vacuums were silent and could hear the guys talking quietly in the other room. I was poised over the worktable, studying the files, entering the details into the computer for more than two hours. Stretching my arms above my head, I moved to the storeroom.

"C'mon, Malone, let's take a break. I'm starving."

"You're a teenage boy. You're always starving. Let's finish that last stack of crates."

"My vacuum is on strike. I think it's overheating. We should let it cool down for a while." Ian was doing his best to be persuasive. I doubted it was having any effect.

"Maybe we should take a break, Malone," I said, leaning against the door jamb.

He winked at me and checked his watch. "If we take a break now, you'll have to finish up with the kid. I've got just enough time to grab something fast then head to work."

"Food at last!" Ian said, clutching his stomach in exaggeration. "Where are we going?"

Malone propped his broom against the wall and winked at me. "There is only one place around here that will be able to tame a teenager's stomach."

Ian looked puzzled. "Where's that?"
"Lafayette," I said.

****

Smack dab in downtown Detroit is an institution that has been there forever. Well, maybe not forever, but it sure seems like it. Lafayette Coney Island is a narrow building that fronts Lafayette Street on one side and Michigan Avenue on the other. The place has been serving up the very best Coney Island hot dogs for as long as I can remember. A true dog comes with a generous scoop of chili, without beans, a shot of yellow mustard, and a soupcon of freshly chopped onions. It's not for the faint of heart. But it's a tradition for people who work downtown or those coming into town for a sporting event or a convention. A smattering of tables jam the small floor space and a counter runs down the middle of the joint. In the big window on Lafayette, you can see the crew putting together the dogs in a matter of seconds.

We grabbed a table near the back. The menu is limited. Before we had warmed our seats a waiter appeared, swiping at the table with a wet cloth. He wore a T-shirt with the restaurant logo and jeans partially hidden by a white apron. He took our order without writing anything down, shouting it out to the guys behind the counter. He returned in a moment, dropping icy cans of soda on the table. After a moment's hesitation, he slid forks and knives on the table as well. In a blink he returned and set our meal before us.

I went with one Coney Island and an order of fries. Malone was having two dogs. Ian had ordered two Coney dogs and a bowl of chili. Forgoing the silverware, I picked up the hot dog and ate it the way man intended, with my fingers. It made a snapping noise when I bit into it.

"This place is so cool," Ian said between bites. "Did you see that guy with the Red Wings cap when we came in?"

Malone nodded and shot me a wink. "He's one of the players. Many of them live in the area year-round."

Faded posters and pictures lined the walls. Some reflected championship sports teams, others big news for the area. I glanced down and realized Ian was sneaking fries from my plate. Teenagers! Where does he put it? I took a few, placed them next to the remnants of my hot dog and slid him the rest.

"I'll drop you two off at the studio and head for work. But I won't have time to stop at the house and let Logan out."

"That's okay, Eric. We'll work a couple more hours and call it a day. You guys made a lot of progress with the dirt. Tomorrow we can focus on opening the crates."

Malone leaned back in his chair and was thoughtful for a moment. "Are you planning on bringing pieces out to the studio or keeping them in the storeroom?"

"I haven't given it much thought. Why?"

"The storeroom is more secure. Few people know how to access it."

"We need to spread things out so we can do an inventory and get it ready for the experts to authenticate everything," I said.

Ian piped up. "If we flip the crates over once they're opened, we could set the sculptures on top of the crate. Then we can make narrow aisles or group the work any way you want. We can leave enough space between crates so people can view the pieces from each side."

Malone and I stared at each other. "The kid's right. That will work."

"What about the piece we looked at today?" Ian asked.

"For now, let's leave it in the studio."

I would never have imagined that someday I would regret that decision.

****

Ian and I worked together the rest of the afternoon. We tackled the last of the dust from the storeroom. The kid took the vacuums out and emptied the drums in a dumpster. When he came back, I was rubbing lemon oil into one of the oak file cabinets. Without a word he grabbed a cloth and began working on the rolltop desk. I had yet to unlock it. Something told me to take these discoveries slowly.

We secured the storeroom. I was about to lock the file cabinet when Ian pointed at the camera bags.

"Are you going to lug these back and forth every day?"

"I may want to view the photos and the video when I get home."

He rolled his eyes. "Jamie, you can just send the files. Why carry all this stuff if you don't have to?"

The laptop was still running. Quickly he pulled the memory cards from the cameras. Ian brought up the files, attached them to an email, and sent them to my home computer. We shut everything down, locked the camera equipment inside the storeroom, and headed for the door. I made sure the deadbolt lock was secured. Ian was running a fingertip over the small brass sign that bore Peter's logo. It was a capital R with a flourish to the stems. Inside the circle at the top was the letters P M done in a similar script.

"You know that was on the statue we saw today?" Ian said.

This kid continued to amaze me. I knew he was bright, but thought his powers of observation were focused on sports and girls. "I didn't notice it."

"It was underneath the base, sort of like he was signing his work."

"That's exactly what he was doing."

****

There was no practice tonight, but Ian went to a teammate's house for a barbecue and to play volleyball. Terri was going to pick him up afterward and drop him off. I'd showered off the dust and grime, taken Logan for a long walk, and was sitting at the picnic table with a glass of iced tea when my phone rang. I didn't recognize the number.

"Jamie, this is Lincoln Banning."

"Hello, Mr. Banning. What's up?"

"Please, call me Linc. I just got off the phone with Vera." There was a sound of frustration in his voice. It was something I could sympathize with.

"Is she coming to town?"

He seemed to choose his words carefully. "Not right away. She's in the Mediterranean."

"I thought she was in Florida!"

"That was last month," he said with a chuckle. "Apparently she's traveling with some friends who decided it was a perfect time to go to Europe."

Vera can be exasperating. All I could do was shake my head. "So she's not coming."

"Not right away. She said her friends were planning on leaving in a few days and going to Hawaii to see the volcano. I explained that the estate would pay for her airfare if she wanted to return directly."

"What was her reaction?"

"She laughed. Vera said her friends have a private jet and she will be flying with them to Hawaii. It's possible she might come to town sometime next week."

I gave my head another shake. "Did you tell her about our plan to examine the contents of the studio and the storeroom?"

"I did. When I explained that you had taken charge of the project, she seemed very pleased. Vera stated that just proved there was no reason for her to rush back here. Everything is in your very capable hands. Those were her words."

"When did she call?"

"Just now," Banning said. "She was going out for a late dinner with her friends and there was mention of a casino. There's a six hour time difference so it's late night where she is."

"Vera has been known to party late and sleep even later. She probably didn't get up until the sun was setting."

Banning asked about the project. I gave him an update about the dust removal and the opening of the first crate. He sounded very pleased with our efforts. He told me the curator for the DIA had made several calls, asking to view the works. Banning told him when we were ready, we would be in touch. He suggested I email him the video files each day so he could keep up with our progress. We ended the call. Sometime during the conversation Logan came over and put his snout on my leg. Without realizing it, I'd been scratching his head. He only pulled away when I stopped.

"At least you're here, which is more than I can say for Vera."

I fed the dog and put together a salad for dinner. After we ate, I went to the computer and pulled up the files Ian sent. Staring at the work of art that Peter created, I wondered why those talents never surfaced in me. The idea that I took after Vera was no consolation whatsoever. Her only talent seemed to be her ability to cultivate her social contacts. That was not something I aspired to do.

Ian came home around ten, smothering yawns with both hands. He wrestled with Logan for a bit, then gave me a wave and headed off for bed. To my surprise, the dog followed him. Wasn't he supposed to be my companion? Grabbing a fresh glass of tea, I went outside to look at the stars.

I was still there when Malone came home. He pulled me to my feet and wrapped me in his arms and just stood there, holding me.

"Welcome home, Eric."

"It's nice to be home, Jamie." He sounded tired.

With my cheek resting against his chest, we were content to hold one another. My eyes roamed the yard. There was a nice spread of grass beyond the picnic table and two stout trees near the rear about twenty feet apart. An old chain link fence with wooden posts and thick wire surrounded the yard. "Do you like our backyard?"

"Sure. But I keep thinking we need something else."

"What else could there be, Malone? We've got the picnic table, the barbecue and plenty of room."

He tickled my ribs and pointed toward the trees. "I keep seeing a nice thick hammock back there, under the shade of those branches. It could be a very relaxing spot."

"Somehow I never pictured you as a hammock guy, Malone. That sounds so sedentary."

"That depends on who I'm with, Jamie."

I told him about the call from Lincoln Banning and the latest escapades of Vera. Malone stifled a yawn and turned me toward the side door of the house.

"So I may have a week's reprieve before I meet the infamous Vera."

"Be careful what you wish for, Malone. You may want to keep your distance from that crazy woman."

"Something tells me she's not as bad as you make her out to be, Jay."

As we went inside, Malone checked the doors, making sure everything was locked up tight for the evening. We got ready for bed. It had been a very long day. The idea was to get another good day of work at the studio tomorrow. Sleep sounded very good right now. Malone slipped beneath the sheets and drew me into his arms. I wondered how I ever managed to sleep without him before. Yet his last comment was circling my brain.

"You're really looking forward to meeting Vera?"

"Yes, I am. She may be a little different, but she must have some redeeming qualities. After all, Bert married her."

"That's true."

"And she is your mother. It will be interesting to see how you two interact."

I pushed him onto his back and slid on top of him. "Right now I'm more interested in how you and I interact."

"There's only one way to find out."

CHAPTER FIVE

Tuesday was an awe-inspiring day. The guys were excited about opening the crates and discovering what secrets lay inside. It was gloomy outside, overcast and spitting rain despite the near eighty-degree temperature. We had the overhead lights on in the storeroom. Some meager light was coming in through the high windows that faced north. I set the tripod up. Ian was the treasure hunter. He used the list of the first ten files I'd reviewed yesterday to find the next crate in sequence. Together he and Malone muscled it into a clear spot on the storeroom floor.

"This one is a beast," Ian said, sliding the crate into position.

"Think of it as strength training. You don't need to go to the gym this week," Malone said with a grin.

"After a day of lugging these crates, I won't be able to lift my arms."

"Do all teenagers complain like this, Nigel?" I asked.

"Wrong again, Jamie. And it's only the boys who complain this much."

This crate was larger than yesterday's. It was almost waist high on me, and about three feet across. I stood behind the video camera and watched. Whether by design or discussion, I didn't know, but the guys had a system worked out. Malone took a crowbar and a hammer and would start to loosen the nails in the lid, moving slowly down one side. As he turned the corner, Ian followed with a second crowbar, wedging it under the lid and prying it up in stages. When all four sides were free, they dropped the hardware on the floor and together lifted the lid. I moved from behind the video camera and started snapping pictures.

"You think we can lift that, old man?" Ian asked with a grin spreading across his face.

"Who are you calling old man?"

"Well, there are only three of us here. And Jamie certainly isn't old or a man, so…"

Malone glanced up at me. I was surprised to realize that Ian's comment had me blushing. "Better be careful there, kid. It's a long walk home."

"But I can always ride with Jamie."

"Bend with your knees, not your back. I don't want to hear any whining tomorrow at the game that you're too sore to play."

They both reached into the crate and at Malone's command, they lifted together. Here was another burlap covered piece. Earlier Ian rolled one of the worktables into the storeroom. They placed the sculpture on the center of the table. Malone cut through the fabric with his pocket knife and Ian carefully pulled it free. The guys stepped back so I could take more pictures.

"I'll get the video," Ian said.

I circled the piece, clicking away, before taking a moment to look at it. Malone gently tugged my elbow, pulling me back beside him so Ian could zoom in for some more footage.

"This is amazing, Jamie."

"It's called "Grace." It's some kind of stonework."

What we were staring at was a spherical shaped piece of

brightly colored stone, with an oblong hole in the center. Under the glare of the overhead light, I could see soft shades of rose and lavender, yet if I turned, there were flecks of gold in my peripheral vision. Somehow the piece was attached to a thick black onyx base that included a pedestal. Ian stopped filming and reached a fingertip to the stone.

"It's smooth," he said. "Your finger glides right off it."

I followed his lead and let my fingers trail across the surface. "It's amazing. I have no idea what kind of stone that is or how he was able to create something like this."

"Your father was an incredibly talented man," Malone said.

This was going to take some time to sink in. That was one thing about this project that I knew was the right way to handle it. We were not going to rush through the storeroom, ripping open every crate in ten minutes time. These were works of art. Peter's legacy was in this room. I intended to give each piece its due. Malone sensed this and I think Ian did too.

After a while they folded the burlap and put it back in the crate. Together they carried it over to a far corner and flipped it upside down. Then they rolled the worktable next to it. Carefully they lifted the sculpture and eased it down on the center of the inverted base.

"This is going to work," Ian said with delight.

"Two down, a hundred more to go," Malone said.

"That's fifty-six to go."

We both looked at Ian. He shrugged. "I counted the crates yesterday. There were fifty-eight altogether. We opened one yesterday and this one."

Malone nudged him with an elbow. "You ever consider there might be more than one item in some of these bigger crates?"

"No."

"But it is a possibility?"

Ian flashed another grin. "I suppose, but we still have

another fifty-six crates to open. That means at least another fifty-six sculptures."

"Nobody likes a smartass," Malone muttered.

I cleared my throat. Being a smartass was one of my most redeeming qualities. At least, I'd always thought so.

"Let's look for the next crate," I said, handing Ian a slip of paper with the code number on it. Malone leaned against the wall and winked at me.

"Nice way to change the topic. And you are the exception to the rule."

"What rule would that be, Nigel?" I asked innocently.

"That would be the smartass rule. You can get away with it. At least, you can with me. But don't encourage the kid. He's not as cute as you are."

I rewarded him with a kiss. Hey, he said I was cute.

It wasn't long before the guys fell into a routine. Ian would hunt down the crate. He and Malone would then pry off the lid. I would film their efforts. While they were preparing each one, I would quickly enter details into the computer. When we stopped around one o'clock for lunch, four more crates were open. So far there was a sculpture made out of bronze, two from steel and glass and another stone piece.

Knowing that eating out every day would be costly, Malone had come prepared. He'd packed a cooler with fruit, cheese, bread, rare roast beef, salami, and turkey. We gathered stools around one of the worktables in the studio and spread out our feast. Malone mentioned that we could get a small refrigerator and put it next to the desk. I liked the idea of keeping some fresh fruit and things close at hand. Especially when I considered how much food Ian could eat.

After lunch Malone helped with one more crate before leaving for work. Ian was straightening up the storeroom while I started looking at more files. He was hoping to find the next couple units. We weren't planning on working tomorrow. I needed time to catch up on some other things and Ian had a travel game. Malone was off work the next two days, but he was coaching tomorrow. I pulled two more files from the cabinet.

Maybe I was becoming accustomed to the sculptures we'd seen, but the drawings and details on these pieces didn't leave me as breathless as my first few. But seeing the actual works displayed in front of me was still stunning. I was reaching for another file when someone knocked loudly on the outer door.

"Are you expecting anyone?" Ian asked.

"No, and I'm hoping it isn't some snoopy reporter." The irony that I used to be a snoopy reporter wasn't lost on me.

"What should we do?"

"Let's close up the storeroom. I don't want anyone going in there until we're ready for a full blown display."

He grinned. Quickly he doused the lights and pulled the door panel shut. As I walked to the outer door, Ian busied himself with a broom.

I opened the door part way, not sure what to expect. Thinking of the newscast last week, I anticipated the worst. What I saw caught me by surprise. He was a stocky man, probably in his late sixties, with a thick gray beard that reached down to his chest. A full head of gray hair rolled to his shoulders and was pulled into a ponytail with a leather strap. He was wearing worn khaki pants that bore splatters of paint and a denim shirt that had seen better days. As I stood in the doorway, he raised his face and his eyes lit on mine.

"You have got to be Jamie. I'd know those green eyes anywhere," he said in a deep booming voice. "It's been too many years. Do you remember me?"

I shook my head, unable to find my voice. The guy looked like a gray-haired version of Santa Claus, only a bit trimmer in the gut.

"Sorry," I said at last, "do I know you?"

"I'm Krippendore. But everyone calls me Krip. The

last time I saw you, you must have been six years old."

"Odon Krippendore?" Ian materialized at my elbow.

"That's right," he said, thrusting a massive hand through the doorway and gripping Ian's quickly. "I'm a resident painter and the building manager, although I'm not sure which one is more important these days."

Now I remembered the name. On the asset list with Peter's will, Lincoln Banning included the names of managers at each building who made sure the rent was paid, repairs and maintenance were performed, and any other necessary functions. All were employees of the management company Peter created. All of that was part of the estate.

I stepped out of the doorway and led him inside. He stood in the room for a moment, letting his gaze run to the walls, the windows, the desk and files, before coming to rest on "Spring Dance." Krippendore moved slowly to the table. He slid onto one of the stools and reached a stubby forefinger out and slowly rubbed the tip of his finger across the marble base.

"Dear God," he said softly, "how many years since you've seen the light of day?"

"I'm guessing it's been a while," I said.

Without moving his head, Krippendore raised his eyes to me. "Your father was a very good friend and an even better artist. I saw him working on this piece. It was one of his best. His attention to detail and his ability to coax images out of the materials was amazing."

"You say we met before?"

"I was here a few times when your mother would bring you by for a visit. It was as if your father could tap into your youth and draw energy from you. Those were magical days."

I slipped onto a stool across the table. Ian hesitated. I motioned for him to join us. "When did you meet Peter?"

Krippendore tugged at his beard. "It was probably thirty years ago. I was making a decent living, selling my paintings, getting a few commissions, when Peter moved into this studio. Back then this place was as run down as an abandoned tomb. But the lighting is exceptional, with those high windows. The studios were cheap. Half the place was empty. We would bump into each other in the halls." A slow smile crossed his face as he recalled the memory. "One afternoon, I was about to leave. There was a voluptuous woman in Grosse Isle whose husband was away on business. I was going there on the pretense of painting her portrait. Peter appeared at my door with a bottle of cheap wine and a kitchen sink pizza."

"What's a kitchen sink pizza?" Ian asked.

Krippendore roared a laugh. "As in everything but the kitchen sink. Kids today don't know much at all!"

"Go on with your story," I urged.

"Peter was in the mood to celebrate. He just received a huge commission for a piece out at Oakland University. The critics were singing his praises. Life was good. He wanted to share his good fortune. He wanted to learn about my art. He was…alive.

"From that point on, we became colleagues. Often I would stop in to see what he was working on. He would extend the same courtesy to me. I also got some work that surprised me. Later on, I would learn it was due to his recommendations. He was a good man. He was an even better friend."

I sat there, absorbing his words.

"Do you still paint, Mr. Krippendore?" Ian asked.

"Call me Krip. Yes, I still paint. Come up to the third floor and you can see my studio. It's a little dingy, but it's been my home forever now."

"We'll do that," I said.

His eyes dropped to the floor. "I can only imagine the dust and dirt that was in here. The company said this area was always off limits. I could have the crew clean these floors if you'd like. Get them as shiny as the ones in the hallway."

"I'll think about it. So how did you end up managing the property?"

He ran his finger across the base of the sculpture again. "Some suit came to my door one day and made me an offer. A management company had purchased the building. I would keep an eye on the place, get a check each month and no longer have to pay rent for my studio. It wasn't long after that they put good money into the place, fixing it up. Artists kept coming. Space always gets rented out. It's a haven for us bohemians."

"Sounds like a good situation."

"It is. Whoever bought this property recognized the importance of having a place like this for artists. The proper venue can make all the difference in the world when one is trying to create something beautiful, something memorable."

Krip swung off his stool and pulled his gaze from the sculpture. I noticed his eyes went beyond me to the desk and the file cabinets.

"Have you opened the desk yet?"

I shook my head. "We've been cleaning."

He reached over and gently took my hand. "You really should look in that desk, Jamie. I've got to run. I do hope you'll stop by my studio for a visit. And if there is anything you need down here, just let me know."

"I will. Thanks, Mr. Krippendore."

"Just call me Krip. It's much easier."

He shook hands with Ian and headed out. Ian followed him and bolted the door behind him. I turned and studied the desk. The kid stood beside me.

"How did you know his name?"

He shrugged. "There's a listing on the wall by the entrance. Every time I took one of the vacuum barrels out to the trash, I'd read a few. Some of them are the artist names, others the names of their studios. His was unusual. I checked it out online. The guy's got a pretty cool website. Some of his paintings are wild."

This kid was full of surprises. "How wild? Don't tell me we're talking about nude women!"

"Relax, Jamie," Ian said with a grin. "There were some portraits and some landscapes but he had a few surreal ones I thought were cool. Here, I'll show you."

Ian grabbed the laptop and logged into the Internet. Within a minute Krippendore's site was on the screen. He scrolled through the history and biography section and brought up the images he just described. Ian was right. There was a surreal quality to many of the newer paintings.

"I wonder why he only recently started doing these," he said.

"You should ask him. It could be that this style is more accepted now. Or maybe he just got bored painting portraits."

"I will. Next time we're here, I'd like to check out his studio. How much time do we have before we leave? I don't want to be late for practice."

"We've got about an hour."

"Good. You can look at that desk while I go finish up."

I turned on the stool, watching him switch open the secret door and disappear into the storeroom. Turning halfway around now had me facing the desk. Krippendore's comments got me curious. Digging the keys out of my bag, I found the one that unlocked the lid and rolled the top open. Some dust had filtered through the tracks over the years, but it wasn't nearly as bad as I anticipated. There was an old towel on top of the file cabinet. Carefully I gathered up the dust in it. I sat in the creaky wooden chair and ran my hands slowly across the writing surface.

It was a beauty. The oak boards had been carefully stained years ago and the ornate brass fittings across the front gleamed. Beyond the writing area were a dozen little cubbyholes. Some held notebooks and papers. Others contained small paper clips and business cards. Front and center of the desk was a row of slots, big enough to hold a book. There were seven identical books in a row. Each was about two inches thick and encased in a leather cover and binding. My fingers seemed to spark as I rubbed a nail across them. There were several small drawers on either side. Flanking the kneehole were three deep drawers. But what caught my eye from the moment I sat down was a small picture frame on the left.

In that frame was a photo of Peter and me. I must have been about five years old. We were cheek to cheek, staring at the camera, eyes dancing with laughter, wide smiles on our faces. He had the same red hair and green eyes that I do. Okay, maybe his hair wasn't exactly the same shade, but it was close. I didn't remember the photo. There was so much about him I didn't remember.

Pulling the frame to me, I wiped a few dust motes off the glass. We looked so happy. I started to put the frame in my bag to take with me. But it didn't belong with me. It belonged here, in the studio. I laid it face up on the desk and grabbed the camera. Technology made it so easy. I took a couple of shots, then put it back where I'd found it. I pulled the first book on the left from its place and opened it. Once again I was taken by surprise. Instead of notes about sculptures or drawings, I discovered these were journals, written in cursive. It took me three tries to read the first entry.

I have found a new muse, a source of inspiration never before imagined. Gazing upon her features is like opening a door to an undiscovered land. I am seeing things now as if for the first time. Perhaps this truly is the first time. From this point forward, everything I create, everything I design, everything I dream, I will owe to her. It is her approval that I seek. She is the one who brings new purpose to my days, to my art, to my being. I live for her. I have a daughter. And her name is Jamie.

****

On the way to Ian's practice, I swung by the house and picked up Logan. He was happy to see us. The skies had cleared so we went for a long leisurely walk around the neighborhood where the baseball diamond was. Logan easily matched my pace, wandering to check the trees and shrubs, scenting other dogs and the occasional chatty squirrel. I kept thinking about the day's events. I wanted to share this news with someone. But Malone was at work and Linda was on vacation. I pulled out my phone and made the call.

"Hello, Jamie Rae."

"Hello, Bert. Got any dinner plans?"

His laugh always sounded like a snort. "Are you broke again?"

"No, I have money. But I realized that you might be interested in what we've uncovered at the studio so far. We could talk more over dinner. I could cook something."

He laughed again. "You are not known for your culinary talents. If you're cooking, I think I'm busy."

"You're such a smartass, Bert."

"I learned it from you."

"Okay, I won't cook."

"Suddenly my calendar is clear. How about Thai food? I can pick some up on the way over, if that's easier."

"That sounds great. Better bring enough for four. Ian is staying over."

"You'll soon go broke feeding him. What time works for you?"

"How's six-thirty?"

"I'll see you then."

By the time Ian got out of the shower, Bert showed up with enough food for six people. He brought yum talay, a seafood dish with salmon, shrimp and crab meat, lemongrass steak, curried duck, and sesame chicken. There were containers of tom yum, a Thai hot and sour soup, and lots of noodles and rice. We gathered around the kitchen table and passed the cartons around.

Ian wasted no time filling his plate and making the food disappear. Bert and I ate slowly, watching him with amusement. I was still working on my first helping when Ian went for seconds. Bert chuckled and watched. When he was done, Ian took Logan out for a walk down to the park. Those two were becoming inseparable. I put the extra containers away then led him to the office and my desktop computer.

"Malone mentioned that you've made some good progress."

"Yes, I'm pleased with what we've done. There's still a lot of work to do, but it's coming along well. And I thought you'd like to see what we've uncovered."

I let Bert take the desk chair and I stood to the side. Clicking on the files, he watched the videos from the last two days. At one point he stopped the file, moved it backward, and played it again. He took his time going through the photos.

"It's like finding a king's ransom," Bert said. "How many more do you have to open? I know I saw the room, but the scope of this is too much."

"There were fifty-eight crates altogether. We've opened seven crates so far."

"This really is amazing, Jamie." He looked at me closely. "How are you doing with all of this? You seem…nervous."

"Just opening the artwork is one thing. And looking at the drawings, the attention to detail he put into each piece before he ever started working on it, shows a great deal of planning and patience. I don't know how he could do that."

Bert shrugged. "He probably had an image in his mind and planned it out before he began. The cost of the materials may have been a factor. No room for mistakes."

I hadn't considered that. But Bert was still watching me closely.

"What else did you find?"

"Peter kept a journal. I just read the first entry. It's not really about his art. It's more personal," I said quietly. "I brought one home to read, but I'm not sure I should."

Bert got up and hugged me. "I think you'd better read it. Because my guess would be that you're the one he was writing to."

CHAPTER SIX

Wednesday morning was a chance to return to normalcy. Or as close to normal as my life usually gets. Malone seemed to sense my nervous state last night when he came home. He refused to let me talk about the afternoon's events. Instead he found a very satisfying way to occupy my body and my mind until sleep overtook me. In the morning he put together some gigantic western omelets before packing Ian in the car and heading off for a game. Now it was just me and Logan. The sun was shining and there was a gentle breeze keeping it comfortable outside. We walked a couple of miles.

With all the windows open, the house felt fresh. I got to work. There were revisions that needed my attention, email messages to respond to, and even a couple of phone calls to make. I caught Shannon, my literary agent, on the first try.

"Jamie, I was beginning to think you'd disappeared again."

"Sorry. There is a new project that popped up and it's got me preoccupied."

She made a clicking noise with her teeth and tongue. "Don't tell me Malone swept you away for another romantic weekend."

"That's wishful thinking on my part," I said with a laugh.

"So is this going to cause a delay in meeting the deadline?"

"I don't think so. The revisions were almost done before this happened."

"That's good, Jamie. You've been on a roll. I'd hate to see you slide backward. Between the promotions for 'Tightrope Twist' and the drafts of your next two books, I think you're really hitting a good stride. The important thing is to keep it going."

"As long as the ideas keep coming, I should be fine."

Shannon's laughter, a light, frilly sound, trickled across the line. "These last two books weren't from your imagination. You're starting to attract trouble like a redheaded magnet."

"What can I say?"

My second book, which had the working title of "Greed" was a fictionalized version of a true event – a police officer staged his own shooting in order to prevent being laid off due to a budget cut. The third book, which I called "Gone", was the story of Linda's kidnapping. Since I was involved in the investigation and resolution of both cases, it gave me the inside track.

"So, are you going to tell me about this project that's distracting you?"

"It's a little complicated."

That got me another trill of laughter. "Jamie, everything about you is complicated."

I was about to argue the statement when an idea struck. Shannon lives and works in New York City. While a savvy veteran of the publishing business, she also knows people in all walks of life. So I gave her a brief rundown on Peter Richmond, his art, his untimely death and the recent discovery of the studio.

When I was done there was no immediate response.

For a moment I thought the connection was broken. Then I heard Shannon draw in a deep breath and let it out slowly.

"Jamie, you're talking about a potential fortune in artwork."

"I know. That's where I've been recently. We're unpacking things slowly, putting together a catalog so we can get it appraised. Everything belongs to the estate. There are enough crates there to keep us busy for weeks."

"You do realize that you're way ahead of schedule on the drafts for 'Gone'?" Shannon said. "The publishers aren't expecting copy from you for another month."

"That's good to know. But talking to you brings up a question. Or more like a favor."

"What do you need?"

"You seem to know everyone in New York City. And anyone you don't know, I'm sure you could get an introduction in a heartbeat."

"Flattery will get you anywhere."

"Shannon, all you have to do is wiggle a bit more when you walk down the street and men will fall all over themselves to do your bidding. And a few women would too. Some of us have to work a lot harder than that."

Now her laughter was loud. "It's very hard to wiggle when you're wearing a pencil skirt. Are you insinuating that I use my beauty and my body to an unfair advantage?"

"Yes, it's unfair to other women who aren't blessed with your looks. And I sympathize with the men who trip all over themselves to be near you."

Shannon is a knockout. She's about five-foot-eight, with a size two body that she refers to as tall and tiny. She packs a lot of curves in that frame and has shapely legs that she likes to accentuate with short skirts and high heels. Shannon reminds me of a taller but tinier version of Linda.

"I'm wondering if you know any art experts. I have no idea who the lawyers may bring in to view the collection, but I think there would be more experts in New York City than in all of Michigan."

"There are a number of galleries and museums in Manhattan alone. I'll have to give it some thought and see if there is an expert I can recommend."

Before ending the call, I gave her Peter's website information. My knowledge of the art world was very limited, but I trusted Shannon. I expected she could find an expert or two. That might give Lincoln Banning peace of mind when it came time for the appraisals.

I spent several hours on the computer. There were a number of requests for online interviews, a couple of reviews on my first book, and even a few emails from fans. I also spent some time writing up notes on the crates we'd opened. This wasn't for the estate. This was for me. I wanted to have a diary of my own, with my thoughts about Peter's work and my reactions to each day's discoveries.

Logan kept nudging me. We went outside. He wandered the backyard, taking care of business. I realized it was after five. We'd skipped lunch. Malone and Ian were due around six. Knowing how limited my skills were in the kitchen, Malone was planning on cooking dinner. Before leaving, he'd put some chicken in a marinade so it would be ready for the grill when they got back. I went inside and put together a big garden salad. There was a bag of fresh green beans. I cleaned them and set them in a pan just as the guys came home.

"Honey, we're home," Ian yelled as they came up the driveway. He was caked in grime. His uniform was stained with sweat and his hair was plastered to his skull. Logan bounded out the door and bowled him over. A wide smile split Ian's face as he hugged the dog.

"Now that's what I call making an entrance," I said.

Malone stepped over and gave me a kiss. "They had a great game. It went the distance, but we walked away winners."

"How did you do, Ian?"

"I went three for four. A homer, a single and a double

and I grounded out. Malone thinks I need to spend more time in the batting cage."

"Really, Nelson, you don't think he's hitting well as it is?"

Malone shook his head. "Nelson? Jamie, when are you going to give up?"

"I am a very determined woman. I may never give up."

He pulled me close and slid a hand down to squeeze my ass. "Sometimes," he whispered in my ear, "it can be fun if you give up."

"I'll keep that in mind for later."

****

After dinner, Ian started pestering Malone to play catch. This kid lived for baseball. I wondered if part of that passion stemmed from his late father's love of the game. Malone hesitated, content to sit beside me on the picnic table and run his fingers up and down my bare leg.

"Nelson, go and play catch."

"You don't mind, Jamie? We've been gone all day."

I leaned my head against his shoulder. "It's fine. You just cooked us a wonderful dinner. I've got some reading I should do. Besides, you can make it up to me later."

He leaned in and gave me a soft kiss. Under the table, his fingers skittered up my thigh. My body shuddered.

"Oh gross. Get a room! You two aren't going to do that while I'm out here! What about the poor dog! Logan shouldn't be subjected to this kind of behavior."

Ian was standing on the other side of the table, holding two baseball gloves. Logan was at his side. Malone was laughing as he pulled away.

"Someday kid, you will appreciate how special it is to kiss a beautiful woman."

"I can appreciate it now. But I'm not going to do it with witnesses around."

"Ian, do you think Logan doesn't see this kind of

behavior when he's with Linda?" I asked.

The kid blushed and suddenly became very focused on getting his glove on. "I never really thought about it."

"Trust me, Ian. Logan has seen her kiss a man."

"Like I said, I never thought about it." With that he hustled to the far end of the yard. Malone moved away from the picnic table and they started a game of catch. There was a loud smack of the ball striking the leather when Ian was throwing.

I brought out the first volume of Peter's journal. As I read, it became obvious that Bert was right. Peter had been writing this for me. There were no dates in the book, but I could guess from the entries that there were gaps of several weeks or more. Peter wrote about some of the new works he wanted to create. He wrote about things he wanted to share with me. New experiences for me might give him a different perspective. He was anxious for me to grow big enough so we could begin this journey together. And while each passage was compelling and opened the door a little wider on my history, these were not as emotional as that first entry had been.

Engrossed in the book, I hadn't realized the guys were no longer in the yard. Malone appeared beside me with two tall glasses of iced tea. He explained that Ian and Logan were out for a walk. I set the book aside.

"Is that interesting reading?" Malone asked.

"It is. It's like I'm discovering Peter for the first time." I opened the book to the first page and handed it to him. Malone read it and silently handed it back.

"I think I would have liked Peter."

"Me too."

We sat there for a while, just sipping our tea and leaning against each other. Earlier today Malone shared an idea he had for Thursday. Now he confirmed that everything was in place. I realized it was the kind of thing Peter may have done if he was still alive.

"You're a good guy, Nelson."

"Thanks, Jay. Do you think we should hold back on the kisses when Ian is around?"

I laughed. "Not a chance, Malone."

We walked out to the front of the house. Ian and Logan had been gone a long time. Malone was holding my hand lightly. He guided me to the front porch. The concrete was still warm, even though the sun was setting. As we sat there, I heard Logan give a friendly bark down the block. Malone swung his head in that direction. Another dog started barking. I could see two people walking slowly toward us.

"No wonder he's taking the dog for long walks," Malone said quietly.

"What do you mean?"

"Looks like Ian found a girl. And I guess that explains why he took the long shower when we got home and the fact he's wearing clean clothes."

Malone has very sharp eyesight. Even in the fading light, he could see details beyond my abilities. I squinted, trying to bring the images into focus. That didn't help at all. With a sigh, I leaned against Malone and waited.

It was a long five minutes before they reached the house next door. Fortunately the streetlight there illuminated the walk, making it much easier for me to see. Logan was playfully bumping against a black dog almost his size. Ian gave his leash a quick tug and the dog obediently stepped back alongside him. I shifted my gaze from the dog to Ian's companion. What I saw was a cherub's face with a crown of jet black hair pulled into a long ponytail. She was shorter than Ian, but not much. She was wearing a white T-shirt and a pair of very tiny blue shorts. I could hear the slow slap of flip-flops. She and Ian were talking.

I nudged Malone. "Should we go over and say hi?"

"Jamie, let's not embarrass the kid. If he wants to, he'll introduce us."

We waited a few minutes more. The dogs were pulling

at the leashes, so there was still some forward motion. Without hesitating, Ian turned up the driveway. She continued to walk with him. Malone gave my hand a squeeze.

"Be still and be polite."

"I'm always polite," I muttered.

"Except when you're being a smartass," he said as he gave me a knowing glance.

He had me there. "I get your point. I'll be nice."

Logan dragged Ian across the grass to the porch. The dog nuzzled my face, so I scratched his ears. He collapsed in a heap at my feet.

"I want you guys to meet Brittany," Ian said. "These are my friends Jamie and Malone. This is their place."

We stood and shook hands. Up close I could see Brittany was about the same age as Ian. She had a trim athletic build, like someone who spent a lot of time swimming. Her legs were very shapely and tanned. I don't think there was an ounce of fat on her. Did I ever look like that when I was fifteen?

"Ian and I kept bumping into each other when we're walking the dogs. This is Lucy. She's a bit overprotective, but she's real friendly once she gets to know you."

Malone eased a hand out in the dog's direction. Lucy tentatively sniffed his fingers. She jumped back and when Malone didn't move, she eased forward for another sniff. Satisfied that he seemed safe, Lucy allowed Malone to scratch the top of her head.

"Malone, I think you made a new friend," Ian said with a grin.

He nodded. "What kind of dog is Lucy?"

"She's a German shepherd," Brittany said. "Most of them have some tan coloring as well. She's the first one I've ever seen that was all black. We got her a couple of months ago. She was a rescue dog. Sometimes you'd think she's just an overgrown puppy."

Lucy moved on from Malone and was now sniffing my

hands and my legs. Apparently I passed muster as well. From the corner of my eye, I saw Ian smother a yawn.

"It's getting late, kid," Malone said. "You've got practice in the morning."

Ian shot a pleading look at Malone. "I was going to walk Brittany back home. You know, just to make sure she gets there safely."

"It's only about a dozen houses," Brittany said with a hint of anticipation.

Malone glanced at me. Suddenly I found this situation very interesting. I winked at Malone. This was his call. He was the parental figure.

"Okay, but leave Logan here."

We said our good-byes. I took Logan inside. He went right to his water dish, then collapsed on the floor beneath the kitchen table.

Malone appeared behind me. I leaned my head back against his chest as his arms circled my waist. He dipped down and his lips found my neck. Shivers ran the length of my spine as he worked his way up my neck with soft, light kisses. I bit back a moan.

"Want to bet the kid gets a kiss?" Malone whispered.

"Not from me. You're the only guy I'm kissing tonight, Nelson."

He chuckled softly. "I'm thinking Brittany. She'll probably initiate it. You know how demanding those Irish girls can be."

I spun around in his arms. "Wait a minute. I'm Irish."

"Are you saying you're not demanding?"

"Well…"

"…or are you saying that you don't initiate certain behaviors when it fits your mood."

"Nelson, we're talking about Ian, not me."

He had one of those smiles going, just a little bit on the mouth, where the corners are turning up, but his eyes were beginning to spark. It's one of those moments where I lose my train of thought and my resistance vanishes.

"I seem to remember a night last winter when you took the initiative. There was something about a pink negligee, pink nail polish, freshly shaved legs and just a touch of perfume. I'm pretty sure that was you."

Malone had me blushing with the memory now. It was in the early days of our relationship and I was still living in an apartment. My efforts led to a very passionate night. As if reading my mind, Malone drew me close for a kiss. I felt his right hand slide up to caress my face. His left hand slid between us and undid my shorts. The fact that he could do this so easily while kissing me never ceased to amaze me. I felt the cool night air on my buns as Malone slipped my shorts and underwear down. Suddenly I wondered how quickly Ian would return.

"Nelson, what about Ian?"

"With any luck, he's getting that kiss right about now."

I tried to pull away, but Malone's power over me was too strong. "I don't want him to come in and see me like this."

Malone's left hand was now cupping my bare ass. "I suppose I could let you go to the bedroom. That might be a bit safer."

"That's a good idea, Malone."

But he didn't release me. With his right hand, he tilted my chin up. "Do you still have that pink negligee?"

My voice left me. I nodded.

"It's been a long time since I've seen that. I think a fashion show is in order."

At that moment I heard the side door open. With a laugh, Malone released me before Ian entered the kitchen. Somehow I grabbed my clothes and raced down the hall to our bedroom. As I closed the door, I could hear the guys talking quietly. I slipped into the bathroom to freshen up. If Malone wanted a fashion show, I was going to give him one.

Ten minutes later he came into the bedroom. The lights were off. Jazz music floated softly from the clock radio. Three small candles were lit on the dresser, the flames reflected in the mirror, giving a tiny amount of illumination. I was in the doorway that led to the bathroom. One dim light was on behind me. Crooking my finger, I beckoned him toward me. Malone made sure the bedroom door was closed tightly. He took a couple of steps in my direction. I raised my palm to him. Malone stopped. Placing a finger to my lips to indicate quiet, I swayed in his direction.

I was wearing the same silk pink negligee, with the spaghetti straps and the plunging neckline. On my feet were spike heels. A very liberal spritz of perfume was on my wrists, behind my ears, on my neck, and where my panties would have been if I was wearing any. In these heels, I could look Malone right in the eye. Stepping forward, I placed my palm against his muscular chest and pushed him back. He complied. I took another step and pushed again. The back of his legs hit the foot of the bed.

Moving my head to the side, I slid in close, grazing my lips across the stubble of his beard, kissing my way to his ear. My freshly applied lipstick left a dark red trail. I sucked on his earlobe and gave it a tug.

"I want you naked on your back on the bed," I whispered. It was a true act of willpower to step away, but somehow I managed it.

Malone complied. His clothes became a small pile on the floor. He kicked them over to the wall so I wouldn't trip on them. How considerate. Malone slid onto the bed on his back. Pillows piled beneath his head gave him an excellent view. He'd asked for a fashion show. I was damn sure going to give him one.

With an exaggerated swing to my hips, I backed toward the doorframe. I could hear the music. Hoping there was just enough light from behind me and from the candles, I began to dance. My hands slid over my body, imitating the way Malone often touched me. With my fingers at my waist, I began to pull the fabric up, revealing more leg.

Leaning against the doorframe, I pulled one foot off the floor and pressed it against the door. I flexed the muscles of my calf, then eased my foot back to the floor. Turning my back on him, I swayed to the rhythm of the music. Looking in the mirror, I could see Malone's expression over my shoulder. His eyes were wide and the look of wanton desire filled his face. I bent over, as if to touch my toes. Then I stood up quickly, my red hair whipping back and forth.

"Jamie," Malone whispered.

I spun to face him, a finger to my lips again. He reached for me. I moved closer to the bed, trying desperately to walk gracefully in those shoes. I hesitated for a moment before kicking them off. Now I was next to the bed. Malone reached for me again. I shook my head. Instead I teased the strap off my right shoulder. It slid down my arm, flashing him a glimpse of my breast. I caught the strap and slowly put it back in place. I repeated the movement with the left strap. Malone's eyes followed. They gleamed when I flashed him again.

Kneeling on the bed beside him, I took his hand and raised it to my lips. I kissed the back of his hand. Then ever so lightly, I slipped his forefinger into my mouth. A low groan escaped him. Pulling my mouth back, I took his hand and laid it on the pillow beside his head. Reaching across him, I lifted his other hand. Once again I kissed the back of his hand. And once again, I slipped my mouth around his forefinger. Placing his hand by his head, I leaned in close to his ear to whisper again.

"Taste me, Malone."

Still wearing the negligee, I moved on top of him. Malone knew what I wanted. He guided me up until my hands gripped the headboard. The silk gown floated beyond my waist, draping to mid-thigh. I could feel Malone's hands on the fabric, on my thighs, on my ass as he pulled me to him. Now it was my turn to fight back the groans as he began to work his magic on my, kissing me, licking me, coaxing me.

My impromptu fashion show was as much of a turn on for me as it was for him. I've never behaved like this with anyone but Malone. It was easy to see the effect I was having on him during my dance. Now with my body shuddering in delight with his attentions, I pulled one hand free of the headboard and reached back, finding him fully at attention. As the spasms overtook me, I slid down his body and straddled him quickly.

One sensation overtook the other. Malone's body reacted with mine. We quickly found a stride, racing each other to the finish line of pleasure. Moments later I collapsed on top of him. I vowed to have a fashion show more often.

"You are an incredible woman," he whispered in my ear.

"You bring out the best in me, Nelson."

"Promise me one thing."

He was lightly stroking my body, his fingers trailing across the silk fabric. It was starting to get me heated up once again. I pulled him closer.

"What's that?"

"Next time you want to put on a show, let's do it when the kid's not here."

"Do you think you can handle a next time?"

Malone flipped me onto my back. He paused as he was sliding on top of me to respond. "Bank on it."

CHAPTER SEVEN

We didn't go to the studio Thursday morning. Ian's team was practicing for a couple of hours late that morning. Since Malone was off work, he took him there and then to the batting cages to work on his swing. I focused on my writing and doing some more reading of Peter's journal. It was getting to the point where I could get through more than a few pages without getting misty eyed.

Malone and Ian returned around three in the afternoon. After taking a quick shower, Ian poked his head into the office and said he wanted to take Logan for a walk. The dog was sprawled on the floor by my feet.

"I took him for a long walk this morning," I said.

A forlorn look crossed Ian's face. "But that was hours ago. The poor dog rarely gets to have fun."

Malone was leaning against the wall in the hall. "We're leaving here at four-thirty."

"See," Ian said, somewhat desperately, "the poor guy is going to be here all alone for a few hours. The least I can do is take him for a walk to the park."

"I don't suppose this has anything to do with Brittany," Malone said.

The kid's face fell. "Well, she babysits a family down the block. She's supposed to be done by now. So there is a chance we might bump into her."

Malone attempted a scowl, but I could see the smile playing at the corners of his mouth. "Don't make me come looking for you. Be back here before four-thirty."

"Yes! C'mon, Logan, let's roll!"

The dog let out a bark and scrambled out the door. I rocked back in my chair and folded my arms across my chest.

"You are so bad," I teased. "Does he know about tonight?"

"No, I only told him that we were going to the studio late and we were meeting some VIPs. And I said we'd probably grab dinner downtown."

"This will be quite a treat, Mordecai."

He pushed off the wall, giving his head a slow shake. "I don't think I've ever heard that name before, Jay. But you do get points for creativity."

"Are we talking about the name or last night?"

"Both," he said, reaching down to draw me up into his arms.

"That's a good answer, Mordecai."

Before things heated up too far, I pushed him away and returned to my computer. I had a few things to finish before we headed downtown. Malone disappeared into the living room. Since we started dating, I noticed he was reading a lot of mysteries and thrillers. Sneaking a peek, I found him sprawled on the 'aunt' with the latest James Rollins novel. I ducked back into the office.

Just before four-thirty, Ian and Logan returned. I shut down the computer. As I entered the living room, a car parked out front. Ian was about to head for the door when I caught his arm and turned him toward me.

"You'd better go wash your face, young man, unless you want to do a whole lot of explaining in a hurry."

Malone chuckled behind me. Ian just stared at me with

a blank expression.

"You have lipstick on your cheek." I caught a faint whiff of perfume, too.

He bolted down the hall. Malone rolled off the 'aunt' and went to open the front door.

"You are right on time," he said.

Ian's mother, Terri, and his sister, Caitlin, walked inside. They had visited the house a few times before so Terri would know what the living arrangements were like when Ian stayed over. Logan wandered around the visitors, checking them out.

"Where's Ian?" Caitlin asked. At thirteen she was almost as tall as Ian. She was hovering between tomboy and womanhood, with a thick head of dark brown hair like her mother's drawn back into a loose plait. She was wearing a white tank top and bright red shorts, showing off a lot of leg.

Malone cracked a grin. "He's just getting cleaned up."

At the mention of his name, Ian appeared. He gave his mom a quick hug. "What's going on? I thought we were leaving to go to the studio."

"We are. Jamie and I thought your mom and Caitlin would like to see what you're working on. And since we're going to be downtown anyway, I thought we'd take in the Tigers game."

Both Ian and Caitlin lit up like a Christmas tree.

"Are you serious?" Caitlin asked.

Malone pulled the tickets from his pocket. "Let's go!"

****

Unlike a traditional office building, there was still a lot of activity at the studio. Many artists work when the inspiration strikes them, so they don't keep nine-to-five hours. Others were gearing up for a season of art shows, where they would travel to different parts of the country for exhibits. I unlocked Peter's studio and guided everyone inside. After Malone secured the outer door, I let Ian be the tour guide. Malone drew me over to the desk, watching the delighted expressions on Terri and Caitlin as they viewed "Spring Dance". They followed Ian into the storeroom. Although their conversation was muted, I could still hear the amazement in their voices.

"This is a good thing you're doing tonight, Mordecai."

He pulled me close. "It's no big deal, Jamie."

"Yes, it is. You know how tight things are for Terri. Both these kids are baseball fanatics. This is the kind of outing they're rarely going to enjoy."

"They are a family, Jamie. They should get a chance to do fun things like this."

"I think we're making them part of our family, Mordecai."

He gave me a soft kiss. "We keep adding to the family, we're gonna need a bigger house."

"Family doesn't necessarily have to live together."

"Good point."

Ian brought the others back into the studio. He secured the storeroom and we headed out, making sure the outer door was locked. It was a short drive from the artist building to the stadium. Malone parked in the deck and we joined the crowd flowing into the ballpark. It was early, but we didn't want to rush it. Our tickets were on the third base line, only about five rows up from the field. The kids rushed down to the seats so they could watch batting practice.

"Malone, I want to pay you for our tickets," Terri said as we settled in.

He was next to me on the end of the row. Terri was beside me and the kids were next to her. Malone looked at me for a second, gave me a slow smile then raised his eyes to Terri.

"No."

"Malone, I insist. I can't expect you to buy our tickets."

"No."

She turned to me. "Jamie, talk some sense into him. These tickets aren't cheap, especially this close to the field. We could have gotten bleacher seats."

"I've learned not to argue with Malone," I said with a straight face.

A wave of laughter greeted this comment. "And I've learned how to be stubborn from Jamie. Just relax, Terri. This is our treat. You can invite us over for a barbecue the next time I have the weekend off."

"You've got a deal, Malone."

I glanced past her at the kids. Caitlin and Ian moved down to the railing where they could see the players up close. Several of the Tigers were stretching and playing catch. I realized that more than one was looking in our direction. We watched them warm up. The kids moved back to the seats as the Tigers were finishing up. Caitlin had just sat down when one of the players whistled and lobbed a ball in her direction. She bounded out of her seat and snagged the ball in mid-air. With a grin she brandished it at her brother.

"He threw it to me," she said gleefully.

"Yeah, but he was looking at Mom."

Terri blushed at the comment. "It's more likely he was looking at Jamie."

"Maybe Caitlin reminds him of his sister." I wasn't sure what else to say.

"Who wants some food?" Malone smoothly changed the subject. "This place has everything. Hot dogs, pizza, burgers, ice cream and anything else your heart desires."

Caitlin gave her mother the ball for safekeeping. She joined Malone and Ian in search of food. I had a feeling no one was going hungry this evening.

It was a perfect night for baseball. The Tigers did their part, beating the visiting Cleveland Indians by a score of 9 to 3. The kids were hoarse from cheering by the time we headed for the car. On the way home I glanced over my shoulder and saw Ian and Caitlin slumped against Terri, sound asleep. She had a very contented look on her face. For a moment, I envied her.

****

Friday morning found us back at the studio. The guys were ready to go as soon as I got the video equipment set up. Maybe it was because we'd been gone for the last two days, but we all felt a sense of anxiousness, an anticipation that I couldn't quite describe. Pulling up my list on the laptop, I called out the next crate number.

"How about a change of plans, Jamie?" Ian said.

Was this kid getting cocky? Maybe he was getting too comfortable with our arrangement? "What's wrong with the way we've been doing it?"

"The next three crates on the list are all kind of small. Those are ones you and I can open on our own. I just thought we should take advantage of Malone's muscles and have him help open the bigger crates, before he goes off to work."

I smacked him on the arm. "I've got muscles."

"I didn't say you didn't. But Malone's got more."

"The kid's got a point," Malone said.

"Fine, Alphonse, you can pick out a big crate and I'll go pull the details from the file cabinet. That way we can still keep the catalog accurate."

"Alphonse? Jamie, you need to get a better list." He handed me a scrap of paper with a code number on it.

"Shut up, Malone."

Both guys were grinning as I went back to the studio. By the time I returned, they had positioned the large crate in front of the tripod. I quickly logged the number and the name into the computer and got behind the camera. This crate was over five feet tall. Rather than pry off the top, Malone elected to work on the front, wedging his bar in from the side. The guys followed the same pattern that had been so successful earlier, with Ian moving slowly behind

86

Malone, prying off the wooden panel. Once the wood was free, Malone swung the panel out of the way and propped it against the wall. Ian pulled out armloads of straw, piling it to the side. Malone slit the burlap covering. Together the guys eased the sculpture out into the light.

This was a brass piece, titled "Limber", and it was a variation of the "Spring Dance" work. Three characters, each over four feet in length, were joined at the hands. Each head was tilted at a different angle, as if the dancers were laughing in delight at their circumstances. I let the video run and moved around snapping pictures. Once I was done the guys moved the sculpture back into a corner and left the crate alongside it.

We made steady progress. With Malone's help, the guys opened six more large crates. The time flew by. After a brief stop for some food, we got right back to it. Malone assisted with one more crate before dashing off to work. Ian lined up four more crates, smaller in size but just as challenging to open. I set the video camera, then followed him with the smaller pry bar as he mimicked Malone's efforts. Each piece was carefully viewed, photographed and videoed. Together we would lift them from the packing crate to the worktable, film all the details, and arrange it for display.

It was after four o'clock when I decided we'd done enough for one day. All told twelve crates had been opened, their precious cargo revealed to the light of day for the first time in over two decades. Ian was sweeping up the last of the straw. I had just sent the video files to my home computer and to Lincoln Banning when someone knocked on the outer door. Quickly we turned off the lights in the storeroom and swung the secret door shut. Ian was closing up the rolltop desk as I went to open the door. Releasing the lock, I pulled the door open partway, letting it rest against my shoulder. It's a good thing I did that, because what greeted me was so stunning that I almost fell over.

She was standing there with a gentle smile on her face. Wearing modest heels, she was still an inch shorter than me. Her hair was the color of sand, with a few blonde highlights sprinkled in for good effect. She was wearing a linen suit in an ivory color, the skirt not quite reaching her knees. The silk blouse shimmered in the light, giving me the impression she was sparkling with energy. Her face was free of wrinkles or shadows. Her makeup was perfect. Even from three feet away, I caught a whiff of her delicate perfume.

Vera.

"Well, Jamie, are you just going to stand there or are you going to invite us in?" Her voice was strong, with just a hint of annoyance.

I hadn't noticed there were other people behind her. Lincoln Banning and Helen Gaines flanked her. Drawing a breath, I pushed the door open and stepped back. Vera reached up and put her hands on my shoulders. She leaned close, but not near enough for an embrace and did the air kiss routine toward each cheek. Then she swept past me into the room, trailing the attorneys. She canted her head in Ian's direction.

"And who is this handsome young man?" she cooed.

Ian wiped his palms on the back of his shorts and came forward. I introduced him to everyone. Vera was sizing him up like a pony at the rodeo.

"I didn't think you were coming to town for a week or more."

Vera fluttered a hand at me as if she were shooing away a pigeon. "Well, once my friends heard about the discovery, they insisted on expediting our trip. We flew to Hawaii. Another friend suggested I use his private jet to come to the mainland. I'd forgotten how tedious international travel can be."

"We did try and call you, Jamie," Lincoln Banning said, "as soon as I knew Vera was in town. I left several messages on your phone."

"It must be in my bag. We've been busy."

Vera walked around the studio, stopping in front of the worktable with the lone sculpture on it. Slowly she brought one hand up to her mouth. No one said a word as she stared at it. Vera reached out and delicately ran her fingers over the figures.

"I remember this one. The lines were giving him fits. He just couldn't seem to get it right. Peter was such a perfectionist."

"That he was," Lincoln said. "Even after all these years under wraps, this is an amazing piece of art."

Vera spun to face me. "Linc said there are many more. I'd like to see them."

"They are in the storeroom." While we'd been talking, Ian moved over by the hidden switch. I nodded and he unlocked the door and swung the panel open.

Vera led the way. I followed with Lincoln right beside me. Helen Gaines walked a few steps further back. Ian stayed by the doorway.

"Linc said you are making a catalog," Vera said, speaking softly.

"We are."

I explained the process and the videos we had taken so far. The group slowly made its way down the aisle, taking the time to examine each piece. Helen remained out of the way. I glanced over my shoulder in her direction. Her face was etched in wonder. I could relate.

"There are so many," Vera said breathlessly. "I had no idea."

"We've opened nineteen so far. We'll resume work on Monday. If we can stay on schedule, we should have them all open and ready for the experts in two more weeks."

"Once we have everything documented, I can have the videos professionally edited and we can make a very detailed catalog," Lincoln said.

We moved back out to the studio. Ian switched off the storeroom lights and secured the door. Once again we gathered around the worktable. I was studying Vera. It looked like her energy was fading.

"I'm afraid jet lag is catching up with me," Vera said. "I'll have Benjamin drive me out to the hotel."

"Who's Benjamin?" I asked.

Vera gave me a gentle smile. "He's the limousine driver. My friend insisted that I use his private car and driver while I am in town. I'm staying at the Hotel Baronette in Novi. Come for dinner. Eight o'clock. The hotel has an excellent restaurant."

All I could do was nod. With the two attorneys flanking her, Vera made her exit. Ian appeared alongside me.

"Are we all done, Jamie?"

"Yes, I think we've just been dismissed."

****

We were almost back to the house when I heard a phone ring. I'd been so preoccupied with thoughts of Vera's sudden appearance that I'd forgotten Ian was with me. It took a moment to realize it was his cell phone ringing. Sheepishly, he pulled it from his pocket and glanced at the screen. A flush of crimson colored his cheeks as he answered. I tried not to eavesdrop. The conversation was brief. I glanced at him as we exited the freeway.

"That was Brittany. She just invited me and Logan down for a barbecue."

"And I suppose her parents will be there?" I tried to make my voice sound stern.

He fidgeted in his seat. "C'mon, Jamie, be real. Her whole family is going to be there. They have a pool too. I'm sure you can come, but I thought you were going to dinner with that Vera lady."

"That is no lady. That's my mother."

"You call your mother by her first name?" His expression was questionable.

I blew out a breath and eased the car into the driveway. "It's a long story. What time is this barbecue? Does your mom let you go to things like this?"

"Brittany said six. And my mom is cool with it. She and Caitlin are doing some movie thing tonight, just the two of them. I've got time to get cleaned up and take Logan for a walk." He was giving me the same kind of hopeful, sad puppy look with those big brown eyes that Logan would use when he wanted a treat.

"Okay, you can go. But I want to meet this family before I leave."

Shortly before six, we walked down the block to Brittany's house. I met her parents and her younger brother and sister. An above ground swimming pool dominated the backyard. Tucked into a corner by the rear of the house was a large charcoal grill. A thin ribbon of smoke rose from the chimney.

"Don't worry about Ian, we have enough food for an army," Brittany's father, Tom, said.

"That's good to know. I'm still getting used to how much this kid can eat."

He nodded. "With three kids of our own, we always stock up. What time does Ian need to be home?"

I was unaccustomed to this maternal role. But I knew he had a game in the morning and he needed a good night's rest. "Eleven. I should be back by then as well, but he has a key."

"We'll take good care of him," Tom said. He glanced over at Ian. He and Brittany were standing close, petting the dogs and talking quietly. "I'll keep a close eye on him."

"Now that sounds like a very good idea."

I was heading out the gate when Ian called my name. I turned as he approached with Logan tagging along. Without a word he wrapped his arms around me in a quick hug. I hesitated for a moment and felt my arms go across his back.

"Thanks," he whispered in my ear.

"Have fun, but not too much fun."

Walking away I realized that was the first time he'd ever hugged me.

Two hours later I was in the Hotel Baronette's dining room. Recalling Vera's reaction to my shorts and T-shirt ensemble earlier, I'd taken some time to get ready for dinner. I was wearing a sleeveless linen dress in a pastel shade of turquoise along with a pair of black leather sandals and gold dangling earrings Malone gave me for my birthday. I'd curled my hair, applied some lipstick and a touch of makeup, and spritzed on just a little perfume. This was about as feminine as I get. The restaurant manager, acting as host, steered me to a special table and informed me Vera would be down shortly. She appeared ten minutes later.

"Jamie, darling, you look so much better. But where is this new man I've heard about? I expected him to join us for dinner."

"Malone's working. He's on afternoons."

Vera perused the menu. As if by magic, a handsome young waiter appeared at her elbow. She flashed him a smile, ordered a vodka martini and the Lake Huron trout. I opted for tonic water with lime and the farm salad, which included apples, walnuts, and cherries. She raised an eyebrow at me as the waiter departed.

"No wine or alcohol with dinner?"

"I don't drink anymore, Vera. And before you ask, I don't miss it."

She considered it and gave me a slow nod. "Very well. You do look good, Jamie. I think your life agrees with you."

"I'm happy with the way things are. Are you happy, Vera?"

"Yes, I am. I get to live the life I've always wanted. I'm surrounded by friends, by people who share many of the same interests and desires. Some of them are very generous. They enjoy my company."

My eyes flicked to her dress. It was probably from some French or Italian designer and worth more than my entire wardrobe combined. It was a soft red number, with a tightly cinched waist and a flared skirt. I didn't know if it was a combination of diet and exercise or the result of a plastic surgeon's knife, but she wore it well.

We were quiet until the waiter returned with our drinks. Vera sipped hers and nodded her approval. The dining room around us was busy, but there were no occupied tables close by. She was staring at me with what could only be described as a smirk on her face.

"Go ahead and ask me, Jamie. It's obvious that you have something on your mind."

"How come you never told me more about Peter?"

Vera took a moment to choose her words. "It was too difficult. He meant so much to me, and to have him taken away so suddenly, I've never been able to get over it."

"Even after all these years, you're still not over him?"

"People deal with grief in different ways. You might say Peter ruined me for other men. I think that's why I could never stay in a relationship very long after that. I was always afraid of having my heart broken again."

"What about you and Bert? You were married to him for more than five years."

The mention of Bert brought a genuine smile to her lips. Her entire face glowed. "Bert was my favorite man. He captured a special place in my heart. I think he still has it."

"So you never talked about Peter because it was too hard. But why didn't you ever tell me about the estate?"

She paused as our entrees were placed before us. The waiter hovered while Vera tasted the trout. After bestowing a smile on him, he disappeared into the background.

"Lincoln Banning helped with the estate. Once he assured me that there was enough money to take care of us each year, I never gave it much thought. Until you turn thirty-five, everything remains in the trust. I have no idea how much that is worth or what impact these new works will have on it. That's still three more years before we have to know.

"Once you were off to college, I thought about telling you. But you'd earned a partial scholarship and I was pleased to see you willing to work for your spending money. I just told you the rest of your tuition was covered. The estate paid for it. When you graduated and started working, I didn't see the need to burden you. Peter would have wanted you to earn your own way."

"So you were protecting me?"

She reached over and took my hand. "No, Jamie, I was protecting me. I can't think about the estate without thinking about Peter and our lives together. He was everything to me. You were everything to him. His whole spirit lit up whenever he saw you."

"Will you do something for me, Vera?"

"Of course I will."

"Will you tell me about him now?"

What looked like tears formed in the corners of her eyes. "I'll tell you everything."

CHAPTER EIGHT

Ian was sitting on the front stoop with Logan when I turned into the driveway a little after eleven. Once out of the hotel, I'd kicked off my sandals. Something about driving barefoot always relaxes me. I slung my purse over my shoulder and grabbed the sandals, letting them dangle by the straps. Walking barefoot across the lawn toward the porch, I couldn't help but smile.

"And where have you been, young lady?" Ian said, using a deep comical voice.

"I was with my mother. When did you get back?" I sat beside him on the stoop and scratched Logan's head.

"About five minutes ago."

I took a closer look at his face. He was struggling to hold in a smile, but his eyes looked merry, as if he'd discovered the secret identity of a superhero.

"Did you have a good time?"

"We had a great time. Mr. Murphy grilled chicken, potatoes and corn on the cob. After dinner we played catch for a while then got into a crazy game of pickle."

"What's pickle?"

He gave me a look like I was crazy. "Basically it's two people playing catch with a runner between the bases, trying to go back and forth and not get tagged out. Everyone was playing, so we had three bases and three runners. It was hilarious!"

"That sounds like fun."

"It was. After that, we went for a swim and horsed around in the pool. Brittany and I took the dogs for a walk. Then Logan and I came home."

I turned to look at him more closely in the dim light. "Did you kiss that girl good night?"

"She kissed me."

"Are you complaining?"

A sheepish grin crossed his face. "No way! I'm just hoping she'll do it again."

"It seems likely." I stood up and brushed off the backside of my dress. "I'm going inside. The mosquitos must love redheads."

We ducked inside. The house was cool, with the ceiling fan turning slowly and the air conditioner on. Logan went down the hall, heading for Ian's room. The kid stifled a yawn. Then to my surprise he gave me another hug and followed the dog.

Malone was due in a little while. I checked the doors, left a light on in the kitchen, and went to get ready for bed. Thoughts of my conversation with Vera were still running through my head. After scrubbing off my makeup, I pulled on a little satin negligee that barely reached my hips. The dark green color was one of my favorites. Turning down the bed, I slid between the cool sheets to wait for Malone. I didn't have long to wait. As if summoned by the thought, he appeared.

"Good evening, Alphonse."

He gave me a long, soft kiss. "How was dinner with Vera?"

"It was better than I expected. We had a nice meal then went up to her suite and talked for quite a while."

After Vera's surprise appearance at the studio, I'd called Malone to alert him. Seeking moral support, I'd tried getting in touch with Bert as well, but he wasn't available. With Linda and Vince still out of town, that was the extent of my support group.

"I guess Vera can easily afford a suite," Malone said as he sprawled beside me.

"The funny part is she rarely pays for anything."

Malone hesitated. "How does that work?"

"It's her social circle. One of Vera's friends owns the hotel, or at least, a large part of it. Somewhere along the line, he offered to put her up at any one of his hotels. In exchange, she does a very glowing review of the venue, the restaurants and the accommodations."

"Vera's a writer?" Malone asked with an incredulous look on his face.

"No, she phones it in to a columnist at one of those exclusive society sites. The columnist cleans it up, and Vera gets credit for it, using a code name. But all of her high society friends know it's her, so they wine her and dine her, give her free lodging and the use of their private jets and limos."

"That's remarkable."

"Yes, it is. Apparently she can go wherever the wind takes her and she has friends. She got into town today and tomorrow night, she's going to some formal society fundraising event. She'll get fitted with a gown tomorrow, wear it for the event and send it back. She'll give the boutique some rave comments and help promote the fundraiser with a little publicity and never think twice about it."

During my discourse, Malone propped himself up on one elbow. Now he was slowly tracing a finger along my side, tickling me through the satin fabric. I realized he was still wearing jeans and T-shirt.

"You sound a little envious, Jamie."

I shook my head. "No way, Alphonse, I work hard at my writing. I covered society events when I was with the newspapers. Some would say Vera is taking advantage of her friends, but as long as her comments are favorable, I guess they don't mind."

"I guess they don't. But I think you could make a comparison between her writing and yours." He leaned in and kissed me again.

Maybe he was being playful, but I was too impatient. Twisting onto my side, I knocked his elbow away and rolled him onto his back. Still kissing him, my fingers clutched the T-shirt and aggressively pulled it up to his shoulders.

"Shut up, Malone. I don't want to discuss Vera. It's been a long crazy day. I want sex and I want it now."

I was about to slide on top of him when Malone took charge of the situation. Just that quickly, he reversed our positions. Now my hands slid underneath his shirt, feeling the warmth of his skin, the rigidity of his muscular chest. He silenced any comments, pressing his mouth firmly on mine.

No matter how many times we've had sex, or how recently it's been, Malone somehow triggers desires in me that border on animalistic. This was a perfect example. Ten minutes after he'd come home, my body was responding to his presence, to his touch, to his kiss. I could feel my heartbeat increasing, my temperature rising, my skin flushing with anticipation. My hands slid across his chest until I was clutching his back.

Somehow Malone managed to lose his jeans. I felt the negligee slide up.

"Jamie," Malone whispered, "I've been thinking about this all day."

Wrapping my legs around him, I drew him closer. "Stop thinking about it, Alphonse, and start doing."

"Yes ma'am."

I shuddered as he entered me. This was not a time for foreplay. We both wanted it this way. I clutched him to me, urging him faster. Malone was quick to respond, driving me to the point of no return. The start of a scream reached my lips and he quickly mashed his mouth on mine. The last thing he wanted was for Ian to come banging at the door to check on me. My fingers twined in his hair as my body bucked in delight. I peaked. And before my heart could even begin to catch up, I did it again. Malone slipped a hand beneath me to squeeze my ass as he reached his own peak. Slowly he pulled his lips from mine. When I could breathe I started to laugh quietly in his ear.

"You sure know how to shut a girl up, Malone."

"When the kid's gone, Jamie, you can scream all night long."

"That sounds like an offer I'll take you up on, Alphonse."

"I consider that to be a promise."

****

Logan and I were just about to leave late Saturday morning when the doorbell rang. Brittany was standing on the porch, wearing a Tigers T-shirt and a pair of skimpy white shorts and a wide smile.

"Hi, Miss Jamie, I'm glad I caught you."

I cringed at the formality. "Just call me Jamie. Caught me for what?"

"Well, Ian mentioned he had a game today and that he and Mr. Malone were going early for practice but he thought you'd be going to watch. So I thought I'd surprise him and go cheer him on, if that's okay."

Such youthful enthusiasm was infectious. "That's fine with me."

We hustled Logan into the car and swung by her house to alert her parents. Once we got to the field I went to find a seat in the bleachers. Brittany took Logan up near the backstop. Within two minutes half the guys on Ian's team were staring in her direction. Ian came over and looped his fingers through the chain link fence. Brittany put her fingers on his. They talked for a moment until the coach called his name. Sheepishly Ian trotted out into center field. Brittany walked up to the bleachers and took a seat next to me.

"Can I ask you a question, Jamie?"

"Sure."

"Are you and Mr. Malone married?"

A smile touched the corners of my mouth. "No, we live together. We moved in together at Christmas time. We'd dated a little while before that."

"He seems like a really nice guy. Ian told me about how he's known Mr. Malone for a long time and how he's helped him since his dad died."

"Malone's a good guy. And you don't have to call him mister. It makes him feel odd."

"I'll try and remember that. Ian said he really likes spending time with both of you, that you treat him like an adult, not like a kid."

I thought about that. "Well, I look at him as a little brother. I think Malone does too."

"Whatever it is, he seems to like you both a lot."

"That's good."

As the game got underway, I discovered that Brittany was a tomboy. She understood the game and loudly cheered the action. When Ian got a double at his first at bat, Brittany put two fingers in her mouth and whistled shrilly. The kid tipped his helmet at her. I glanced toward third base where Malone was in the coach's box. Even from the bleachers I could see the grin on his face as he slowly shook his head.

Ian's team played well and by the sixth inning had a four-run lead. The coach rotated some players, making sure everyone got a chance to play. Even though Ian was no longer in the game, Brittany watched with the same level of enthusiasm. After the game, the team went their separate ways. Malone took us out for a leisurely lunch at a burger shop near the field. Ian reluctantly went to his house, where Terri had a few dozen chores for him. Malone dropped him off on his way to work. I took Logan and Brittany home.

With the house empty, it was a perfect time to do some domestic chores. I ran a couple of loads through the laundry, and put together a grocery list. I left Logan behind and went to stock up on food. He was ready for a long walk when I returned.

Before leaving for the game this morning, Malone had fixed up a vegetarian pasta salad, filled with rotini noodles, fresh veggies, and large chunks of cheese. I filled a plate and sat at the picnic table, enjoying the meal. Logan patrolled the yard, chasing a couple of squirrels who knew exactly how far he could go. After all the activity of the past week, this was exactly the kind of quiet evening I needed.

****

I was nervous about brunch Sunday morning. Vera insisted that we meet her at noon. I couldn't even decide what to wear, changing my outfit twice. Malone finally took me by the shoulders to halt my jitters.

"Jamie, you need to relax. We're going for a nice meal and some pleasant conversation."

"That's easy for you to say, Elwood. You don't know what Vera is like."

He stepped into the closet and pulled out an ivory colored shift trimmed in lace. I'd been pacing back and forth in my underwear for the last ten minutes.

"Wear this and some heels and you'll be perfect."

I was about to argue when I realized he was right. Since when did Malone become so knowledgeable about ladies fashions? I glanced at him. He was wearing a gray silk blazer over a white dress shirt and navy blue slacks. There was a little flash of navy in the jacket that tied it all together. Malone looked like he just stepped out of a men's catalog. I realized that while most of the time he was in jeans or his uniform, the dressier clothes he owned were very sharp. When the occasion demanded it, Malone could step up.

"You've got five minutes, Jay, and we have to go."

"Shut up, Elwood."

He merely stood there, dangling the dress in front of me. Attempting to give him a disgusted look, I pulled the shift from the hanger and slipped it on. I stepped into some modest ivory heels and was ready.

We arrived at the restaurant right on time. It was an upscale place in Bloomfield Hills, known for the talented chef and the five-star cuisine. It wasn't uncommon to spot some of the movers and shakers from the area here. The hostess beamed a smile and guided us to a table for four. On the way I saw two media personalities, a retired athlete, and one of the county executives. I'm sure there were other famous people about, but I didn't recognize them.

Malone had been holding my hand since we got here. Now he gave it a squeeze as we sat down. "Jamie, you really do need to relax. I can't remember ever seeing you this tense."

"Elwood, there is something I have to tell you."

"You can tell me anything, Jay."

I took a deep breath. I should have warned him about this before, but I thought there was more time. Clutching his hand, I let the words tumble out. "I've never brought a guy to meet Vera before."

"You're kidding?" What could have been a playful look crossed his face.

"No, Malone, I'm not. She left when I started college and the guys from high school never stuck around very long. It's so rare that Vera comes to town, it's just happened that I have never been dating anyone seriously when she was here."

Of all the reactions I expected, laughter was not one of them. Yet that was exactly how Malone took the news. He just stared at me, letting a quiet chuckle escape.

"So I am the first guy you're bringing to meet your mother."

"Yes. Now do you understand why I'm so nervous?"

"No, I don't."

"Malone…"

"Jamie, what we have is very strong. Despite some challenges—"

"What challenges?"

"—like your stubbornness, I think we have a pretty good thing here. You're an independent woman. So despite what Vera may think of me, I don't see things changing between us."

Malone leaned over and kissed my cheek. "So breathe, Jay. Let's just be ourselves and enjoy this nice meal."

He was right. I was worried about nothing. Suddenly all the tension left my body. I was reaching for my coffee cup when I sensed someone coming toward us. Glancing up I saw Vera slowly passing other tables, pausing to chat with patrons as if they were old friends. And linked on her arm was a familiar figure.

Bert.

I shot Malone a quick glance. "Did you know he'd be here?"

"No, I didn't. Does it matter?"

"Actually, it might make things easier."

They reached the table. Vera did the air kiss thing with me and turned her full attention on Malone. She took both his hands in hers, leaned up, and actually kissed him on the cheek. Bert pulled out a chair for her. After she sat, he shook hands with Malone. I got a quick paternal bear hug and kiss.

"Well, isn't this a lovely place," Vera cooed. "It came highly recommended and it looks like the reputation is well deserved."

"Surprised to see me?" Bert asked me with a grin. Vera was talking quietly to Malone, no doubt doing an interrogation.

"That's an understatement."

There was a mischievous glint in his eyes. "She called me late Friday, in dire need of an escort for that society thing last night. When she mentioned brunch with the two of you, I thought I'd tag along, just in case you needed a buffer."

"She was always easier to deal with when you were around, Bert."

"I can keep her distracted."

I realized now why there was a gleam in his eye. "Are you telling me you were a booty call?" I whispered.

He didn't respond, merely picked up his coffee cup and sipped it. I knew for a fact that Bert still had strong feelings for Vera. Apparently it went both ways.

Vera expertly steered the conversation around the table. She ordered a variety of entrees and cajoled the waitress into bringing extra portions so we could share. We heard about last night's soiree, which sounded like every high roller in the three metropolitan counties surrounding Detroit was in attendance at. The food was outstanding. The waitress paused at our table with a bottle of champagne. Vera peeked at the label, nodded her approval, and accepted a fluted glass. Bert hesitated a moment, his eyes flicking across the table at Malone. I caught the tiniest inclination of his head. Bert took a glass as well. The waitress hesitated until both Malone and I declined.

"I understand you and Jamie have become quite close," Vera said, gently placing her champagne flute on the table.

"Yes, ma'am." Malone reached over and took my hand. "Your daughter is a very special and talented woman."

"That she is," Bert said.

"I must admit to being a little worried about her with these recent—escapades," Vera said, her voice taking on just a hint of urgency.

"You know, I can hear what you're saying. And Malone isn't the one to blame. If anything, he's been there to help me when things got serious."

Vera fluttered her eyes at me. "I am very thankful for that. Still, it seems that you've started taking chances recently. I just hope this isn't going to be a habit."

"Jamie is very intelligent and extremely resourceful," Malone said. "I don't think she goes looking for trouble."

Bert cleared his throat. "Look at it this way, Vera. If Jamie hadn't followed her own intuition, she and Malone might not be together now."

"That is a very good point."

The conversation returned to more mundane topics. We lingered over extra cups of coffee and some miniature pastries. Bert asked for the check. The waitress explained that it was already taken care. We all looked at Vera. She offered a sweet smile and daintily patted her lips with the linen napkin. Bert and Malone both left a generous tip for the waitress. Together we went outside.

As the valet was bringing the cars around, Vera leaned close. This time she pressed her cheek against mine and whispered in my ear. "He's adorable."

Bert and Malone shook hands. Vera stepped back as Bert enveloped me in a hug. As he walked toward his car, Vera took both of Malone's hands in hers.

"So you really only use your last name."

He nodded. "That's all I need."

She looked him up and down for a moment, then leaned in and kissed his cheek again. "I think you're right."

****

We were home enjoying a few minutes together before Malone left for work. He was sprawled on the 'aunt' and hooked his fingers around my wrist as I was walking by. The sofa worked its magic and I was suddenly in the arms of a very passionate man.

"Well, you survived meeting the parents, Elwood. Although I must admit Bert's arrival was a welcome

105

surprise."

"Vera is an attractive woman, Jamie. I doubt she spends much time without an escort, unless she wants it that way."

"I think they were rekindling a few passionate flames last night."

Malone shifted, drawing me up until he could look me in the eye. "I can think of a few flames I'd like to rekindle."

"How much time do you have, Elwood? Because lately, having a quickie has not been in the cards for us."

Malone didn't respond verbally. Instead he drew me closer and began kissing me. First it was a gentle kiss at the corner of my mouth. Then it was stronger, more heat, more passion full on the lips. His hands were on my waist, holding me close. My eyes started to go out of focus. I felt one hand slide up my back and tug the zipper of my dress down in agonizing slowness. I didn't care that it was mid-afternoon that the sun was shining, the curtains were open, and the dog was sprawled beneath the windows. I wanted Malone and I wanted him right now.

As if reading my mind, he caressed the exposed bare skin of my back. Deftly, he unhooked my bra. He traced the ladder of my spine down to my tailbone with a solitary finger. My heart was racing. My arms were wrapped around his neck. I could feel his body responding in my favorite way. I reached down and unhooked his belt and opened his slacks. Just as I was reaching for him, Malone pulled his head back.

"I really should go to work, Jay."

"Malone! You can't be serious!"

"I am. You're not a 'quickie' kind of woman."

My eyes flicked to the clock on the mantle. "What the hell, Malone. Today I'm exactly that kind of woman. Don't leave me like this!"

"We could rekindle this later."

"Bullshit, Malone. We're kindling now!"

A devilish look flashed in his eyes. "A quickie you want, a quickie you will get."

I started to move off him, but he held me in place astride him. Malone snaked a hand under my dress and yanked my panties to the side. From his attentions moments before I was definitely ready. Crying out, I felt him slide into me. Now both of his hands were beneath my shift, clutching my ass. We found a rhythm in a heartbeat. Twenty yards beyond the window, cars were driving by. Neighbors were walking on the sidewalk or riding bicycles. All they had to do was turn this way to see me riding Malone. That knowledge drove me over the edge. I peaked, clenching my lips together. Malone thrust higher, digging his fingers into my ass. He let out a low moan. I was still riding the crest of my own orgasm when I felt his wash over me. Gasping for breath, I collapsed onto his chest.

"One quickie as requested," he whispered.

"Thanks, I needed that."

"You weren't the only one."

Tenderly his hands were stroking me, caressing my ass and the back of my legs. One hand drifted up from under my dress to find the exposed skin of my back. My heart was finally slowing down, but I realized it was no longer mine. I thought back to the comments he made at brunch.

"Do you really think I'm a special woman, Malone?"

He turned and kissed me. "Yes, I do. You are a very special woman, Jay, with many talents. Sometimes you take chances, but that's part of you."

"You're pretty special yourself, Elwood."

A sly grin touched his lips. "Thanks. But I meant what I said."

"That I'm also intelligent and resourceful?"

"Well that too, but I meant that I have to go to work."

CHAPTER NINE

Monday morning came way too soon to suit me. After Malone went to work Sunday, I had just enough time to change into some shorts before Linda and Vince stopped by. They looked incredibly happy and relaxed. The week in Montreal had done wonders for both of them. Logan practically did backflips when he saw Linda. She thanked me repeatedly for taking care of her guy. I declined an offer to join them for dinner. It was obvious they wanted to be alone.

Ian returned after seven. He unpacked his clothes, grabbed an apple from the refrigerator, and scowled at me. He slumped into a chair at the kitchen table.

"Logan's gone."

"Yes, Linda and Vince came home this afternoon."

He gave me an exasperated look. "But Logan's gone."

"Of course he's gone. He was only staying here because she didn't have time to put him in a kennel before their vacation."

Ian's gaze went to the floor. He started bumping his foot against the table leg. I knew what was going on. He looked so sweet I couldn't torment him for long.

"She's waiting for you."

His head snapped up. "What?"

"Brittany is waiting for you. She stopped by before you got back. I told her Logan was gone but that you were due anytime."

"Why didn't you tell me?"

"I just did."

"But I thought, you know, without Logan, I didn't have a reason to go by there."

He was so cute. I reached across the table and punched him in the shoulder. "She likes you, Ian. The dog was just your wingman. Go see her."

"She likes me?"

"Be home by ten."

He bolted from the table. Halfway across the kitchen, he whirled around. "Can I stay until eleven?"

"We've got an early morning. Let's make it ten." I got up and went to the sink.

"C'mon, Jamie, how about just a little bit later?"

"Ten-thirty. That's my final offer."

Ian stepped over and gave me a hug. "Deal."

With a bang he was out the side door and jogging down the driveway. I rinsed my glass from the iced tea and started to laugh. I had seen four different men that day and been hugged by each one. This was very unusual for me. But I was starting to like it.

When Malone returned after work, he was very amorous. Apparently our afternoon quickie had been replayed in his mind during most of the shift. He was not to be denied. I would have even considered it, since I was just as aroused as he was.

Now it was a sleepy trio headed down to the studio. We were taking two cars. Ian was slumped against the passenger door in my car, sound asleep. I wondered if he was dreaming of Brittany.

Arriving downtown, Ian grabbed the cooler with our lunch and drinks. Malone and I followed. I unlocked the door and stepped inside. Ian followed and Malone swung the door shut, twisting the lock in place. I was almost to the desk when I realized something was different. Before I could say a word, Ian dropped the cooler with a crash.

"It's gone!"

"Spring Dance", the first sculpture we'd unpacked, the one that had graced the worktable in the studio since that moment, was gone.

****

Someone was banging on the outer door. Ian remained perched on the cooler. I sat at the rolltop desk, my arms folded across my chest. Malone unlocked the door and swung it open. Lincoln Banning walked quickly inside, his eyes flashing around the room in disbelief.

"I called the Detroit Police. A detective from the robbery division should be here shortly," he said. "Is anything else missing?"

"We checked the storeroom. The other sculptures we'd unpacked are all there," I said quietly. I was having a hard time speaking, whether from anger or frustration I couldn't tell.

"What about the crates you hadn't opened?"

"We counted them," Ian said. "We have the right number and as far as I can tell, nobody moved them. They must not have been able to find the release switch for the door."

"That's assuming whoever took the sculpture knew about the storeroom," Malone said.

Before anyone could respond there was another knock at the door. Malone stepped over and opened it. There was a tall black man wearing a black suit with a narrow pinstripe and a stocky Hispanic man wearing khakis and a navy blue sport coat. Both were holding up identification wallets that included their badges. Malone motioned them inside. We all gathered around the worktable.

"I'm Detective Rayburn and this is Detective Suarez."

He looked around the room at the four of us and his eyes came back to Malone. "You want to be the spokesman?"

Malone showed his own badge and handled the introductions. Detective Suarez pulled out a notebook and jotted down our names. He also dug out a digital tape recorder and placed it on the table. After identifying himself and his partner, he read all our names into the record. Banning took over and gave a rundown of our recent activities. He stopped when we got to this morning's discovery.

"Let's start with the easy stuff," Rayburn said. "Who has access to this studio?"

"Only Jamie and I have a set of keys," Banning said. "Oh, and the building manager, Krippendore, has a set as well, but he's only supposed to access this area with my permission first. I don't know if he's here today or not."

"When was the last time you saw this piece?" Rayburn asked.

"It was Friday afternoon around four. Jamie, Ian and I were here, along with Mrs. Richmond, that's Jamie's mother, Vera, and my associate, Helen Gaines."

"Can you describe the piece that's missing?"

"We can do better than that," I said. While we were waiting, I'd pulled the camera equipment from the file cabinets. The pictures of "Spring Dance" were cued up and waiting. Both cops looked at it closely and noted the details. "I don't have a printer here, but we can send you the file."

Banning raised a finger. "I have the files too. I'll have color copies made and delivered to the detectives."

"That will work," Rayburn said. "So you're telling me that there are only three sets of keys to this place. What about the other tenants? Were they around this weekend?"

Surprisingly, Ian piped up. "There was a big gallery exhibit on Saturday. Most of the different artists in the building have works on display. They usually draw a steady flow of people all day long."

"How do you know that?" Rayburn asked with obvious curiosity, not expecting the kid would have such information. It reminded me not to discount Ian's observations because of his youth.

"There were posters on the doors last week advertising it. I asked Krip about it and that's what he told me. It started at noon and lasted until about six."

Malone grinned at the kid. "Why don't you run upstairs and see if Mr. Krippendore is around?"

"You got it, Malone." Ian pushed off the cooler where he'd been perched and headed out the door.

Rayburn looked at Malone. "Want to take a look at that door?"

The two of them walked over and inspected the door from both sides. I looked at Banning. He was slowly drumming his manicured fingertips across the table. Suarez was over at the exterior wall, gazing up at the windows where they met the ceiling. He stepped back to the worktable and pointed a stubby finger at the camera.

"You mind if I use that for a second?"

"Go right ahead."

He pointed the camera at the windows high up on the wall and used the zoom feature to bring it into focus. Slowly he panned across the windows. Satisfied he dialed it back to the previous setting and gently placed the camera back on the table.

"You'd have to be a scrawny-assed Spiderman to get through that glass. And there's no evidence those windows have been opened in my lifetime."

Rayburn nodded as he rejoined our group. "There are no signs of forced entry on that outer door. No scratches, no indications that anyone tried to get inside without a key."

"So what does that mean?" Banning asked indignantly.

The three cops exchanged a look, but no one said anything. Suarez merely shrugged his shoulders and raised his palms slightly. "Right now, we don't know what it means."

I was about to comment when Malone caught my eye. He didn't have to say a thing. His expression said it all. Now was a good time for me to keep my mouth shut. So I did, with some degree of difficulty.

Malone had left the door ajar. Ian pushed through it, followed by Odon Krippendore. The burly man stepped into the room and hesitated. At the sight of Lincoln Banning, he stopped, as if searching his memory for a name to go with the face.

"I didn't tell him anything," Ian said, "just that we needed him down here."

"Good move," Malone said.

Banning walked over and shook the painter's hand and gave his name. Krippendore relaxed a bit, his eyes on the two detectives. Banning explained who they were and that the statue was missing. Krippendore looked at the empty table. His eyes searched out mine.

"When was the last time you were in here?" Rayburn asked.

"One day last week, when I met Jamie and young Ian."

"So you haven't used your keys to come into the studio? Maybe you wanted to check on their efforts, see what else they found?"

Krippendore shook his head. "No. I hoped that when everything was unpacked that I'd have a chance to view the collection. Many of us in the building are curious."

"Tell us a little about this weekend. Did you see anyone unusual hanging around? Was anyone asking questions about this studio?"

"The building was swarming with people on Saturday. It was like an open house. Many of the artists put out food, even a little wine for the patrons and visitors." A soft smile played on his lips. "We get our share of regulars and more than a few hangers on. It's a regular exhibit, the third Saturday of each month."

"Who handles the security for the building?" Suarez

asked.

"I'm always the last one out. It was around eight o'clock Saturday night."

"I thought this exhibit thing ended at six," Suarez said.

"It did. But there's about a dozen or so artists who like to get together afterward and talk about the day. We brag about the number of works we sold, how many beautiful women flirted with us and any inspirations for new work. So it was close to eight when we left. I'm the last one out. I make a round, check to make sure all the windows are locked and all the entrances are secured before I set the alarm. It was a normal night."

"Who has access to the alarm system?" Rayburn asked.

"Only Mr. Banning and I do."

"What are you getting at, Detective?" Banning asked. I saw his shoulders go back as if he were getting ready to fight.

"That if your security system is any good, chances are someone broke in here during the day on Saturday."

Rayburn asked for a list of all the tenants. Krippendore offered to provide that and to show the cops where each artist studio was. After the cops left, Malone and Banning had a quick conversation. The lawyer just kept nodding his head in agreement. Then he checked his watch and hurried out for an appointment. Malone made a call. A solemn Krippendore returned. Ian and I took Krip into the storeroom to show him the other pieces we'd already unpacked. Some of his gregarious spirit returned as he wandered around the room. He left when Malone ended his call.

"What's going on, Cassidy?"

Both Ian and Malone laughed. "Cassidy? What's next, Sundance?"

"Hey, I'm not giving up on this. Besides, it helps break the tension."

Ian boosted himself up onto the worktable. Malone pulled a water bottle from the cooler and threw it to the kid. He snagged it in midair without really looking at it. Malone brought me one to share. I realized how hot and stuffy the studio was. Maybe it had been that way all along, but today it seemed worse.

"Mr. Banning agreed that we need a better security system. The one for the building doesn't have any video cameras, beyond the front door and the parking area. The system only tracks the two access cards. So we're going to have the storeroom and the studio monitored. There's too much at stake here not to do it right."

"So who did you call, Cassidy?"

"There's a service I've dealt with before. The company is very reputable. The owner himself will be down within an hour and he'll get everything in place quickly. Outside of the three of us, no one else will be able to tell what kind of security measures you've added."

None of us were in the mood to work. Ian and I ran over to Pegasus, a restaurant in Greektown, to pick up an early lunch. We came back with kabobs, fries, Greek salad and a few treats from Astoria Bakery for dessert. We pulled stools up to the worktable and were just about to start digging in when the security guys arrived.

Malone handled the introductions. "Jamie, this is Wyatt Donohue. He's going to make sure everything is taken care."

Wyatt looked like something out of central casting. He was almost six foot tall with wavy brown hair, chocolate brown eyes and a thick, muscular build. He had a chin that looked like it was chiseled from granite. The only feature that was odd was his nose. It appeared to have a ninety-degree bend to it.

"Malone wasn't kidding when he said this building was old. But don't worry we'll have it set up in no time." His voice was creaky like a door hinge that needed oil.

"You're setting this up with battery backups as well?" Malone asked.

Wyatt gave him a wounded look. "Do I tell you how to

chase bad guys?"

Malone laughed and showed Wyatt the rooms. Ian and I moved back to the table and started on lunch. Wyatt pointed at one of his guys who carried an extension ladder and a toolbox. The guy jumped to work. The others quickly followed. Malone joined us.

"These guys look serious," Ian said.

"Yes, they are. But when they get done, we'll know if anyone sneaks in here."

"What exactly are they doing?" I asked.

"Although we don't think anyone got in that way, they're wiring contacts on all of the windows. You can still open them during the day. Just close them at night in order to set the alarm. Wyatt is going to install cameras that will focus on the door areas and cover the storeroom and the studio. The idea isn't to scare away intruders with an alarm bell, but to catch them in the act on video."

"How complicated is the code?" Ian asked. "In the movies you always see someone break it quickly with a four digit code."

"This isn't the movies, kid. Wyatt has something better than a keypad with a code. He's got a remote control unit that looks just like the one for your car."

"Okay, so what's the cameras gonna be hooked to?"

Malone grinned at the kid. This kind of bantering between them had become a familiar scene since Ian started spending time with us. It was enjoyable to watch.

"Wyatt is going to set the cameras up with a recorder here. He's also installing a system where he can access the live feed at his office. And it will be uploaded to a remote server every twelve hours."

"But only if the system is on?" I asked.

Malone must have read my mind. I was flashing back to the first day we'd been here and when passion interrupted our work. He shot me a sly wink and nodded. "Yes, only if the system is activated."

Blushing, I focused on lunch. If Ian noticed, he didn't

say anything.

****

Wyatt Donohue and his crew were gone. Malone was on his way to work. There were two remote units for the video surveillance system. I'd given one to Malone and hooked the second one on my key ring. Malone told me he didn't explain what he had in mind to Banning. Given the situation, the attorney agreed that he didn't need to know what was going on, as long as he could still access the rooms if necessary.

Ian polished off the last of the macaroons from the bakery. "Are we going to do any work today? Since we're already here, we should do something."

I swiveled around to look at the file cabinets and the rolltop desk. "I just don't have the heart to unpack any crates. But there are drawers I still haven't opened."

"What do you have in mind, Jamie?"

"You take the laptop into the storeroom. Enter the crate numbers in the sequence that makes the most sense to you."

"Like the ones you and I can open on our own, and the ones we can have Malone help us with?"

"Yes, that's it exactly. Then you go to the file cabinet, find the corresponding file and enter in the details. Arrange the files in the same order."

"Okay. What are you going to do?

"I'm going to look through Peter's desk."

Ian beamed me a smile. "Let's get to it."

His energy and enthusiasm could be contagious. I spun to the desk and began slowly going through the drawers. One was a double drawer, perfect for hanging folders with invoices, correspondence, and notes not related to a particular piece of art. I read some of the correspondence, trying to recall Peter's voice. It wasn't happening.

Another folder had some yellowed newspaper

clippings. I saw the familiar banner of the Detroit Free Press on several of them. These referred to art exhibits Peter participated in when his career was just taking off. Another stack mentioned pieces he had been commissioned to create. There was also an article describing a collaborative effort with several artists who were trying to revitalize the downtown Detroit area. I took my time and read them all.

After going through all the drawers, I didn't know if I was any closer to Peter or not. It was like doing research for a character. There were some traits I could recognize and a few glimmered in my memory. From my conversation with Vera the other night, I had a few bits more. But could I ever really know him? He'd been gone forever. I rocked back on the chair, lost in my thoughts.

"Did you go through the whole desk?"

I spun around. Ian was at the worktable with the laptop in front of him. I'd been so engrossed in my thoughts, I hadn't noticed him there. He drew a stack of files from the cabinet and began putting them in order.

I swept my hand toward the old oak desk. "Every drawer has been examined."

"Yeah, but did you look in those little cupboard things?" He gestured toward the back of the desk where the lid rolled up.

"I'm guessing he stored paper clips and stamps there."

"Boy, some detective you are. Those could be perfect hiding places for clues."

I flipped a pencil at him. Ian laughed and caught it. He turned his attention back to the files. With a shrug I began to open the small cupboards.

"Rubber bands in this one, and oh, what a surprise, paper clips. This one has plain white envelopes with his logo on the left corner. And this one here…"

The cupboard was about six inches high and six inches across. When the door popped open, I froze.

"What is it, Jamie?"

I didn't answer. My voice left me.

Ian appeared beside me. Gently he reached into the cupboard and drew out its contents. Turning slightly to the side, Ian blew on it, sending a little cloud of dust toward the floor. He wiped the edges with his fingers, then wiped his fingers on his T-shirt. With great care he set it on the desk between my hands.

It was a square box, wrapped in the type of paper you'd use for a child's party. The paper was faded, yet you could still see the images of colorful balloons floating around a white script that read "Happy Birthday". With trembling fingers, I picked it up and turned it around, looking at each side as if expecting a clue to the contents.

"Aren't you going to open it?"

I gulped to get my voice back. "It might not be for me."

He reached into the cupboard and pulled out a small envelope that had been beneath the package. My name was written across the front of it. I set the box down and worked a fingernail beneath the flap of the envelope. The front of the card was an explosion of colors, like a fireworks display. Inside was a simple message.

"May all your birthday wishes come true. You are the sparkle in my eye, the warmth of my smile, the glow in my heart. Love always, Daddy."

Ian had stepped back to let me read the message in private. I wiped my eyes with the back of my hand and passed him the note. From the center drawer I pulled a letter opener. Carefully I slit the tape around the wrapping paper. Inside was a cardboard box. I pried open the lid and slid the contents out.

"It's a wooden box," Ian said, peering over my shoulder.

"Not just any box. This is a puzzle box. I used to love to put puzzles together when I was small. Peter would sometimes help me." I handed it to him.

He tried to open it without success. He shook the box lightly and we could hear something rattle inside. "So how do you open it?"

"That's the trick. Some of these boxes require a number of pieces being moved in the right order before the lid slides off. This may take some time."

"I'm curious what will be inside."

"Yeah, I'm wondering too."

CHAPTER TEN

After dropping Ian at practice, I swung by Linda's place. This was her week off before the summer school classes started. She had chased Vince off to work and spent the day cleaning her house and doing laundry. I found her on the deck in her backyard, sipping a glass of lemonade. She poured me a glass while I told her about the day.

"That's unbelievable! How could someone break into the studio?"

I shrugged. "That's what I can't figure out. Malone has some suspicions, but he's not sharing yet. It's frustrating."

Linda tossed her thick head of curls back and studied me for a moment. "What are you thinking, Jay Kay?"

"I'm just thinking of doing some research."

"What type of research?"

I looked down and scuffed the toe of my tennis shoe on her deck. Logan came over and rubbed his head against my leg. "The usual kind of research where I make a few phone calls, reach out to my old contacts and see if anything makes sense."

"Why don't you wait and see what Malone finds out?"

"His way might not turn up anything. I can't just sit

still."

She shook her head and laughed at me. "You are so pathetic. Why can't you just admit that you're too damn stubborn to wait?"

"All right, I'm too damn stubborn to wait. Are you coming to the studio in the morning?"

"Of course I am. I'm dying to see all of these beautiful pieces your dad created."

"Well, you might like this one." I reached into my bag and pulled out the puzzle box and the card. Linda's eyes grew soft as she read it. Twenty-five years later, the sentiment on the card was still powerful. I handed her the box.

"I've seen these at art shows. Some of these are easy, maybe one or two moves. But this one is incredible."

I studied the box while she held it. There were at least four types of wood, determined by the different colors. Each side formed a pattern. I watched Linda slide one strip of wood on the right side forward. It moved about two inches and stopped. She pushed the strip beneath it in the opposite direction but it wouldn't budge. Linda fiddled with it a few minutes before giving up and handing it back.

"What do you think is inside, Jay Kay?"

"I hope it's not chocolate."

We made plans to meet in the morning. I picked up Ian and went home. Ian hit the showers, then disappeared to Brittany's house for dinner. After that big lunch, I wasn't hungry at all. I went to my computer and pulled up my contact lists.

When I was working as a reporter, I'd made it a practice to keep the details on any of the people I interacted with on a regular basis. I'd broken it down into folders with different professions. There were attorneys, judges, cops, business people, contractors, editors, and other reporters. Flipping through the lists, I started making calls. It was interesting how quickly I fell back into reporter mode. I was chasing an idea, just a glimmer of a thought.

Two calls later, I had a new lead. Three more calls and I found someone in the know. Not only that, but they were willing to make an introduction. Now it was time to hurry up and wait. I spent the time online, doing more research. It took an hour before my phone rang.

"I would like to speak with Miss Jamie Richmond," a deep, cultured voice said when I snatched up the phone.

"This is Jamie Richmond."

"A mutual friend suggested it would be our best interest to meet. Are you familiar with the Townsend Hotel?"

I bit back a smartass reply. Everybody in Motown knew that swanky spot in downtown Birmingham. "Yes, I've been there before."

"Tomorrow evening at six-thirty you will find me in the Rugby Grille. I will have an associate present. You may have one hour."

"How will I know you?"

There was a pause and a dry chuckle. "That will not be necessary, Miss Richmond. I will know you. Will you be alone?"

I couldn't help but mimic his tone. "I will also have an associate present."

"Very well, I will see you tomorrow evening."

With a click, he was gone. Before I could lose my nerve, I hit the speed dial number for Linda. She answered on the second ring.

"Bring a change of clothes with you tomorrow. We have a meeting in downtown Birmingham after six."

"With who?"

I gulped. "We're meeting with Harrison Mundy."

"Is that a name I'm supposed to know?"

"Sorry, sometimes I forget we don't always swim in the same information pools. Harrison Mundy is alleged to be one of the greatest art thieves of all time."

"Jamie!"

"Bring a dress and some heels. I'll see you in the morning."

I knew better than to say anything to Malone about my meeting. It was entirely possible nothing would come of it. And the last thing I wanted to do was have Malone get upset with me. By the time he came home, Ian was fast asleep, a gentle snoring emanating from his room. Images of Brittany were probably dancing in his head. I was in bed, wearing just a sheer slip of a nightie and a splash of perfume. Malone eased quietly into the room.

"Hey, Jamie."

"Hello, Cassidy. How was work?"

"A little quiet for a Monday," he said. The room was dark, with only a little moonlight coming through the blinds. "What are you wearing?"

"Not much. Do you think I'll get chilled?"

"Somehow I doubt that very much." He shed his clothes like a magician and slid beneath the sheet. I expected him to slide on top of me but Malone had other ideas. We were on our sides, facing each other as he started kissing my neck.

"Wow, Cassidy, have you been thinking about this all night?"

He paused and moved his lips to my ear. "Jamie?"

"Yes, Cassidy?"

"There are times for talking and there are times for love. Which one do you think this should be?"

Before I could answer he nibbled on my earlobe. Malone knows the effect that has on me. If he does it long enough, I can't even remember my own name.

"No more talking," I gasped.

"Good answer."

Malone rolled me onto my back. He balanced his weight on his knees while his hands were busy sliding up the nightie. In the pale moonlight, I could see his smile as he touched my bare skin. Slowly he lowered his body onto me. My arms and legs automatically wrapped around him, drawing him closer until we were one. He was right. We didn't need to talk. Our bodies knew exactly what to do. Soon we were racing together, dashing toward the finish line and victory. It was too close to tell for sure, but I think I got there first.

We fell asleep afterward, curled up in each other's arms. That was how I wanted every night to end.

****

Tuesday morning was bright and hot. Linda arrived wearing a pair of shorts and a bright red T-shirt. She hugged me first, then gave Malone a quick squeeze. She hesitated when she stood in front of Ian.

"Oh, why not," she said softly. She threw her arms around his shoulders and rewarded him with a brief hug too.

The kid flushed as red as her shirt. "Wow."

Malone poked him with an elbow. "If you ever expect that to happen again, you'd better keep that to yourself."

"Yes, sir. But I don't think any of the guys would believe it anyway."

Ian loaded the cooler into Malone's Jeep and then climbed aboard. Linda got in my car and we headed downtown.

"Did you tell Malone about our meeting?"

I shook my head. "I want to see if Mundy knows anything. There's no sense getting Malone riled up if it turns out to be nothing."

"How did you find this guy anyway?"

I explained to Linda about the rumors that often circulate courthouses and police stations. Legend had it that Harrison Mundy was a third generation master thief. Supposedly his training was from both his father and grandfather, who were notorious for planning the most elaborate robberies anyone could imagine. No security system was safe from them. They covered the globe, looking for new adventures. Many of the capers were bankrolled for a large percentage of the goods value from a fence. Others went into private collections at an exorbitant fee. A few were reported to remain in the family, a legacy to be shared by the trio.

"How long have these guys been in the thievery business?"

"No one knows for certain. I think Harrison is in his late sixties. His grandfather passed away years ago. No one knows about his father."

"Weren't any of them ever caught?" Linda asked.

"I don't think so. There may have been suspicions, but no charges were ever filed. That's part of the planning. The story is that they were meticulous."

"It sounds like this is going to be a very interesting day."

"You could say that."

At the studio, Ian was the tour guide. He showed Linda the secret panel for the storeroom and slowly walked her to each of the pieces we had unpacked. Malone and I set up the cameras and the computer.

"Ready to go to work, Noel?"

He gave me one of those low voltage smiles. "That sounds like one you should save for December, Jay. Let's get to it."

I'd given Linda instructions on the way down. She picked up the camera while I focused the video camera. The guys started on one of the crates, following their pattern. Soon another piece of art was brought forward into the light of day. Linda stood there in awe.

"What is it called?" she whispered.

"This is called 'The Lovers'. It's a sandstone carving. You can see the two figures, drawn together in a kiss." I nudged her and pointed at the camera in her hands.

Linda began to slowly circle the worktable, taking pictures from each angle. "You could tell that just by looking at it?"

"No, that's the description and the details that are in the files."

The guys moved the crate to a position along the wall. When the filming was done, Malone carried it over and settled it on top.

"This is like Christmas morning," Linda said.

"Yes, it is."

With the extra set of hands, the guys quickly opened another crate. As soon as the sculpture was displayed on the worktable, Ian would grab a broom and gather up the old straw and any splinters of wood. Then he and Malone would prepare the crate along the wall and move to the next box.

By early afternoon we had unpacked ten crates. We broke for lunch, digging out pieces of cold roast chicken, fresh fruit, and cheese from the cooler. By following Ian's strategy, the guys opened the largest crates. When Malone left to work his shift, I stepped in with Ian while Linda handled the cameras.

"Each one is completely different," Linda said as we hoisted a forty pound bronze statue from its resting place.

"Some of the files include notes as to how Peter created them. That sandstone carving we opened this morning was something he worked on slowly from a large block of stone. Some other pieces he started working with a mold to get the general shape he wanted."

"Jay Kay, you're starting to sound like an art expert."

I smiled at the comment. "I'm no expert. But it's intriguing to find out more about the process. I'm also learning more about Peter."

"He was a very talented man."

Ian snagged the camera and moved around the sculpture, framing his pictures. When he was done he gestured at the next crate. "Should we keep going?"

"You're such a slave driver," Linda teased.

He grinned. "Jamie's paying me. I don't want her to complain if we don't get enough work done today."

"Let's open two more and then we'll pack it in," I said.

"That sounds like a good plan to me," Linda agreed.

We opened fourteen crates in all on Tuesday. Linda helped Ian sweep up the excess straw and put the tools away while I sent the video files to my home computer and to Lincoln Banning. After locking up the cameras and the desk, we headed for home. I made sure the security system was on before locking the deadbolt on the outer door.

I mentioned to Ian that Linda and I had to go out for the evening. I was about to offer to drop him at his mother's house when he raised a finger with a smile.

"Have you told my mom yet?"

"No. What evil plans are percolating in that teenage brain?"

"It's nothing evil. Brittany's parents were supposed to be going to a concert, so she was going to be babysitting her kid brother and sister. I could go help her out."

Linda winked at me while doing her best to hold back a smile.

"Call her, but I want to make sure this is okay with her parents."

In a blink, he had Brittany on the phone. I could hear the conversation going back and forth for a minute. Ian handed me his cell phone. There was much laughter on the other end as I spoke with Mrs. Murphy. She agreed that Ian could stay there and help out entertaining the younger kids. Apparently their next door neighbor was an honorary grandmother who would also keep a close eye on things.

"Looks like our evening plans are set," Linda said.

"Let's hope it's worthwhile."

****

We arrived at the Townsend Hotel five minutes early. Something told me that Harrison Mundy was not the type of man who would like to be kept waiting. The receptionist directed us to the Rugby Grille. As we approached, I could see the place was about a third full. Maybe it was too early in the evening for society's elite to have dinner. There was also a bar at the other end of the hotel that seemed to be doing a brisk business. At the hostess stand, an attractive young woman wearing way too much makeup and perfume gave us a vague smile.

"Are one of you Miss Jamie Richmond?" she asked in a breathy voice, as if she'd just run up two flights of stairs wearing stiletto heels.

"That's me. We're supposed to be meeting someone."

She nodded twice. I noticed that her hair didn't move when she did that. "Your party has already arrived. Right this way."

We followed her across the room to a private corner table. I noticed there was no one else within twenty feet of it. A distinguished looking man with a full head of silver hair was already seated. As we drew closer he rose smoothly and extended his hand.

"You must be Miss Richmond."

"Please, just call me Jamie," I said, lightly taking his hand.

"Thank you, Jamie." He turned smoothly to Linda. "May I presume that you are Miss Davis?"

She took a step back in surprise before taking his hand. "I prefer Linda."

He flashed a charming smile at both of us. "I would be pleased if you will call me Harry. Let us sit down."

I noticed the place setting that was to the right of his chair was disturbed. Linda took the seat on his left and I took the one opposite him. Before we were settled, an exotic looking beauty with silky black hair came over from the bar and took the empty seat.

"This is Jocelyn."

She smiled and nodded. A waiter appeared with a tray of food.

"I took the liberty of ordering a few simple dishes to go with our conversation." He glanced up at the waiter.

"What did you bring us, Phillip?"

The waiter gave a quick nod. "We have chilled prawns, foie gras and duck tacos. These are specialties of the house. I'm sure you'll enjoy them."

"Perhaps a drink would be in order?" Mundy said.

I ordered tonic water and lime. Linda asked for a glass of chardonnay.

"How did you know who I would bring along?"

Mundy flashed a smile at me that was almost blinding in its brightness. "I prefer to know as much as I can about the people I am meeting. Even though I am retired, I like to keep my senses sharp."

"So you've retired from a life of crime?" I asked.

"Really, Jamie, you know I am not a criminal. I was never convicted or even accused of an illegal act. I have many interests that have been cultivated over the years. Is there a particular area of my expertise that appeals to you?"

I took a moment to study him while phrasing my response. He was very handsome, with the dazzling smile, smooth complexion, and thick silver hair. He was fit and trim, perhaps a little taller than me, which would put him about five-foot eight-inches tall. I had no doubt the suit he was wearing was tailor made for his frame. He spoke with an educated tone. His nails were manicured. Jocelyn motioned to Linda at the food before us. She sampled the foie gras.

"I would like to know about art thefts, particularly the best way to do it. Did you always have a buyer in mind?"

He chuckled dryly. "Jamie, what makes you think I know anything about thievery?"

"Perhaps in your studies of the subject, you learned how thieves work."

"That is a very good answer," he said. "May I presume your interest stems from the recent discovery of your father's work?"

"He really did do his research," Linda said quietly.

"You may," I replied somewhat sullenly. It dawned on me that I was mimicking his precise way of speaking. This wasn't like me at all. And it was obvious that Mundy was in complete control of the conversation and the situation. Disgusted with myself, I speared a prawn with my fork and focused on sawing it into bite sized pieces.

"Miss Davis is quite correct. Before I accepted your inquiry, I researched your background. It is somewhat unsettling to discover how much information can be so readily available on the Internet."

While nibbling a chunk of prawn, which was incredibly good, I saw Jocelyn carefully put a sample of each appetizer on a plate and hand it to Mundy. He smiled his thanks, gently squeezed her hand, and set the plate squarely before him. Before tasting anything, he sipped from a highball glass filled with a clear liquid and ice. I caught a whiff of juniper.

"How's the gin?" I asked.

"Smooth as always." He tasted a duck taco and lightly patted his mouth with the linen napkin. "Shall we dispense with the formalities and the subterfuge?"

"What the hell. I'd appreciate that."

"Then tell me what it is you are really interested in?"

"If you were going to steal some of Peter's artwork, how would you do it?"

Mundy leaned back in his chair. He took another sip and carefully set the glass down beside his plate. He glanced at Jocelyn. She held his gaze and gave a tiny nod of her head.

"Suppose I give you a hypothetical example of the theft of some artwork. Would that be helpful to your situation?"

"That's exactly what we want to know," Linda said. "If you were going to do it, how would you manage it?"

Mundy began to weave a tale that sounded like something out of Hollywood. After being trained by his father and grandfather on the basics, he utilized technology to beat the latest security systems. Mundy turned his attentions to insurance companies and collectors, using his skills to recover stolen pieces of priceless art and jewelry and return them to their rightful owners. It was his claim that such work was in high demand and that the commissions on the recoveries paid him well. There was still a great deal of risk involved, since many of the people he'd retrieved pieces from were less than honorable.

"So hypothetically, how would you get away with it? I mean, surely the people you stole from would be suspicious when the artwork or jewelry that was supposedly safe in their possession suddenly disappeared," I said.

Linda had been engrossed in his tale and was anxious to join in. "In some situations, it would be weeks after a recovery before the person would realize the item was gone, if it was jewelry locked away in a vault or a painting stored at a summer house. But that couldn't have been the case every time," she said.

Mundy took his time studying each of us before turning to Jocelyn. "Your perceptions were extremely accurate. Not only are they both beautiful, but highly intelligent as well."

She flashed him a delighted smile. "It would be in your best interest not to underestimate them, especially Miss Richmond. I understand she can be quite…determined."

Mundy gave me a gentle nod. "I must admit a certain degree of pleasure in meeting you. I have read some recent accounts of your escapades as they were described in the media. The actual police reports were very enlightening as well."

"How did you get copies of police reports?" I asked.

Mundy smiled and lifted his palms lightly from where they rested on the table. Maybe it was his version of a shoulder shrug. "My network of resources is quite extensive."

"So if you were hypothetically going to steal some of

Peter's artwork, how would you go about it?"

"There are many ways to execute a perfect crime. But each one takes a great deal of careful planning and preparation. Contingencies must be calculated as well." Mundy paused to sample the foie gras. He gave a single nod of approval. "Tell me about the building."

Linda and I took turns describing the structure. I was surprised how much detail she was able to give, knowing she'd only been there today. But Linda is extremely observant. I described the minimal security system. Before I could tell him what had been stolen, Mundy raised a hand.

"Pardon me, Jamie, but I do not want to know what is missing. You are asking me to postulate a hypothetical robbery. I will need some time to consider various options. I must ask your indulgence."

Puzzled, I glanced across the table at Jocelyn. She smiled and rose smoothly from her chair. I realized Mundy was now on his feet as well.

"You're leaving?"

Harrison Mundy dropped his linen napkin on the table. I noticed his glass was empty and the appetizers were gone. He shot his cuffs.

"Our meeting was for one hour. That time has passed. Jocelyn and I have another commitment." He turned slightly toward Linda and lifted her hand. Smoothly he bent forward and grazed his lips across her knuckles. "It has been a delightful pleasure to meet you both."

Linda's cheeks flared red. "Thank you," she stammered.

Mundy turned to me. I was standing now, trying to figure out how to prolong the conversation. His eyes were twinkling as he looked at me.

"Your reputation is well deserved, Jamie. I must admit to be intrigued by your—situation. When the time is right, I will be in touch." With that he gently, but firmly, took my hand and did the knuckle grazing kiss. I felt a flush run through me. Who was this guy?

Dumbfounded, I stood there, watching Jocelyn and Mundy leave the bar. Automatically she linked her arm through his. Linda appeared beside me.

"What just happened?" Linda asked.

"It beats the hell out of me."

Phillip appeared and began to briskly clear the table. For a moment I thought Mundy had stuck me with the bill, but the waiter only smiled and shook his head.

"That was taken care of before you arrived."

Linda stared at me. "Who was that guy?"

"He certainly wasn't what I expected."

We headed for the door. There was no sign of Harrison Mundy or the exotic Jocelyn. We exited the hotel lobby and stood for a moment on the sidewalk, waiting for the valet to bring up my car.

"I don't know about you, Jay Kay, but I'm starving. Those tasty little treats inside just woke up my appetite."

"You expect me to feed you now?"

She fluffed back her curls and struck a pose. "I am all dolled up and we are in downtown Birmingham. The very least you could do is take me to dinner."

"I think there's a hot dog place nearby."

"You're not getting off that easy."

I shook my head as we got into the car. "You're such a pricey broad."

"You'd better believe it."

CHAPTER ELEVEN

Malone was due any time now. It was a little after eleven. Ian was sound asleep, fresh from another evening with Brittany. When he came home, he sheepishly snuck down the hall, absently rubbing his neck. I wondered for a moment if the kid had a hickey. Was this attraction with the beautiful young girl down the block moving too fast? I couldn't really compare it with my own teenage years. I was definitely a late bloomer. I hoped it didn't get him in trouble with Terri. She might not be pleased with her son growing up so quickly. Shaking off those thoughts, I turned my attention back on the evening.

Linda and I discussed it in great detail and I decided not tell Malone about our meeting with the infamous thief. It may turn out to be nothing more than an interesting conversation. Mundy was reputed to be an international crime wizard. It was highly unlikely that the works of Peter Richmond ever crossed his radar before hearing about me.

Just before departing, Linda made a mischievous comment. She was on her way home to get ready for a nightcap with Vince. Her preparations included a bubble bath, some expensive perfume and a very skimpy piece of silk that she'd found in Montreal. That was all. With her fashion model figure, her luxurious crown of thick curls, and her traffic-stopping beauty, I knew it was more than enough. But it did get me thinking.

So I had spent the time getting ready for Malone. I hoped he appreciated it.

I was sitting on the edge of the rocker with my legs crossed when the lights of his truck swept up the driveway. It took all of my strength to wait until he was in the kitchen, framed in the archway with the soft light from the counter.

"Hey, Jamie."

"Good evening, Donatello." I uncrossed my legs and pushed smoothly to my feet. The living room was dark, with only some meager light coming through the window. Slowly I swayed in his direction. I paused in front of him.

Malone's eyes traveled up and down my body. The tip of his tongue came out and moistened his lips.

"Do you like my ensemble, Donatello?" I said quietly.

"Like isn't a strong enough word, Jamie. You look amazing."

It was nice to hear that my efforts weren't in vain. I was wearing a silk negligee in a deep dark shade of blue. It had tiny spaghetti straps on the shoulders and it dipped dangerously low in the back. There was lace trim around the edges and down into my cleavage. It ended at my hips and there was a pair of loose skimpy tap pants that came with it. I'd brushed out my hair and put a little curl to it. I was wearing makeup, fresh lipstick, and black high heels. But that wasn't all.

"That's a very nice response, Malone." I put a hand to his chest and pushed him back.

He took a step into the kitchen, a quizzical look on his face. Malone started to bend down to kiss me, but I pushed him again.

"Patience, Donatello."

"I will try, Jamie, but it has been a very long day."

One more step and his legs made contact with the

chair. Malone glanced back and got the hint, settling onto the heavy kitchen chair that was facing away from the table. I stepped closer and took his hand in mine. Very lightly, I rubbed the back of his hand down the outside of my thigh. The smile on his face widened in delight.

"I missed you today, Donatello."

He released me and rotated his hand so his palm was now sliding down my leg. I moved closer still and raised my leg, placing my foot between his legs on the chair.

"These legs are freshly shaved, Jamie. Do you know what your smooth, sexy legs can do to me?"

"I'm hoping they can give you some ideas."

He was running both hands up my leg. My heart rate was beginning to double. As his fingers tickled the back of my knee, Malone dipped his head and placed his lips on my thigh. I felt his tongue dart out for a taste. I bit my lips to hold back the moan building rapidly inside me.

"Is that my favorite perfume?" he asked hoarsely.

I could only nod. His fingers were now stroking my thigh, moving higher. It was only a matter of seconds before my legs would weaken. I didn't want to break the moment, but I knew if I didn't move now, I'd fall on my ass. Drawing a deep breath, I slipped my foot from the chair. Before Malone could shift, I stepped forward and lowered myself into his lap. I clutched his head and tilted his face up for a kiss.

"Do you want me, Donatello?"

"More than life itself, Jamie."

His arms were wrapped around me. There was no mistaking the effect I was having on him as Malone's body was pressing against me in all the right places against the thin fabric. He started to rise with me in his arms, hesitating when I shook my head.

"Right here, Malone. Right now, just like this."

"Are you sure, Jamie?"

"I can't wait another second."

Hurriedly we pulled the fabric out of the way. When his

fingers brushed against me, I almost exploded. Malone lifted me up. Then he was inside me and we quickly found a rhythm. His hands clutched my ass. I squeezed him, locking my arms around him. Our mouths were hungry, searching, probing for each other. I could feel the chair rocking beneath us. My body shuddered in wonderful delight. Before my heart could begin to slow, I felt Malone's climax. We slumped together, gasping for breath, whispering to each other. Malone released his grip on my ass and used one hand to tilt my head back.

"Jamie, you are an incredibly beautiful woman."

"Thank you, Donatello. But I may not be able to walk tomorrow."

He drew me close for a kiss. "I'll carry you anywhere."

"I'll keep that in mind."

****

Wednesday morning was controlled chaos. It was another game day for Ian, so he and Malone left the house around nine. With no plans to go to the studio, I focused my energies on the computer. After a couple of hours of writing, I found myself drifting into research mode. I read a lot about controversial art heists, about priceless collections that disappeared during the wars in Europe, insurance company recoveries and swindles galore. There were stories about paintings and sculptures. I even found a few additional articles about the Mundy family. The more I read, the more uncertain it became as to whether these guys were actually as good as the legends described, or if they were the result of some extravagant publicity campaign. It was entirely possible they received credit for the work of other thieves who pulled off elaborate crimes.

Linda called twice, curious to learn if Harrison Mundy had contacted me. Her disappointment grew with each call.

"Why are you so anxious? Are you thinking about

trading in Vince?" I teased.

She greeted that with a whoop of laughter. "Jay Kay, that guy isn't for real. He's a player. He knows how to be mysterious, how to raise your hopes, how to get your attention. But I'd bet you lunch at Toot's Deli that he'll disappear like a puff of smoke when things get too complicated."

"But some of these capers were extremely complicated."

"Jay Kay, he may have been a great cat burglar, but when it comes to matters of the heart, he's not the kind of guy to stick around and fight for the woman he loves."

I sat back for a moment to consider that. "You mean like Vince?"

"Yes, just like Vince and Malone. And don't forget Bert too. Our guys are real. Harrison Mundy isn't the type of guy who will hold you when you're feeling down, who still thinks you're beautiful when you covered in bandages and bruises and never misses an opportunity to sweep you off your feet."

"Algae…"

"Yes, Jay Kay?"

"Let's go to lunch."

****

Thursday morning the four of us returned to the studio. Linda was anxious to see what treasures lurked inside the remaining crates. By my count, we still had twenty-five to open. In no time at all we had the cameras set up and running while the guys maneuvered the first large crate into position.

I watched from behind the video camera as Malone and Ian pulled the burlap off the sculpture. This one was a marble titled "Fleeing Beauty". It was the body of a woman caught in the act of running. Tendrils of slender marble in various lengths and thicknesses extended from her head, as if they were locks of hair billowing out behind her as she ran. Part of her face was obscured, turned against her shoulder as if attempting to hide her features from whoever was chasing her. The woman's body was voluptuous, full of dangerous curves. There was something haunting about this piece. The guys became quiet, which was unusual. Linda slowly moved around it, taking pictures with the other camera.

"Holy shit," Ian muttered.

"Watch your language," Malone said, cuffing him lightly on the back on the head.

"How did he do that?" Ian said, taking a step away. "She looks real."

"She looks alive," Malone said.

"Check the file," I suggested.

Ian ducked back into the studio. The three of us were now leaning against the worktable that held the laptop computer. None of us could take our eyes off the sculpture. After almost two weeks of doing this, I thought I was becoming accustomed to unveiling these incredible works of art. But this one stopped me in my tracks. And it wasn't just me. Linda and Malone were staring at it as well.

"He used a model," Ian said, holding up the file.

We spread the file out on the worktable. There were pictures of a woman standing in front of a drop cloth. She was blonde, with an impish smile on her face. She could have been in her early to middle twenties. It was impossible to tell how tall she was. Her figure was eye catching, with a tiny waist and round hips. Most of the pictures showed her in a one piece bathing suit. There was one where she wore a sheer negligee. There were shots of her standing on a pedestal, others with her arms outstretched, and still others where she was looking over her shoulder. In a couple of photos he must have used a fan to blow her hair back from her face. She had bottle green eyes that were very expressive.

"She's a doll," Ian said softly.

"I wonder who she was," Linda said.

Pushing the pictures toward Malone, I started flipping through the other papers in the file. There were sketches and notes in Peter's now familiar handwriting. Across the top of one page was a name. Meredith Bell. I showed it to Malone. He turned over one of the pictures and pointed. The same name was written across the back.

"Jay Kay, I think this is the most beautiful thing I've ever seen," Linda said softly.

"You'll get no argument from me."

We stood there for another minute or so, just studying it. Finally Malone gave his shoulders a shake and nudged the kid. Together they moved the crate to the back wall and resumed working.

Just after noon we were taking a break when Malone's phone rang. He took the call, listened for a minute, gave a quick laugh, and winked at me. Ian popped open the cooler and began spreading food containers on the table. A minute later Malone joined us.

"What's going on, Jameson?"

He shook his head slowly. "That's kind of tame for you, Jay."

I gave him a coy smile. "Got to keep you guessing, Malone. So what's going on?"

"That was Sergeant Roscommon. He's in a bind. His wife misread his schedule and thought he was off tomorrow night. She got tickets for the whole family to a concert. It's their anniversary."

"So he can't go?" Ian said around a mouthful of bagel.

"Friday and Saturday were my days off. Roscommon was off for Sunday and Monday. So he'll take Friday off and I'll take his Sunday."

"A weekend free? What will I do with you, Malone?"

"I'm sure you'll think of something."

****

By the time Malone left for work, we had opened twelve crates. Looking around the storeroom made me realize we were close to the end. Ian had grown quiet. His smile that usually shined was dimmer. Linda mentioned it as well. She wandered out to the studio. I lifted myself up onto one of the large crates and dangled my legs. Ian was pushing a broom, sweeping some straw into a pile.

"What's going on?" I asked.

He shrugged, guiding the broom across the floor in front of me. "Nothing."

"You're a terrible liar."

"It's no big deal."

I flicked my foot at him and knocked the broom out of his hands. "Talk to me, Ian. It's obvious something's bothering you."

"Look around us." His voice was low and sorrowful and his eyes were locked on the floor. "We're almost done."

I let my eyes scan the room. There were only about a dozen crates remaining.

"You should be proud of this. We've gotten a lot done already."

"Yeah," he said with another shrug. "I guess that's the problem. We'll probably be done tomorrow and you won't need me anymore."

"What are you talking about?"

Finally he looked right at me. "Once we open the last crate, my summer job is done. I'll just go back home."

I pushed off the crate and stood in front of him. "For such a smart guy, you can be kind of dumb. Just because we have the crates open, doesn't mean we're done. We'll need to group the art so the experts can view it. This place needs more cleaning. There's more to do. We might even build some pedestals or racks to display the smaller pieces on. I still need your help, if you want to keep working."

"Of course I want to help you, Jamie."

"Then stop moping like someone stole your lunch

money."

"You bet!"

I left him to finish up and walked into the studio. Linda was sitting at the desk, looking at the different cupboards and nooks. As I approached she tapped one that had a little door with a keyhole on it.

"What was in there?"

"I don't know. I never opened it."

She gave me an exasperated look. "Do you have the key?"

I pulled the ring from my purse and handed them to her. Linda flipped through them and found one that fit. There was a loud clicking noise as she turned it and eased the little door open. Inside was a small cardboard box. She rolled back from the desk and looked at me.

"Here we go again," I muttered, reaching for the box.

"You sound like it might be bad news."

"Everything we've found here comes with history. I'm not sure how much more I can handle right now."

The box was maybe four inches square. It was heavier than I expected. I set it on the center of the desk and lifted the lid. Inside was something made of brass. It felt solid when I picked it up. There was a short stem that was battered on one end. The base was flared out and circular. Turning it over in my hands, I realized the bottom bore Peter's trademark.

"That's what he used to sign his work," Ian said, appearing beside us. "I'll bet it's on the bottom of each piece."

I hefted it and passed it to Linda. She held it for a moment and gave it to Ian. A look of wonder crossed his face as he turned it over in his hands.

"Can I check?" he asked.

"Let's all look."

We went back into the storeroom. Lifting some of the smaller pieces, we turned them over to look at the bases. Sure enough, each one bore the imprint from the trademark stamp.

"How would he do this?" Linda asked.

"It was probably the finishing touch. Once the work was done, he'd hit this into the base before attaching it," Ian said. "I'll show you."

He fetched a hammer from the tool box. Then he centered the stamp on a broken piece of wood from a crate and struck it once with the hammer. There was a loud ring as it hit. Ian pulled it away and all three of us stared at the wood. Imprinted in the center was Peter's trademark, the large cursive R with the letters P and M in smaller script inside the circle of the R.

"Now that's an autograph."

Ian handed me the stamp and the piece of the wood. He put the hammer back in the toolbox. Linda was watching me closely as I turned the wood over in my hands.

"Jay Kay, I think we should call it a day."

"Good idea."

I watched her turn toward the studio and had to smile as she wiped her hands on the back of her shorts. She now had little fingerprint smudges on her buns. I'm sure Ian would notice as she went passed. I followed her out to the studio as he finished up in the storeroom. She closed up the desk and locked it, handing me the keys. I was still holding the stamp and the chunk of wood. I dumped them in my bag.

"Looks like your conversation with Ian helped."

"He thought I wouldn't need him to help once all the crates are open. There's still a lot of work to do."

She stared at me for a moment, then slowly shook her head. "Jay Kay, it's not the work he was worried about."

"What are you talking about?"

"He's fifteen years old. He's been spending his days either playing baseball or hanging out with you and his buddy, Malone."

"That's right."

Linda leaned against the desk and crossed her arms beneath her breasts. "But where has he been spending his evenings?"

Now I got it. "He's been with Brittany every night when he's at our place. Now wonder he was in the dumps."

"Honestly, Jay Kay, sometimes the most obvious things sail right by you."

"Shut up, Linda."

****

We finished Phase One, as Ian was now calling it, on Friday. The last of the crates were opened, the contents captured on video and still photos and the digital files were sent to my home computer and to Lincoln Banning. I called Vera to see if she wanted to view the complete collection. She was busy until Tuesday. Linda decided not to join us on Friday, so Ian and I were there alone after Malone went to work.

We were sitting on stools beside the main worktable in the studio. The laptop was in front of us with the spreadsheet open. I kept scrolling up and down on the page.

"Okay, kid, let's talk about options."

"Far as I can tell, Jamie, we can do it a couple of different ways. We could group all of the similar works together. Or we could set them up based on when he did them."

"Chronologically might be interesting. What do you mean when you say similar works?"

He gave me a shrug. "You put all the bronze pieces together. All the sandstone ones can go in one section. You take the steel ones and set them apart. And the ones where he used several different elements…"

"…I think that's called mixed media."

"Yeah, mixed media could be in another spot."

"Do you think we should keep them all in the storeroom? With the crates right with the works, or should we make it more of a display, like in an art gallery?"

Ian looked at me as if I'd suddenly lost my mind. "Why are you asking me? I'm just a kid. Linda or Malone would be more help on this stuff."

"Don't sell yourself short. You're a bright guy. It has nothing to do with your age. I want your opinion. You've been here for this whole project. What would you do?"

He was thoughtful for a few minutes, letting his eyes flick back and forth between the storeroom and the computer. "I think we need to go see Krip."

Ian led the way upstairs. We found Odon Krippendore's studio at the opposite end of the hallway on the third floor. He had a large space divided in half. One side was the gallery, where many of his finished pieces were displayed on easels and framed on the wall. The other side was his studio, where the natural lighting was the best. Sinatra was singing softly from an old stereo tucked in the corner. Krip was working on an abstract painting. A broad smile lit his face when he saw us. He dropped his brush in a jar of paint thinner.

"It's Jamie and the young apprentice! Come in if you can stand the fumes of paint and turpentine!"

"This is quite a setup, Krip," I said, doing a slow turnaround.

"That it is. Come on the other side, it's far more comfortable." He led us to the gallery, where a battered loveseat and chair commanded a view of his efforts.

I spent a few minutes bringing him up to date. Ian moved slowly along the wall, gazing at the paintings on display. There was a small portrait, maybe an eight-by-ten, in a thin wooden frame down near the corner that held his attention for a while. I watched him start to move away, then go back to it. He turned and waved me over.

It looked like the same woman who had posed for the "Fleeing Beauty" statue. Krip appeared beside me, staring wistfully at the painting.

"She's the love of my life."

MARK LOVE

CHAPTER TWELVE

"I can't tell you how many offers I've had to sell that painting," Krip said. "There is something haunting about her beauty. I'd swear it burns right into my soul every time I look at it."

"Did she pose for a lot of artists?" Ian asked.

"No. Peter discovered her. She was a secretary for some firm downtown. He met her by chance. I think he went for a meeting about doing a sculpture for their offices. Meredith brought him coffee." Krippendore chuckled at the memory. "It took him months to persuade her to pose for him. He had to assure her that she could keep her clothes on. Peter was much more disciplined than the rest of us."

He guided us back to the sofa. I noticed Ian chose a spot where he could still see the painting. Was this typical behavior for a teenager?

"Tell us about her."

"She was one of those women who didn't realize how beautiful she really was. Meredith always downplayed comments about her features. She thought it was just an attempt to get into her panties." He flicked a glance at Ian. "Sorry, kid."

Ian blushed. "It's okay."

Krip went on to explain. Peter eventually convinced her to pose for him after he gave her some sketches of works he wanted her to model for. Krip met her once when visiting the studio. He admitted to seeing some of the earlier sketches and conveniently dropping by when he knew Meredith would be there. The more she posed for Peter, the more comfortable she became with the idea. Soon she was in high demand. Other artists in the building, including Krip wanted to paint her, photograph her, and pose her. She deferred. Peter was the only one she would work with.

Krip remembered a gallery show where Peter had several works on display and Meredith was his model. Every piece was sold before the end of the opening night. Meredith was present, shyly talking to patrons about the work. She was very modest. Krip recalled being there, watching how protective Peter was about her and how she never left his side.

"But if she didn't pose for anyone besides Peter, how did you do the portrait?" Ian asked.

Krippendore smiled so widely his eyes twinkled. "I sat in one day when she was working with Peter. I had a sketch pad that I filled with drawings. I used different angles, different lighting, with as many poses as I could capture. She laughed at me. Her laugh was musical, like a delicate instrument running through the scales. Later I came back up here and painted three different portraits." His paint stained hands had been resting on his knees. Now he rolled his wrists and gazed at his palms for a moment. "I sold the first two. That was one of the most foolish things I've ever done. I'll never sell the last one."

"Whatever happened to her?" I asked.

"Some guy with a lot more money and class than the likes of me swept her off her feet. She would show up in the society pages every once in a while, but I don't think she ever posed again."

Ian finally pulled his eyes off the portrait and stared at Krip. "But you said she was the love of your life. I thought that meant you were together."

"No, I was never so lucky."

I didn't want to pry, but I was curious. "Do you mean you've never married?"

A belly laugh ensued. "I've been married four times, Jamie. But I think my heart has always belonged to Meredith."

Now I really didn't want to pry. Instead, I explained what had brought us up there in the first place. Krip was pleased that we would consider his thoughts. He accompanied us back downstairs and slowly walked the room, hands clasped behind his back, taking it all in.

"There are several ways you could present the art. As Ian suggested, you may consider grouping all the bronze together and so on. But I'd be inclined to do it another way."

"What's that?" I asked.

"Some may be more impressed if you can present them by the date. There may be intricacies that Peter was able to incorporate as the years went on. Some little tricks he learned or perfected," Krippendore said.

"Each piece has its own file. I think that includes the date when he completed the project," Ian said.

Krip swung an arm around the room. "The studio is not large enough to properly display all of these works. You want people to be able to study each piece from every angle. Lighting will be a factor to consider as well. Perhaps pedestals of various heights will be helpful. Something sturdy yet in such a way that it won't detract from the work."

"We're not setting this up as a gallery. We only need to arrange these so when the experts come in to appraise and authenticate the collection, they'll be able to do their job," I said. Krippendore's enthusiasm was contagious, but it was giving me a headache.

"My apologies, Jamie, I just naturally picture things in a gallery setting. Even so, it may be helpful for these so called experts to be able to view Peter's works under ideal circumstances. Perhaps you should consider contacting one of the art dealers in the area and asking for their advice on displays."

"That's an excellent idea. Thank you, Krip."

He tugged at his beard. "Anything I can do to help, Jamie, just let me know. Now I'd better get back to my studio."

After he left, Ian secured the storeroom. We locked up the outer door and set the alarm. Together we lugged the cooler out to the car and headed for home. Maybe Malone would have some ideas.

****

Something was bothering me. It took me a while to figure out what. We'd stopped on the way home to grab a pizza. Ian was down at Brittany's house. I was restless, pacing from room to room. Finally I dropped into the chair behind my computer and booted it up. While I waited, I lifted the puzzle box from its place of honor beside the monitor. I fiddled with a couple of sections. So far I had been able to move four pieces before getting stymied. Maybe there was a receipt in Peter's files from a woodcarver. If I could find that, I might get a clue on how to open the box. I rejected the idea. That would be cheating. I set it aside as the computer hummed to life.

I went to the previous day's files and found "Fleeing Beauty." Odon Krippendore's words replayed in my mind. This was a woman who downplayed comments about her beauty. She thought compliments were associated with attempts at seduction. Could Peter have been seducing her? Was it possible my loving father had fallen under her spell? Did he want to do more than idolize her in stone for eternity? I stared at the sculpture. She was even curvier than Linda. Was he tempted? Was there a straight man who wouldn't be?

Part of me didn't want to know the answers to those questions. Part of me wanted to leave the memory of my father intact. Yet I doubted I'd be able to leave this alone. My eyes flicked to the bookshelf beside the window. On the top of the case rested the brass stamp Peter used to punch his trademark into the art. Over the last few days, I brought all the diary volumes home. They filled one section of the case. Flipping to the database, I saw that "Fleeing Beauty" was created when I was five. I dug that year from the shelf and began to read, searching for any mention of the work.

As with the earlier books I'd read, Peter went into great detail on the pieces he was working on. He wrote about the struggles he had to overcome certain obstacles, constantly working to perfect his craft. The entries were mixed with bits of humor. There was mention of a time when Vera and I visited the studio. Peter described my delight playing with bits of clay, molding them into a giraffe. A vague memory flitted through my mind.

Near the end of the volume I found the only mention of "Fleeing Beauty." Peter described the piece quickly, stating only that it was life size and that he felt this was one of his best pieces to date. I read the passage slowly, trying to read between the lines.

"This one has been elusive. The image in my mind is slowly becoming a reality. I've got the perfect model, the perfect pose. Even her expression is exactly what I had in mind. Capturing her energy, her personality is the challenge. Every line, every lock of hair, the playfulness of the model will be perfect. It's close now. Another day or three and I'll be done. When it is finished, I'm going to take a week off. I'll take my family away for a break. I want to spend more time with my inspiration. She is becoming more inquisitive each day."

That certainly sounded like me. But now my inquisitive

nature was going in a different direction. I wanted to know. I needed to know. I punched up the Internet and started searching people. I was going to find Meredith Bell.

****

"You're working late, Jay."

I looked up from the monitor, surprised to see Malone leaning against the door jamb. It was almost midnight. I'd been on the computer for more than four hours.

"I'm just preoccupied, Malone. Is Ian home?"

He nodded his head slowly as one of those low voltage smiles touched his lips. "He's in bed, Jamie, which is where you should be."

Leaning back, I rubbed my eyes with the heels of my hands. Reluctantly, I switched off the computer and pushed myself away from the desk. Malone was blocking the doorway. I moved to him and leaned my head against his chest.

"It's been a long day, Horatio. I just couldn't shut my brain off."

He wrapped his arms around me. "Come to bed, Jay."

I nodded against his chest. "I'm not feeling incredibly sexy tonight, Malone. Do you mind if we just go to sleep?"

"Somehow, I'll control my urges."

At times I tend to forget how strong Malone is. Without seeming to move he lifted me off my feet and swung me up into his arms. This was no easy feat, considering he was in the doorway and didn't bang my head on the walls. He carried me across the hallway and into our room. I was still wearing the shorts and tank top I'd worn all day. When he reached the bed, Malone eased me down on top of the spread. His fingers slid down and unhooked my shorts. Just that easy, he slid them down my legs and tossed them in the general direction of the closet. Malone kicked off his jeans and yanked his T-shirt over his head. Then he was next to me on the bed. He pulled me back into his arms.

"Malone, I should probably take a shower," I whispered.

"Too late, Jamie. We're in bed."

"But my clothes are smelly."

He pulled my tank top over my head, unhooking my bra along the way and pulling that off as well.

"That problem has been solved. Go to sleep, Jamie."

I was about to argue when a yawn overtook me. If I got up to shower, it might wake me up. Right now, all I wanted to do was curl up with Malone. His arms drew me closer. Arguing would take too much energy. I burrowed closer and fell asleep.

Monday morning arrived way too soon. Since Malone had the weekend off, we seemed to run non-stop. Ian played two baseball games on Saturday, which we attended, followed by a barbecue dinner at Terri's house. Brittany tagged along as well. I noticed a momentary glimpse of concern on Terri's face when they first met, but it quickly vanished when she saw how comfortable Ian was with her. Brittany was also a hit with Ian's sister. Together they ganged up on Ian with squirt guns and enjoyed quite a battle.

Sunday we spent on one of the small lakes with Vince and Linda, swimming and horsing around on a couple of wave runners. The weather was perfect, plenty of sunshine, clear skies, and gentle breezes. Malone had been extremely passionate over those two days. At one point he let me drive the wave runner. As he perched behind me with his arms around me, I could feel the vibrations of the machine shooting through my body. When Malone let his hand fall between my legs, I was steering the craft through a sweeping turn. I was focused on keeping the wave runner moving. He began to massage me. Malone managed to pull the fabric of my bikini bottom aside and slide a fingertip inside me. Between his attentions and the vibrations of the watercraft, the orgasm was so strong it had me screaming.

And that wasn't the only time that weekend.

Now it was back to reality. Linda was in the classroom with summer school. Vince was seeing patients. The three of us were sitting in the studio, splitting a box of donuts. Ian had a mischievous look on his face. I wondered what he had been up to on Sunday.

Malone called him on it. "What's going on in that teenage mind of yours?"

"I've got a plan for Jamie."

"What kind of a plan?" Malone asked. He bumped his knee against mine and I saw the flash of humor in his eyes.

"It's a plan on how to display the art. Here, let me show you."

He pulled a folded sheet of paper out of his back pocket and smoothed it out on the worktable. It was a sketch of a long, low box, with two risers in the center. A row of figures proceeded down the box. I was surprised at how clear the picture was. There were several pieces I could identify. I stared at Ian in amazement.

"When did you do this?" Malone asked.

He shrugged. "I had some time at home yesterday, before you guys picked me up. I just started doodling. The cool thing is we can do this with the crates we have. We don't need to buy a set of racks or lumber. We can use what we have."

Ian went on to explain his idea. If we took the largest crates and reattached the panels, we could then lay them horizontally. Then we could take a medium sized crate, lay it horizontally on top of the large one, and create a tier. By covering everything with some inexpensive dark cloth, we now had a display stand. This way we could exhibit several pieces on the same tier. The life-size units we could position along the aisle, either at the end or between some of the crates.

"So you just figured this out in a few minutes yesterday?" Malone asked.

Ian sheepishly gave him a shrug. "Actually, I've been

thinking about it since Friday, when Jamie and I met with Mr. Krippendore. I kept coming up with this. We don't have to do much but rearrange the crates and cover them with fabric."

Malone pulled a tape measure from the toolbox. With Ian's help, he measured the studio and the storeroom. They also measured all the crates. Together they worked out numbers and determined how many of each type crate was available. I listened to their chatter. But I couldn't take my eyes off of Ian's sketch for more than a minute. Like Peter's work, it kept pulling me in. I rummaged in the desk and found an artist sketch pad. The guys were finishing up their calculations when I approached.

"Do me a favor," I said, passing the pad and a couple of pencils to Ian. "Draw "Fleeing Beauty" for me."

He started to argue, but something stopped him. Instead, he took the pad and the pencils and walked over to the corner. Slowly he walked around it, taking it all in. Then he folded himself into the lotus position on the floor with the pad in his lap and he began to draw.

"What's going on?" Malone asked.

"I'm not sure, but I think we're watching a potential artist at work."

Silently we waited. Malone slipped an arm around my waist. I was perfectly content, leaning against him. In less than a year's time, I had discovered how good life could be. Yet every time I got comfortable, thinking I had it all figured out, something would pop up and surprise me. Like Ian's artistic talents. He fiddled with the pad for half an hour before he pushed to his feet and handed it to me.

"It's pretty rough," Ian said.

I gawked at him. In thirty minutes he captured most of the statue's power. He had the shape, the curves, the windblown hair, and the facial features. The eyes looked different, but there was no way to capture the expression of the eyes in the sculpture. Here they looked playful, as if the model was toying with the artist, keeping a secret.

Malone was looking over my shoulder. "Well, what do you know?" He glanced at the kid. "How long have you been doing this?"

Ian seemed embarrassed by the sudden attention. "Since I was young; I was always drawing stuff. I'd copy cartoon characters. I would make little flip books for Caitlin. I'd use the comics and put her in there with the others. It was fun. In school if things are boring, I'm always doodling."

"You do this in all your classes?" Malone asked.

His face went crimson. "I won't in Linda's class. I'll be paying attention."

I couldn't hold back the laughter. "I'm sure it's the subject matter that will keep you alert. Can you do this from memory too?"

"Sure. Those pieces I put on the diagram were some of the smaller ones we unpacked last week. They're just rough sketches, but I can do better if you need me to."

Malone pointed at the pad. "Can you do a sketch of Brittany?"

"I could do that with my eyes closed."

Malone waved him toward the worktable in the studio. "Prove it, hotshot."

Ian grinned and walked into the other room. There was a cockiness in his stride that I hadn't noticed before.

"Wolfgang, what are you doing?"

Malone smiled and shook his head. "What's next, Jay, Amadeus?"

"You could always just tell me, Malone."

He gave me one of those low voltage smiles. "What would be the fun of that?"

While Ian worked, Malone and I talked about options for displaying the works. We both liked Ian's plan. Over the weekend I decided to group the works chronologically. Odon Krippendore was right. You could see subtle differences in Peter's works. Keeping them together might make it easier for the experts to properly evaluate them.

Using the computer, I made up a list by date. Malone calculated how much cloth we would need to get started. He made a few calls and found a wholesaler not far from the studio. I left the guys and went shopping.

By the time I got back with bolts of fabric, there was a row of the largest crates arranged in the studio. Malone and Ian wasted no time measuring the cloth and cutting it into drapes. We used thumb tacks to hold it in place in the corners. Once the base row was covered, the guys began setting medium sized crates in place and trimming more fabric.

I walked over to the worktable. Three sheets of sketch paper lay upside down. While the guys were occupied, I flipped over the first sheet. Brittany's face stared back at me, a coy smile on her lips. There was excitement in her eyes. For a pencil drawing, it was amazingly lifelike. I almost expected her to step right through the paper and talk to me. I wondered what Ian could do with watercolors or acrylics.

Tentatively, I turned the next one over. This one was a profile of her features. Her hair was pulled back into a ponytail. He captured the small, upturned nose, the line of her jaw, the slight pursing of her lips. Ian knew her features well.

I glanced up. He and Malone were busy tacking the fabric on the next level of crates.

The third sheet took my breath away. This was a full body pose. It couldn't have been more accurate if Brittany was standing in the room. She was in a bikini, something with thin vertical stripes. I assumed it was what she'd worn on the night of the barbecue at her house. Ian captured her curves, the illusion of her long legs, her toned arms. The expression was different from the other two drawings. I wondered for a moment if he had pictures of her on his cell phone.

"What do you think, Jamie?" Ian asked. He walked up while I was gazing at the last one.

"If you can do something this good from memory, I wonder how well you could do if she was standing in front of you."

He was obviously delighted with my comment. "So you think these are good?"

"No. I think they're incredible. But if you really want a professional opinion, you should show them to Krip."

Ian paled at the idea. "I couldn't do that. This was just for fun."

"You've got a real talent, Ian."

He turned the pages back over and stacked them. "Let's focus on the displays."

I watched him walk away. Just when I thought I could figure things out, he proved me wrong. Malone looked over at me and shrugged. Rather than press it, I tucked the pages inside the sketch pad and went to help the guys.

Referring to the list, we began to arrange the sculptures on the display. Over the next several hours we moved them into place, turning them in such a way that the natural light from the high north-facing windows shined down on them. Malone and Ian talked about installing some track lighting so small spotlights could be added. By the time we broke for lunch, the second display was beginning to take shape. There was room in the studio for two displays. The others could be set up in the workroom. Flanking the studio displays would be two of the life-size sculptures from the same era.

While I tried to pay attention to the work, my mind kept wandering back to Ian's drawings. Why was he downplaying his obvious talents?

CHAPTER THIRTEEN

Late Tuesday morning Vera arrived with Lincoln Banning on her arm. Or maybe it was the other way around. Malone and Ian were putting the last of the life-sized statues in a row along the back wall of the storeroom. Earlier in the day, Odon Krippendore visited and discussed options for lighting. He and Malone looked at a couple of versions online and came to an agreement on the most practical style. He would order a number of floor lamps with adjustable arms where we could point bulbs of different wattages in the direction of the displays. Even with the large windows allowing plenty of natural light into the studio, the extra illumination would be helpful.

Vera swept into the room, her pale yellow shift flaring out with her stride. "Hello, Jamie. You've been very busy." She did the air kiss thing, coming close to each of my cheeks.

"It's been a group effort. Do you remember Ian and Malone?"

She shot me a withering look. "Darling, I never forget a handsome man, no matter how young or how old he may be."

I smothered a laugh while she went past me. She put a hand on Ian's shoulder and leaned up to brush her cheek against his. He blushed and seemed to freeze in place. When she moved on to Malone, Ian drew in a breath of relief. Malone bent down and received an actual kiss. Over her shoulder, he winked at me. Banning stood beside me, gazing thoughtfully at the display of artwork.

"This is incredible," he said. "I've watched the videos each day, but it doesn't compare with seeing everything in person."

Vera returned. "Tell us how you decided on these arrangements."

We were gathered by the first display in the studio. Malone and Ian were hovering by one of the worktables. I described the process and the groupings. Last night I printed out cards for each piece with the title on it. For now they were pinned on the cloth. I was going to buy a bunch of little frames later to make it look more professional. Banning peeked under the cloth. Malone pointed out that it was Ian's idea to use the packing crates.

"I'd like a tour," Vera said.

I stepped back and extended my arm. "Right this way."

"Lincoln, why don't you join me?"

Banning smiled and took her arm. The guys remained by the worktable. I followed them like a dutiful daughter, answering questions, pointing out my favorite pieces from each group. Vera paused by some sculptures, taking her time to walk around the display, studying the works from every angle. When she spotted "Fleeing Beauty" she stopped mid-stride. The gentle smile that had been playing on her face flickered for a moment.

"I'd forgotten about this one. Peter worked so hard to make it come alive."

"Looks like he did," Banning said.

There was a sharp intake of breath from Vera. "Yes, he certainly did."

"It's haunting. I'd swear she's looking right through

me," he said.

"It was one of the last crates we opened," I said. For a moment I sensed they forgot I was there. "This is a very powerful piece."

"I think it's my favorite," Vera said softly.

We moved back to the studio. Malone's arm went around my waist. He turned his attention to Banning.

"Have you heard anything more from the Detroit Police about the stolen sculpture?"

The lawyer shook his head. "I spoke with the detectives yesterday, requesting an update. There have been no sightings and no leads."

"This is a work of art. It's not likely to end up in a pawnshop."

"I agree. But even with his reputation in the area, few people would be willing to purchase one of Peter's sculptures without a letter of authenticity. Unless the thief wanted to sell it for a few hundred dollars, they will have difficulty finding a buyer."

Ian scoffed behind me. "This isn't a velvet painting of dogs playing poker. It's a freaking masterpiece."

I expected Malone to glare at him. Instead he winked at me and shrugged. "The kid's right. It is a masterpiece. Whoever snatched it is holding on to it."

"One of these days, I'm going to figure out who did it," I said.

Vera gave me a gentle smile. Malone pulled me a little closer. Banning's expression was a bit puzzled.

"I am going to figure it out."

****

Ian and I were alone in the studio. The files were in the cabinet, arranged in the order of the displays. We used the cameras to take video footage of how everything looked. Ian narrated the groupings, giving quick descriptions and titles. I noted that while his voice was not very deep yet, there was a trace of excitement that he was keeping in check. We finished with the cameras and put them back in the travel bag. There was nothing left to film. We were going to take all the camera equipment and the laptop home. The desk and the cabinets were locked up tight. I boosted myself up on the worktable, letting my legs dangle. Ian finished zipping up the camera bag and looked at me. I patted the spot beside me. With the grace of a natural athlete, he swung up and landed lightly beside me.

"Do you want to talk about it?"

He gazed at me for a moment before lowering his eyes to the floor. "It's no big deal."

"I think it is a big deal. You obviously are very talented. Why hide it?"

He gave me the teenager's answer to everything, a shrug of the shoulders. I poked him with an elbow.

"Talk to me, Ian. There's no one else here."

"It was my dad. He always teased me about drawing. He said I'd have more luck making it in baseball than I would with art."

I took a moment to digest that. It was almost a year since the accident that had taken his dad so abruptly from his life. There was no way I wanted to harm the memories of his father.

"From what you and Malone have told me, your dad was a great guy. His whole life was wrapped around his family."

Ian knuckled a tear away. "Yeah, he was always encouraging us, cheering us on at games, taking us on trips and picnics, making us all laugh."

"Do you think people change?"

"I dunno."

"Don't you think you've changed, even in the last six months?"

He considered it. I got another shrug.

"Ian, since we've met, I know you've changed. You are growing, both physically and intellectually. And you're probably growing emotionally as well."

"I dunno," he repeated.

I put an arm around his shoulders. "If you had met Brittany six months ago, would you have been comfortable talking to her. Or kissing her?"

He brought his head up. A grin began to touch the corners of his mouth. "No way could I have kissed her."

"See, you have changed. I'll bet if your dad was around and saw how you've grown, he wouldn't tease you about your artistic talent. There are a lot of career possibilities for someone with an art background. Besides, nobody says you can't play baseball and be an artist." I gave his shoulders a squeeze. "And I'll bet your father would be proud of the young man you're becoming."

"Thanks, Jamie. It's just so hard sometimes. I think about something that happened during the day and want to rush home to tell him. For a minute, I forget that he's gone."

"I understand." I could feel the tears welling up in my eyes.

"I just really miss my dad."

I nodded, the words sticking in my throat. Ian turned and wrapped his arms around me and started to cry. I hugged him tightly. "I miss mine too."

We sat there on the worktable, letting the tears flow, surrounded by this room of artistic wonders. Nothing else mattered.

****

Ian was down at Brittany's house. Once we got home, he'd cleaned up, inhaled some of Malone's leftover barbecue chicken, and disappeared. He seemed to be in a much better frame of mind. I took one of Peter's journals out to the picnic table and read it through. This was another tenuous connection with my father. I wondered if it was better or worse than what Ian had with his.

I tried to write for a while, but nothing could hold my interest. Instead, I did a little more research on Meredith Bell and checked emails. Two messages surprised me. One was from Shannon, my literary agent. She was at a convention in Raleigh, but wanted me to call her cell after nine o'clock. It was already after ten. The other was from Vera. She was going up to Martha's Vineyard for a few weeks or so with some friends. Lincoln Banning knew how to reach her. She planned on coming back when the experts were going to view the collection. Apparently life for Vera just kept on spinning.

Shannon answered on the third ring. There was a trill of laughter in her voice, and some loud background noise. I could hear the strains of country music in the distance.

"Jamie, you're going to have to start coming to these events! There is a great mix of writers and agents and fans here. You'd have a blast."

"Is that what you wanted to talk to me about?"

"No, I'm got a couple of names for you. These are recommendations from people very knowledgeable about the art world."

"That's great, Shannon. Who are they?"

Another peal of laughter greeted my ears. "Seriously? You think I'm hovering around the dance floor with my notebook in my hand, waiting for your call?"

"I just got your message."

"I meant nine in the morning, Jamie. I'm standing here in my little black dress, wearing a pair of dangling gold earrings, two-inch heels and a splash of Chanel."

"What, no sexy lingerie?"

Her voice was a soft purr in my ear. "It's too hot for lingerie, Jamie. Everyone is having a fantastic time. I can't remember the last time I danced this much."

"Are all those dances with the same man?" I teased.

"The same three men. Call me in the morning, Jamie."

I was grinning at that image as she clicked off. With her appetite for handsome men, I had no doubt that Shannon would not end up alone. She thrived on variety. Some might say she had commitment issues. Thinking of her comments brought to mind something Malone had recently said about not wearing panties this time of year. I dashed into the bedroom and took a quick shower. There was just enough time.

****

The house was dark. Ian was sound asleep in his room. I was standing in the kitchen, leaning against the counter when Malone stepped through the side door. A thin shaft of moonlight came through the window behind me. Malone entered the kitchen and stopped, taking in the scene. I pushed off the counter and swayed toward him, giving my hips more wiggle than normal. He was about to say my name when I put a finger to his lips.

The kitchen lights are on a dimmer switch so you can adjust the brightness to set the mood. I reached over and dialed the setting low with my free hand. There was just enough light for me to see Malone's reaction as his eyes took me in.

When Linda was in Montreal, she found a lingerie shop. After buying a few goodies for herself, she picked up a lacy peignoir set for me. It was in a dusty shade of green that almost perfectly matched my eyes. Beneath it was a very tiny silk negligee in the same color. With the soft light behind me, I knew Malone could see right through it. Open toed heels completed my ensemble. I wondered briefly if he could see my makeup in the dim light.

One of my favorite smiles appeared on his face. Without a word, Malone kissed the finger that was still pressed to his lips. His tongue darted out and he sucked my finger into his mouth. I struggled to keep my balance. Malone's left hand found my hip and steadied me. With his tongue he pushed my finger out of his mouth. Malone dipped his head close to my ear and began lightly tracing the shell of it with his lips. I could feel him draw a deep breath as his right hand settled on my waist.

"Perfume?" he whispered.

"Chanel."

His lips traced their way down my neck. Now he was at my throat, nibbling here and there. He paused at my mouth, long enough for a probing kiss. Then he was turning me around, nuzzling my hair out of the way, and kissing my neck, trailing kisses around the top of my spine. I could feel the stubble on his cheeks and chin as he eased the peignoir off my shoulders. It fluttered to the floor. The negligee was almost backless, dipping down to cover my buns. Thin straps held it to my shoulders. I expected him to slide them off at any moment. But Malone had other ideas.

His lips and tongue darted across my spine. His arms were around me now, holding me steady. Strong fingers stroked my breasts, my stomach, and the top of my thigh. My body was shuddering. He moved lower.

I was tossing my head, lost in his attentions. My hair was flying now, falling down into my eyes, brushing against the tops of my shoulders. I felt his teeth nip my buns lightly through the silk. My jaws were clenched to keep from screaming.

Malone spun me around and pressed me against the counter. My knees were going to give out. He nudged the lace hem of the negligee out of the way and pressed his lips to me. I clutched his head, curling my fingers in his hair. The orgasm raced through me. He was everywhere. I could feel his lips, his fingers, his tongue pleasing me in numerous ways. The next wave raced through me.

Malone sensed I was over the edge. He pushed me just a little bit farther then eased back, holding me tightly against the counter. Gasping for breath, I slumped against him. Malone rose from his knees and gathered me into his arms. Without a word, he carried me into the bedroom and laid me gently on our bed. He disappeared for a moment. When he returned he had the peignoir in one hand and my heels dangling from the other. I couldn't remember stepping out of them. In case Ian awoke before we did, Malone didn't want him to find the evidence of my seduction in the kitchen. He flashed me a wicked smile as he closed the door.

My voice was nothing more than a throaty whisper. "Welcome home, Malone. I take it you liked my outfit."

"That's an understatement, Jamie. Let me show you what I really think of it."

****

Wednesday morning the guys left for Ian's game. There was work to be done, so despite the offer to join them, I stayed behind. Malone had given me a hint this morning. With a wicked smile on his face, he pulled a pair of shorts and a dark blue T-shirt from my dresser and handed them over.

"This is all you need for today, Jamie."

"Giacomo, whatever do you have in mind? You're supposed to work this afternoon."

"That's true. But we should be back in plenty of time for a little action before then."

I couldn't help but laugh. "A little action? Really? Is that what I've become, a little action?"

The devil was dancing in his eyes now. "Sometimes, Jamie, you're a lot of action."

There was no argument for that. I got dressed as he requested. Now I was at the computer, working away. It was after nine, so I called Shannon. A groggy voice answered just before it went to voicemail.

"This better be important."

"Shannon, this is Jamie. You wanted me to call."

She groaned. "Hang on, Jamie." I could hear her turn her head away from the phone and speak to someone else. There was a thumping noise and fragments of a conversation were taking place. I waited. My curiosity was growing by the moment. I was about to hang up and let her call me back when she came back on the line.

"What time is it?"

"Almost nine-thirty. Are you okay?"

There was another low groan. "I will be once I shower and ingest half a dozen aspirins and a pot of coffee."

"Hope I didn't interrupt anything."

"Honestly, Jamie, we were still asleep. So it's a good thing you called since I'm leading part of a panel discussion at eleven. We all needed to get going. But let me give you those names. I know this is important for you."

"It is."

I scribbled down the details. Oliver Guthrie was a consultant with several galleries and auction houses, including Sotheby's, perhaps the best-known auction house in the world. Rebeca Sharpe was a curator at the Metropolitan Museum of Modern Art and her specialty was sculptures. Shannon gave me phone numbers, emails, and mailing addresses.

"You could have just emailed me that," I said.

Her voice rasped as she cleared her throat. "I know, but I wanted to talk to you. This project is very intriguing. This would be great material for another book. Of course, I wouldn't want to pressure you into writing something too personal."

"Shannon, my last two books were from personal experiences. You know that."

"Yes, Jamie, but this one may come with too high a price. From what you've told me about your father, this could be too close to home."

In the background, I could hear a voice calling her.

"I'm fine, Shannon. Thanks for the recommendations. I hope it didn't cause you too much trouble."

A trill of laughter floated across the line. "It was no trouble at all. I've got to run Jamie, they're waiting for me."

"They means plural, so I guess you mean the people at the conference."

"No, Jamie, I mean the people in my shower." She broke the connection.

I sat back in wonder.

I spent the next couple of hours reviewing everything I could find on Guthrie and Sharpe. Both had extensive biographies on the Internet. Sharpe had written a number of articles about artists and exhibits that were going to be on display at the museum. She studied in Paris and Rome, as well as California and New York. It looked like her reputation was well deserved. There were several publicity photographs of her, correlating with exhibits at the museum. She was an attractive woman with a wide smile.

Guthrie's background was not as clear. It seemed that he appeared on the scene with a vast knowledge of art. It was rumored that he once studied with several great artists in Europe and had even tried his hand at painting for several years. While he had a remarkable eye for the masters, he did not possess the talent to create his own works. Instead he honed his skills as an expert, studying in many of the great museums throughout Europe. Sotheby's engaged him for their auctions in London and New York and kept him busy.

I knew Lincoln Banning was getting pressure from the curator at the Detroit Institute of Arts to view the collection. While their galleries were impressive in some respects, I knew the city's financial problems would prevent them from making any serious attempt to acquire even a portion of the collection. But that didn't mean the curator couldn't take a look. To my knowledge, Vera was placing her trust in Banning to get the artwork authenticated and appraised. Yet I remembered Bert's advice when this whole thing began. Two experts were better than one. And three would be better than two.

I tried Banning's number, but he was out of the office. Rather than leave the details with an assistant, I emailed him the information about Rebeca Sharpe and Oliver Guthrie. Banning was having the videos professionally edited and a color catalog of the sculptures produced. It was his intention to provide as much information as possible not only to the experts for their appraisals, but for use in the event we decided to auction off the collection. That idea wasn't something I was ready to consider.

CHAPTER FOURTEEN

For the next three weeks, we rarely went to the studio. The attorneys were coordinating the schedule for the experts to appraise the collection. All the promotional materials were ready. Banning sent copies for me and Bert to review. One night when Malone wasn't working, we had taken Linda and Vince out to dinner downtown and stopped by the studio so Vince could see the collection firsthand. His reactions mirrored my own. Every time I entered the studio, it was like discovering these wonders for the first time. I would never grow complacent. Walking through the studio still took my breath away.

As Vince was wandering through with Linda on his arm, someone rapped on the outer door. I swung it wide when I saw Odon Krippendore.

"Hello, Jamie. I've been wondering how things are shaping up down here."

"Take a look and tell us what you think."

Krip ambled into the room, nodding his approval at the groupings in the studio and the light stands Malone purchased. As he entered the workroom he paused, letting his eyes take in Linda. I gave him a nudge to make sure he was still breathing. Malone chuckled as he introduced them.

Krippendore apologized for the intrusion. "You've done a wonderful job, Jamie. The displays are exactly what you want for the experts. I have no doubt that they will be anxious to get their hands on Peter's collection."

"Are you a sculptor also, Mr. Krippendore?" Linda asked. I noticed a little extra sultry in her voice.

"No, I'm a painter." He flashed a smile at her. "My studio and gallery are upstairs. Canvas and paints are much easier to carry up when the elevator is occupied."

She paused at the end of the aisle, standing in front of "Fleeing Beauty". "Tell us more about your paintings."

Krip gave a little laugh and tugged his beard. "I've done a wide variety, from landscapes to portraits to still life. Lately I've been doing whatever catches my eye."

Vince wrapped a protective arm around Linda's slender waist. "Anything in particular catching your eye?"

"I've been doing a series of water scenes. It's a commissioned work for a yacht broker. Nothing very exciting, but the money is excellent."

I followed behind them, listening to Krip and Vince discussing styles of art. The men moved along. Linda and I circled back to "Fleeing Beauty". I realized that I'd neglected to continue my research on the model. Seeing it again made me curious about Meredith Bell. If she was still alive, I was determined to find her. We strolled back into the studio area. Malone was perched on a stool, idly turning pages of a sketchbook. Krippendore and Vince joined us around the table. I watched Krip's eyes narrow at the pad.

He curled two fingers toward his chest. "May I?"

"Sure, it's just some doodles."

Krip pulled the three loose pages from the bottom of the pad. Malone had been looking at them and hadn't pushed them all the way back inside. I realized he'd done this deliberately. We watched quietly while the painter studied the sketches.

"My, my, my. Are you harboring artistic talents, Malone?"

"Not me. Ian drew those a few weeks ago."

Krippendore raised his eyes. "The lad has obvious talents. I sensed a kindred spirit whenever we talked. He shows a great deal of promise. Is it safe to assume a young lady posed for these?"

"It's a girl he met recently. He did those from memory," I said.

"Jamie, that's even more impressive. The next time young Ian is here, I'd like to speak with him. He did a remarkable job here."

"These are really good?" Malone asked.

Vince leaned over my shoulder. "Yes, Malone. They really are. I'm no artist, but I've studied enough art over the years to recognize talent. Ian's got it."

"Don't let the boy squander it," Krippendore said. "Bring him around so we can talk. And for goodness sake, don't leave these drawings laying around. They will be worth a lot of money someday." He tucked the pages back into the sketchbook and handed them to me. "From memory, huh?"

"That's right."

"First kiss?"

I grinned. "I think so. They've become close over the summer."

"If he hasn't shown those to her yet, he should. A young woman would find such talent very flattering. Especially since he did these from memory."

"Imagine what he could do if she posed for him," Vince said.

Krip gave his beard another tug. "Yes, indeed." His eyes flicked toward Linda. "And speaking of posing…"

"Not on your life. That's very flattering, but I'll pass." She smiled sweetly as Vince once again drew her close.

"I understand. But you can't blame an artist for asking. Now I'll have to try and sketch you from memory. And I don't believe I'd do your beauty justice."

Linda patted him on the cheek. "Nice try, but the answer is the same."

"*C'est la vie.* And with that, I'll bid you all good night."

Watching him leave made me wonder if Peter would have been as captivated by Linda's beauty. Would he have wanted to sketch her as well? Could she have become the inspiration for another work like "Fleeing Beauty"?

"So you're not interested in posing," Malone said. There was a wry smile on his face.

Linda coyly batted her lashes. "There is only one man I'm interested in posing for," she said, turning her attention to Vince.

"And me without a paintbrush or even the talent to hold one."

"You could always use a camera, Vince. I'll bet Linda has a few costumes that might be worth a picture."

She scowled at me as we headed for the door. Something told me there was going to be some posing this evening.

****

A few days later Ian was at the house with Brittany. I was just finishing up some work on the computer when I remembered the sketchpad. Taking it from the bookshelf, I walked out into the backyard. Brittany and Ian were at the picnic table with glasses of lemonade. Her dog, Lucy, was lounging in the shade. The kids were sitting close together. As I set the sketchpad on the table Ian's eyes widened in disbelief.

"We bumped into Krip the other night at the studio. He happened to see these and encouraged me to bring them home."

Ian started to reach for the pad, but Brittany was faster. She snagged it and flipped it open, His sketches of her were right on top. She carefully studied the first one, then moved it aside to look at the next. Soon all three were spread out on the table before her.

"I can explain," Ian said. His voice was soft and meek.

Brittany raised a hand to silence him. She kept staring at the drawings.

Ian turned his gaze to me with a pleading look on his face. I shrugged. There was nothing I could say to diffuse the situation. We waited. A minute later Brittany turned to Ian and placed her hands on his shoulders.

"Did you draw these from pictures?"

He slowly shook his head. "No."

"So this is how I look in your head?"

"Don't be mad. I know you're even prettier in person, it's just that Malone challenged me and I…"

He never got another word out. Brittany raised her hands to his face and drew him to her. She planted a deep kiss on his lips that left both of them blushing. The fact that this happened less than three feet from me may have occurred to them only after they separated.

"That is the sweetest thing anyone has ever done for me," Brittany said. "You think I'm pretty?"

Ian shook his head. "No, I think you're beautiful. Pretty was all I could do from memory."

Was Malone coaching this kid in more than just baseball? The thought brought a smile to my face.

"So you think you could do even a better job if I was right in front of you?"

"Brittany, I don't know, but I'd like to try."

She pushed the sketchpad toward him. "Well, let's try."

Ian scrambled into the house for pencils. Brittany looked at me as if suddenly remembering that I'd been there all along. She glanced at the sketches spread out before her.

"He really did these?"

I nodded. "Yes. And Mr. Krippendore thinks he's very talented. Krip is a painter. He wants to talk with Ian the next time we're at the studio."

"Would it be okay if I went to the studio sometime? Ian's told me all about it, but I'd like to see it firsthand."

"Sure, we can go next week."

Ian returned with several pencils and a big gum eraser. Brittany moved to the grass and pulled the dog with her. She knelt down and coaxed the dog to sit beside.

"Okay, Rembrandt, let's see what you've got."

Ian picked up the pad and started to draw. I took that as my cue to leave.

Back at the computer, I pulled up the research I had done on Meredith Bell. What I'd found had stopped abruptly, only a couple of years after she posed for Peter. But there had to be more. I thought about the beautiful young woman. Did she disappear? Did she move away? A search of marriage licenses in the three main counties came up empty. There were no death notices. Was it that easy to disappear back then?

Thinking about disappearances made me reflect on the missing sculpture. The old journalistic mantra floated in front of my mind. Who, what, when, why, where, and how. Who was responsible? How did they break in? When did it happen? What were they after? Where was it now? I had more questions than answers. Hell, all I had were questions.

On a whim, I called the Townsend Hotel. It had been weeks since Linda and I met Harrison Mundy. Surely he would have some information for me by now. But there was no record of him being a guest at the hotel. When we were there, he acted like he owned the place. Maybe he did.

All I had were questions. It was time to start looking for answers.

****

The day dawned bright and clear. This was the moment we'd been anticipating for weeks. It was a Wednesday. I was nervous and should have been running around the house, getting ready. But Malone had other ideas. I was on my stomach with my arms stretched above my head. Malone was slowly massaging my shoulders and back, digging in with his fingers and thumbs. His hands were slick with a scented lotion.

"Relax, Jamie, you're tighter than a guitar string."

"And you're strumming me like a virtuoso, Buster."

He chuckled softly, probing a spot on my shoulder. "You must be running out of names by now, Jamie."

"Nope. I have an infinite list. But you could always just tell me, Malone."

He bent down and nibbled my ear. "That would be too easy. Are you anxious about today?"

"Excited is more like it. We're all meeting at the studio at nine. Bert is picking me up."

Malone rolled onto his back. I slithered on top of him. His slippery hands began stroking my sides and my stomach. The tips of his fingers grazed underneath my breasts. I shivered. "Too bad Ian's got a game and I have to work. Otherwise I would have gone with you."

"It's liable to be pretty boring. A bunch of artsy know-it-alls prancing around the room doesn't sound like much fun."

Lincoln Banning would be in attendance, along with his associate. Vera would also be there, having flown back into town yesterday. There were three experts coming to view Peter's collection. Banning vetted them. While it would be helpful to get a sense as to the monetary value of the work, the idea of selling any of these pieces left me cold. Which was exactly the opposite of what I was feeling right now as Malone's attentions were rapidly getting to me.

Somehow he managed to swing his legs off the bed and stand up. I wrapped my legs around his hips and my arms were cinched around his neck.

"Buster, where are we going?"

"To the shower. Ian and I need to leave in about

twenty minutes and you should get ready for the day at the studio."

As if I were nothing more than a feather, he carried me into the bathroom. Together we managed to get the shower started. Reluctantly Malone eased me to my feet.

"Is Brittany going with you?"

"Yes, apparently those two are becoming inseparable." Malone pushed me under the showerhead and began to work shampoo into my hair. I turned my face to the spray and leaned against him.

"What do you think is going to happen to them when school starts up?"

He spun me around and began to rinse my hair. "I wouldn't be surprised if Ian's here every weekend. And then some."

It became very difficult to talk. We took turns lathering each other up and enjoying the obvious reactions to our attentions. At one point I was directly underneath the showerhead, struggling to maintain my balance while Malone was amorously pressed against me from behind. Hopefully the noise of the shower and exhaust fan muffled my passionate moans. It was only after the water ran cold did we climb out.

Malone quickly dried off, pulled on jeans and a T-shirt, and went to check on Ian. I wrapped my hair in a bath towel and slipped into a terry cloth robe. I heard voices and laughter coming down the hall.

Ian and Brittany were in the kitchen, finishing breakfast. Malone grabbed a bagel and began to guide the kids out to his truck. He turned back, gave me a quick kiss and a squeeze on the ass. Then he was gone. I had just enough time to get dressed before Bert arrived.

****

We were at the studio a few minutes before nine. Bert was decked out in one of his best suits, a charcoal number that accented his stocky build. He wore a striped burgundy tie and shoes that gleamed with polish. Knowing it would be another hot day, I opted for something light, yet classy enough for business. My dress was a jade green wrap that showed off my legs. I was wearing black heels, which clicked loudly against the old wooden floor as we walked down the hall.

"Are you nervous or excited?" Bert asked.

"A little bit of both. And extremely curious. How about you?"

He shrugged his massive shoulders while I unlocked the studio and switched off the surveillance cameras.

"I'm interested in hearing what these experts have to say. Banning's people did a nice job creating that catalog, but it was all of the work that you and the guys did that made that possible. I'm glad you took that upon yourself."

"It just didn't seem right not to be involved. This is a link to my past."

"Do you think knowing more about your past will change who you are?"

I considered that for a moment. "I don't think so. But it might help me understand a little more about who I am and why I behave a certain way."

He snorted a laugh at me. "Jamie, your behavior is a product of your upbringing and your own experiences. What you've learned along the way reflects how you will behave. Like how you get so stubborn at times and determined that your way is absolutely the right way."

"You just can't accept the fact that I'm always right."

He engulfed me in those strong arms. "That's my girl."

I hugged him back. "Yes, I am your girl. You are my father, the man who helped raise me, the man who taught me about life. You're the man who is always there for me, no matter what craziness I've gotten myself into."

Bert pulled back a little so he could look me in the eye. Then he leaned in and gave me a kiss on the cheek. I kissed his as well, leaving a bright red lip print. Someone knocked on the door. I pushed him away and pointed at his cheek. Bert snorted another laugh and pulled a hanky from his pocket to remove the evidence.

Lincoln Banning greeted me with a smile. Vera stood beside him, one arm hooked through his. She was wearing a frock in a pale blue that did her figure justice. Briefly I wondered who the designer was. Wherever it came from, it would be way beyond my budget. Helen Gaines was in the background, adjusting the strap on a large briefcase.

"Hello, darling," Vera said. She swooped in for the air kiss routine.

"Hello, Vera."

She spotted Bert and gracefully moved past me to greet him. I noticed he got a real kiss, not on the cheek, but full on the lips. I wondered if our shades of lipstick would match. The attorneys entered the room. We exchanged greetings as Helen swung the heavy briefcase up onto the worktable. She began to efficiently set out three large portfolios.

"I've scheduled the experts to arrive at separate times," Banning said. "From conversations I had with the curator at the DIA, this is a common practice. That way there can be no collusion between the parties and each will give an honest appraisal of the collection."

In addition to the catalog Lincoln Banning sent to the experts, the portfolios contained more information about Peter. There was a detailed biography, comments from professors and colleagues, and appraisals of other works currently on display.

Promptly at nine o'clock there was another knock at the door. Banning did the honors. On the other side of the door was a tall brunette woman in her early forties. Banning introduced her as Rebeca Sharpe. She smiled warmly at me and gave my hand a firm shake. I recalled that she was from the Metropolitan Museum of Modern Art in New York. This was one of the people Shannon recommended.

"I am a great admirer of your father's work. The opportunity to view his collection is quite a treat."

"Thanks. I hope the collection meets your expectations."

"From what I've seen, I'm sure it will. I've had goose bumps since flying in last night. This is like discovering buried treasure."

I smiled and stepped aside as Vera swept in. They chatted briefly. Rebeca took one of the portfolios from the table and began with the first grouping. Helen Gaines remained by the desk. Lincoln Banning walked a few paces behind the expert. Vera and Bert were talking quietly in the corner. Vera motioned for me to join them.

"What do you think of her?" Vera asked.

"She seems nice. And she spoke highly of Peter. Her background is pretty impressive."

Vera smiled sweetly. "Yes, it is. And it's not every woman who can wear Armani. I'd bet that suit she's wearing cost over a thousand dollars."

"I don't pay that for two suits," Bert said.

She gave him an appraising look. "Yes, dear, we know."

Banning allotted two hours for each expert to view the collection. Rebeca was taking her time, absorbing each piece. I noticed she'd pulled on a pair of white cotton gloves. Certain pieces she would lift and closely examine. She was speaking quietly. There was a tiny microphone with an ear bud poised by her mouth. There was an external wire that ran down to the pocket of her coat. Occasionally she would flip to the portfolio and cross reference something. At one point she caught my eye and gave me a brief smile. Then she resumed her work.

She was done shortly before eleven. Removing the gloves, she thanked each of us for our time and the opportunity. "Breathtaking. Absolutely breathtaking. I would have loved to be here when you were unpacking these."

"It was pretty special," I said.

Rebeca turned back to Lincoln. "I'll have a report to you within a week. There is no doubt in my mind that these are the works of Peter Richmond. If the decision is made to show these to the public, I know the museum would be extremely interested in bidding for at least part of the collection."

"We haven't discussed that possibility," Lincoln said. "But if we do, you'll certainly be on the list."

He motioned to Helen. She escorted Rebeca Sharpe outside. Apparently part of Banning's plans included hotel accommodations and a private car. The driver would take Rebeca back to the hotel and then out to the airport. Another driver was bringing in the second expert. Helen waited in the lobby and brought him in. Once again, Lincoln Banning handled the introductions.

"This is Nicholas Cullen."

I remembered the background on Cullen. He seemed too young to be an art expert. Actually he looked more like a surfer. He was tall and lanky, with bleached out hair that swept over the collar of his suit. There was several days' stubble on his cheeks and chin. Or maybe he only shaved once a month, whether he needed to or not. According to the biography, Cullen was from California. He currently represented two museums and a number of galleries along the Pacific Coast. What surprised me was when he saw Vera.

"Vee, darling, it has been ages!"

"Nicky, is that you? I had no idea you were going to be here."

Bert appeared beside me. Together we watched Vera and Cullen give faux hugs and kisses and chatter away about socialites they had in common. Eventually he took a portfolio and clutching Vera's elbow, went to view the collection.

"How could she not realize this guy was going to be here?" I muttered to Bert.

"You don't think she really read any of that

background do you? Vera trusts Banning to do the dirty work. She also knew that you and I were going to be here. There was no reason for her to do any heavy lifting."

"I'm glad we did. And I'm also glad you're here, Bert. Even if this feels uncomfortable for you. Your opinion means a lot to me."

He winked at me. "Actually, Vera asked me to be here too. I don't know what her reasons were, but I let her believe I was doing it as a favor."

"You didn't mention that I asked you too?"

"What, and pass up having Vera owe me?"

I looked at him closely. "You rat. She came in yesterday. You had another booty call."

Bert looked away and adjusted his tie. "I refuse to comment. And what your mother and I did or didn't do in the privacy of her hotel suite is none of your business."

"I don't believe you for a minute," I said, biting back a laugh.

"Just don't ask me to explain the location of certain rug burns."

"Are those on you, or on Vera?"

He winked at me again. "Yes."

"Whatever. I just hope she doesn't have to pay for the damages."

CHAPTER FIFTEEN

After Nicholas Cullen finished swooning alongside Vera, we ran out for lunch. Banning took us to a private club nestled in the heart of downtown Detroit. Everyone from the valet to the maître d' knew him on sight. We were escorted to a large round table, well away from the kitchen. Two waiters appeared, bringing appetizers and drinks. I nibbled at a chunk of bread and ordered a small salad. Food had little appeal.

Vera held court with a gentleman on either side of her. She guided the conversation effortlessly, paying full attention to whatever either man had to say on a variety of topics. After a while I ignored her. Beside me Helen Gaines was fidgeting in her chair. She poked at her lunch entrée, a broiled fish fillet.

"Is everything alright?"

Her face flushed, realizing I was watching her. "Yes, just a little restless. My knee has been bothering me."

"What happened to your knee?"

"I tore it up in April while running a marathon. Some kind of tendon or ligament damage." She offered me a wan smile. "But it will be okay."

"Was this your first marathon?"

She shook her head. "No, I've been running for years. It's a good way for me to keep in shape. I find it's also good for a stress reliever."

"So do you need surgery or therapy?"

"No, it's just going to take some time. I've had surgery on both knees over the years. Believe me, I know my body. It won't be much longer and I'll be out there running again."

"It must be painful."

Helen shook her head. "I'm used to it."

I realized in every meeting she'd been in with Banning that she always wore a business suit with slacks. There were no dresses or skirts in memory. I wondered if that was corporate policy or just her preference. Maybe she was embarrassed by the surgical scars. Physically she still reminded me of a tomboy. We had just enough time to get back to the studio for our third visitor.

****

Waiting patiently in the building's parking lot was another one of the chauffeured cars Banning's firm used. The driver got out immediately and moved to the rear door as we parked. He must have recognized Banning. From the back seat climbed an elderly man. Banning steered us into the building while Helen greeted the guest. A few minutes later they appeared in the entrance to Peter's studio.

"This is Oliver Guthrie," Helen said.

He slowly made his way around the room, taking a moment to chat with them. He didn't shake hands, explaining that he suffered from arthritis. His hands looked puffy, the knuckles all twisted and swollen. I studied him as he approached Vera. He had to be at least seventy years old, with a head of snowy white hair and a neatly styled white beard. Although he may have been trim in his youth, Guthrie was round now. He didn't limp, but he used an ornate cane as a walking stick, pressing it firmly to the floor whenever he took a step. But it wasn't his body or his handicap that interested me. It was his knowledge of art.

Guthrie was the other expert Shannon recommended. I was more than a little surprised to find out that both Guthrie and Sharpe had been selected. Banning declined the recommendation of the DIA's curator and had gone for experts from both coasts. It made me curious.

This time both Helen and Vera escorted the expert around the collection. Now that I was aware of Helen's knee problems, I noticed her stride was awkward, a lurching motion that made me think she was wearing two different shoes. Perhaps she should invest in a cane. She was carrying the portfolio, opening it to the different sculptures as they moved around the room. Guthrie would slowly nod his head as she gave him the background on certain pieces. His voice was low and deep. Several times he made a comment to Vera that resulted in her girlish giggle. His own laugh was a throaty chuckle. I wandered over to the desk. Bert and Lincoln Banning were speaking quietly by the door. Banning stepped away to take a phone call. I watched Bert watch the others. He gave his head a little shake and came over to join me, leaning against a file cabinet.

"What are you thinking, Jamie?"

"That you shouldn't waste your time worrying about him. Vera's too crafty to fall under the charms of some old art critic."

Bert snorted a laugh. "She'd probably give the guy a coronary. Vera still has a great deal of stamina."

"Please! That kind of information is not something I need or even want to know."

"On the contrary. This could be hereditary. And someday, you will be interested."

I blushed at the thought. The memory of Malone's attentions in the shower just a few hours ago suddenly warmed me from within. Time to change the subject.

"So what's your take on all of this?"

"Honestly, Jamie, I'm still in awe of the whole thing. When Vera and I were dating, I was able to learn a little bit about Peter. There was no Internet back then, but I did some research the old fashioned way."

I gave him an innocent look. "What way was that?"

"Talking to people, as you well know. I asked around. Talked to people in the art community, a few dealers and critics. I looked up articles in the newspapers about him. Even went to see a couple of his works that were on display out at Cranbrook. He was a very talented man. When we married, Vera rarely talked about him. She certainly never mentioned anything about all of this. She only said that there was an estate and a reputable law firm managing it."

"So this sudden fortune is a surprise to us all."

He nodded. "If Vera had any clue, she may have forgotten it. But she's never had to worry about money, so that may have been a factor. As long as her allowance continued, she didn't think about it."

We watched in a comfortable silence as Oliver Guthrie and the women finished. I saw them circle back to "Fleeing Beauty". I realized that if Vera ever wanted to put that piece up for sale, I'd fight her for it. Maybe I'd let them put it on display in a museum, but I'd never want anyone else to own it.

Guthrie proceeded to thank each of us for our time. I was the last one. He paused and nodded.

"Your father was a very talented man, Miss Richmond. You should be very proud."

"I am."

"Perhaps you inherited some of those talents."

I smiled sweetly. It was the second time someone had mentioned inherited traits. Maybe I should start looking into my family tree. "Have you seen a lot of his work before?"

"A few pieces. But nothing in the past compared to what I've experienced today." Guthrie used his walking stick to gesture back into the storeroom. "That last one is perhaps the most imaginative sculpture I've even seen. He captured her spirit along with her beauty."

"Yes, I think he did."

Guthrie's eyes twinkled. "Perhaps this was how envisioned you would be when you reached the model's age."

I glanced down at my own slim figure and gave my head a slow shake. "Nah, Peter would have known better."

"Nonsense, my dear, beauty is in the eye of the beholder. And in a father's eye, beauty holds no bounds." Guthrie gave me a little nod, then turned to let Helen escort him out.

Vera appeared beside me. "What a weird little man."

"You can't charm them all, Vera."

She flashed me a devilish smile. "Want to bet?"

****

It was a week later when I got the call from Lincoln Banning. He had received the last of the appraisals and wanted to meet with us to review them. Vera had disappeared to Traverse City, the posh resort area in Northern Michigan. She would be back in town next Tuesday. Banning was preparing a summary. Not only did he want to discuss the appraisals, but he also felt it was time to consider a sale.

"Interest in Peter's work has skyrocketed with the discovery of the collection. I would be remiss not to suggest we consider a sale."

"But if we flood the market with all of these pieces, won't that drive the prices down?"

"I wouldn't propose selling the entire collection. We could pick one or two sculptures as a trial and see what kind of reaction we get. It would be in the best interest of the estate to explore the option," Banning said.

It was too soon for me. Each piece of the collection was a part of Peter. I wasn't ready to let go of any of them yet. But I wanted to talk this over with cooler heads first. And I also wanted to discuss it with Vera. Odds were she would come back into town sometime on Monday. I sent her an email, suggesting we have dinner Monday night. It was doubtful she'd answer a call from me before then.

Outside the August sunshine was beginning to fade. Malone was working. Ian and Brittany had gone for a walk after dinner. The dog was their chaperone. I'd promised to take them to the studio tomorrow. Reluctantly Ian agreed to meet with Odon Krippendore. I went out to the picnic table.

The summer had been good in so many ways. I'd done nothing to disrupt my relationship with Malone. Linda and Vince were still together and were frequent visitors. Ian was growing into an interesting young man. I think the time he got to spend with Malone was helping him come to terms with his life. Of course, his growing relationship with Brittany may have been a factor too. Thoughts of his father made me think about my own. How different would my life be if Peter was still alive? Would he be happy with me, proud of me? Would he be supportive of the career path I'd chosen? Would he like Malone?

I gave my head a shake to chase such thoughts away. You can't go backward, playing the "what-if" game. Malone taught me that. There was no room in my life for regrets. It's as if I was afraid to be happy, afraid that I might get complacent and then things would fall apart. I was surrounded by good people, those I loved and cared about. Why did I have to make it more complicated?

Ian appeared. He was wearing a goofy grin as he sat beside me. Without a word he wrapped his arms around me in a tight hug.

"Thank you, Jamie."

I hugged him back. "For what?"

"For everything. For giving me the best summer of my life. For helping me deal with my feelings. For letting me stay here so often with you and Malone. For…everything."

"You're welcome." He released me and propped an elbow on the table.

"I know it's a pain having a kid around."

"Two kids. And you're not really a pain."

He looked confused. "Who's the other kid?"

"Brittany. You two are pretty much a package deal."

"Yeah, we are at that. I'm glad you're taking us to the studio tomorrow. I want her to see those beautiful works of art your dad created. And I really want to talk with Krip. It's weird that he thinks I may have talent."

"You are talented. Did you let Brittany show those sketches to her family?"

This was a point of contention. He'd done several more drawings where she posed for him. Each one looked better than the last. Brittany wanted to let her parents see them, but Ian was embarrassed. I knew she'd persuaded him, but never heard of the outcome.

"Yes, last night I took them with me. Her mom was all excited. She talked me into doing the whole family right then. Her dad was a little…quiet."

"Quiet, as in thoughtful, or quiet as in getting angry?"

He shrugged. "I can't tell. But Mrs. Murphy had me do separate drawings of everyone. Brittany wants me to do one of them together. I'm not so sure her dad likes the idea."

"Don't overthink it. Once he sees those drawings and has some time to consider it, he'll come around."

"You really think so?"

I threw an arm around his shoulders. When had he gotten so big? "Yeah, I really do."

****

The kids were anxious Thursday morning. I had every

intention of sleeping in and attacking Malone before he was completely awake. Unfortunately those intentions never got acted upon. About the time I was easing on top of him, a muffled conversation was heard from down the hall. Chuckling, Malone rolled me onto my back, slid out of bed, and pulled on a pair of jeans. He padded down the hall. Young voices floated in my direction. Malone appeared in the doorway. Ian raced by behind him, clad only in gym shorts.

"Apparently we have a peeper."

"You're kidding me."

He shook his head. "Brittany is excited about going to the studio. Supposedly she was taking the dog for a walk and somehow ended up in the backyard. Right outside Ian's window. Imagine that."

"Don't tease her. It was probably perfectly innocent until you barged in."

"At least the screen was still intact. The kids are waiting outside. I told them we could all go out for breakfast since I'm not going to the studio with you."

I reached for him. "Dustin, I am not ready to get out of bed yet."

"Not even close, Jay."

The gleam in his eyes shut me up. I was still mostly under the sheets. Malone sat on the edge of the bed and pulled me to him. As he zoomed in for a kiss, he pulled the linen around me. This must be what it felt like to be gift-wrapped. When I was completely encased in the sheet, he pushed me back onto the pillows and headed for the shower. The rat. By the time I got unraveled he was already under the spray.

When we came out, the kids were at the picnic table. Ian had gone back inside for jeans and a T-shirt. Brittany was wearing a skimpy pair of white shorts and a bright red tank top. She was showing an awful lot of shapely bronzed legs. I noticed they were holding hands.

After breakfast, Malone dropped us back at the house.

He was going to the range for some target practice before work. The kids were chattering as we drove downtown. Brittany rode in the shotgun seat. In the mirror I could see Ian fidget. I didn't know if he was nervous about seeing Krippendore or if it was just the way he reacted around Brittany. Maybe it was a little bit of both.

At the studio, I let Ian be the tour guide. Brittany stood quietly, taking her time to study each sculpture. I flashed back to the three art experts. Perhaps they were jaded by their years of experience, because none of them spent nearly as much time with each piece as Brittany did. We were in no hurry. I settled back in the desk chair and watched.

When they were about a third of the way through the collection, Brittany turned to Ian. She gave him a fierce hug, kissed him lightly on the lips, and pushed him in my direction. He stood there for a moment before walking over. Brittany turned her back to him and resumed her study.

"What's up?" I asked as he approached.

"She wants to look at the rest by herself. And she told me to go see Krip. He's up in his gallery by now."

"Go ahead. If you're not back when she's finished, we'll come upstairs."

He gave me a teenage shrug and turned toward the door. "I'm a distraction."

"What?"

"Brittany says I'm a distraction. I didn't mean to bother her. I just wanted to tell her about the sculptures."

"She wants to see them by herself. Take your book and go see Krip."

He gathered the sketchpad that he'd been using and headed upstairs. I'd told him earlier that Krip would want to see all the different drawings he'd done recently.

When he was gone, I spent a few minutes watching Brittany. She would stand in front of each piece, staring at it as if she was absorbing every detail. Ian had given her a pair of white cotton gloves to put on in case she wanted to handle some of the smaller works. I watched her carefully lift a small sculpture, turning it around so she could see it from a different angle. She even lifted it high and peered at the trademark stamp underneath. Gently she replaced it on the display and moved on.

I pulled a reporter's notebook from my bag. Lately I'd been jotting down ideas on how to incorporate these last few months into a book. Now I did my best to describe some of the statues, the way the sun shined through the high northern windows, the way the shadows danced along the walls. I became so engrossed in my observations and notes that time flew by. I was drawing everything in when I remembered I wasn't alone. Glancing up I saw Brittany at the rear of the workroom. I went to join her.

She stood in front of "Fleeing Beauty", holding one hand over her mouth.

"Pretty amazing, isn't it?"

"I keep expecting her to break the pose and walk over to me," Brittany said.

"Have you seen the whole collection?"

She nodded. "Ian steered me at the beginning, telling me to save this corner for last. Now I understand why. They are all fantastic, but this one takes my breath away."

"We should probably go find Ian. I think you'll like Mr. Krippendore."

Together we locked up the storeroom. I stuffed my notebook back in my bag and we closed the studio door. I remembered to switch on the security cameras before heading for the stairs. As we were coming down the hall, we could hear excited voices from Krip's gallery. At first I thought they were arguing, but as we peeked around the corner, I could hear laughter from the big man.

"The shading, here and here, is the type of detail most people don't even begin to understand without years of study. Yet you captured it!"

"I just thought it made the sketch better," Ian said.

"Better? Lord, boy, you've enhanced it. The subtlety, the lines, and the expression in the eyes alone set it all apart. You can't deny talent like this."

I knocked on the doorframe as we entered. The guys were at a drawing table, with several of Ian's sketches spread out before them. Krip had been gesturing with a stubby finger. They turned to us. A look of relief crossed Ian's face.

"Jamie," Krip boomed. "At last the voice of reason has appeared. Perhaps you can help me explain things to our young genius."

Ian moved around him to Brittany. I introduced her and Krip seemed to deflate. Gently he crossed to her and lightly shook her hand.

"It's a pleasure to meet Ian's inspiration. What do you think of these drawings?"

She hesitated for a moment. "I think they are very good."

"You're absolutely right." He flashed a big toothy grin at her. "They are indeed very good. And to think that Ian has accomplished this with raw talent alone. Imagine how incredible these may be with a little professional instruction."

"Are you offering your services, Krip?" I asked.

"Jamie, I am many things, but a teacher is definitely not one of them. I have neither the patience nor the fortitude to instruct young minds, to help shape their talents."

"But I'll bet you know someone who does."

"I may know a couple of people."

Krip guided us back into the gallery to the old furniture. Ian and Brittany sat close on the old loveseat. Krip dragged a heavy stool over and straddled it. I settled into the chair. Along the way Krip picked up the sketchpad and was slowly turning the pages. After a moment he looked up at the kids with a gentle smile on his face.

"I must apologize, Ian. My enthusiasm for art knows

no bounds. When I see work such as this, common sense and good manners go right out the window."

"But those are just rough sketches. Especially the first few that I did from memory."

Krippendore waved his hands in a calming gesture. "Ian, I'm not trying to tell you what to do. It's obvious to these old eyes that you're talented. I just think it might be something to explore, to get you lessons with a real instructor who can help nurture your talents."

"What are you recommending, Krip?" I asked.

"These drawings may be just the tip of the iceberg, so to speak. There are a few people who would relish the chance to work with Ian." He turned his attention toward the kid. "Have you ever tried painting? Acrylics or watercolors or oils?"

"No, I did do some sketches with crayons when I was a kid, but never anything serious."

I sat back and watched as the two guys discussed art. Ian relaxed a bit when Krip carried the conversation into studying other artists, visiting some of the galleries and museums. Brittany crossed her legs beside him. Her arm was laced through his and I realized his hand was resting on her knee. Ian seemed natural in this pose. Nervously I worried that the physical part of their relationship had gotten too serious too fast for fifteen-year-olds. I hoped Malone had talked with Ian about that.

With a shake of my head, I focused on the conversation. Ian was now asking questions, getting Krip's advice on exhibits to see and people to talk to. Brittany flashed me a wink and a smile. We both could see how excited the kid was becoming, talking about artists and opportunities. Krip bustled around the studio and came back with a couple of small canvases, some brushes, and tubes of paint.

"Let me pay you for the supplies," I offered.

"Nonsense, Jamie. These are just some things I had around the shelves. Besides, I consider it an opportunity to pay it forward. And if Ian does a painting and wants to exhibit it, I'd be delighted to put it on display."

"So someone might buy it?" Brittany asked.

"That's the idea. He could do a portrait of you."

"If I painted her, I could never sell it," Ian said. "She's my inspiration."

MARK LOVE

CHAPTER SIXTEEN

Monday night I met Vera for dinner at a Japanese restaurant called Cherry Blossoms in Novi that Linda and Vince really liked. She was hesitant at first, but when I offered to buy, Vera agreed. Apparently she didn't have any connections at the restaurant. We settled into a little table near the back. Vera looked happy, with a fresh glow of pink on her skin.

"The weather was perfect up at Traverse City," she said, tracing a fingertip across the rim of her wineglass. "We did some sailing and lounged around in the fresh air and sunshine for several days. It was delightful."

"I never pictured you as a sailor."

"Jamie, it's not as if I'm climbing the rigging or hauling in the sails. I find a nice place out of the way, settle back and enjoy it. When it's just the wind powering the boat, it can be very peaceful. And very relaxing."

I shrugged. "Maybe I'll try it sometime."

"I'll bet Malone would enjoy it. He seems like the rugged, outdoor type."

"Down, girl."

She laughed and flicked her nails at me. "He's all yours, Jamie. Now why don't you tell me what's on your mind?"

"I think Banning is going to push us to sell the collection. Since he's received the appraisals, it's like he can't wait to make a sale. It's almost as if he were operating on commission."

"Lincoln draws a very generous salary from the trust as the executor. Yet it is his responsibility to properly manage the assets. I don't think he wants to sell everything."

I waited while the waitress brought our entrees. Vera had ordered a bento box, which included tempura shrimp, teriyaki salmon and some California rolls. I'd opted for a sushi platter, which had a nice variety of fish. I watched Vera take a small chunk of the green wasabi paste and swirl it into a cup of soy sauce. I tried some yellowtail. It was delicious.

"Okay, so maybe he doesn't want to sell the whole collection. But I get the impression he's anxious to put something on the table."

Vera closed her eyes as she savored the salmon. "Lincoln has been researching the market. It's possible that the value of the collection would go up if we did put a piece or two up for auction."

"Do we have any say in the matter?" It was an effort to keep my frustration in check.

"Of course."

"So if we decide to sell something, we'd both have to agree on which piece?"

Vera gently placed her chopsticks on the tray and dabbed her lips with the linen napkin. "Jamie, we don't have to make a decision tonight."

"No, but Banning is anxious to meet with us tomorrow afternoon. And it would break my heart to sell some of those sculptures."

"Well, before anything is sold, we will all discuss it." Vera picked up her chopsticks and resumed eating. "Personally, I think we might consider donating one of the sculptures to a museum for a time."

"I like that idea. It's not that I don't want others to see

Peter's works, I just don't want to sell them all away. That would feel heartless to me."

"Let's just wait and see what Lincoln has to say. Meanwhile, I would like to relax and enjoy this lovely meal."

"You're just enjoying it because I'm buying."

She gave me a bright smile. "Every meal tastes better when someone else is paying."

****

Tuesday afternoon we arrived at Banning's downtown office. I'd offered to pick up Vera on the way, but she had other plans. I suspected they involved Bert. He winked at me when he escorted her into the law firm's conference room.

"Should I be worried about the two of you?" I managed to whisper while buzzing his cheek with a kiss.

"No. We both know this is just like watching a favorite old movie. We're enjoying the steamy parts and we already know how it's going to end."

"Yes, with Vera riding off into the sunset on some private jet."

Bert nodded wisely. "She wouldn't want it any other way."

One of the staff brought in a sterling silver coffee urn and was handing out bone china cups and saucers. They fussed over Vera as Lincoln Banning and Helen Gaines entered the room. Helen efficiently handed us a leather folder. Banning took a chair beside Vera. She immediately turned her attention to him.

"I think you'll all be pleased with the results," Banning said. He took a moment to make eye contact with each of us. "Each of our visiting experts rated the collection very highly. While there were some minor disagreements on a few sculptures, they were all duly impressed with Peter's work and the breadth of the collection."

Banning walked us through the folders. Each expert had submitted an itemized value for the individual artworks. This was followed by a grand total and a recommendation as to how best to preserve the collection. Suggestions were also made as to potential displays and auctions where Peter's works would receive the greatest reception. While Banning was discussing the recommendations, I shifted my gaze to Vera. She was paying close attention to the attorney, as was Bert. My eyes darted to the end of the table. Helen Gaines sat there primly, a notepad open before her. She was busy jotting down comments that any of us made. She reminded me of a court reporter, taking in every statement and question in some form of shorthand. I looked back at Banning.

"So the experts value the collection at a little more than ten million dollars. It's not uncommon for significant works of art like this to increase in value over time."

Vera straightened and preened. I was speechless. It was difficult to wrap my mind around numbers like that. Bert sensed my discomfort.

"Isn't it customary that an artist's works become even more valuable after his death?" he asked.

Banning bobbed his head. "Yes, that's very true, particularly if the artist has been successful and well received. Peter had a gift. Many of his works are priceless."

"They are to me," I said. Somehow my voice had come back. "So what would you recommend our next steps be?"

"We have a few options," Banning said. "I've taken the liberty of contacting two auction houses, just to take their temperature." He gestured to Helen.

She touched a control panel on the conference table and a hidden projector came to life. A screen silently rolled down from the ceiling behind Banning. The image of a world famous auction house in New York appeared. The screen changed, showing a number of works of art recently offered and the amount of the winning bid. I recognized several paintings, including a Monet and a Chagall. The numbers listed beneath each one were staggering.

"Given the opportunity, the auction house would promote the work well in advance. As a result, they are quite confident any piece approved for sale would attract a significant number," Helen said.

"Significant my ass," I muttered.

"Jamie!" Vera cast me her version of a furious look. Beside me I could hear Bert chuckling.

"Sorry. It's still a challenge to be seriously talking about this kind of money."

Helen's fingers danced across the control panel. Another house, this one in California, appeared on the screen. Again we saw a brief parade of recent events, with some very impressive works and even more impressive numbers.

"There are complete backgrounds in your portfolios for your consideration. I would be happy to answer any questions you might have," Helen said. Her tone was brisk and professional. I noticed that she failed to make eye contact with any of us. Her eyes were locked on the control panel as she turned off the system. The screen rolled silently back into the ceiling.

Vera turned her attention on Banning. "Do you have a recommendation?"

"I would suggest choosing two items, perhaps one of the larger pieces and a medium size one, something from his earlier days. We could send one to each of the auction houses for consideration and sale."

"If it was your decision, which it isn't, which ones would you send?"

Vera snapped to attention. "Jamie! You're being difficult."

I ignored her, never taking my eyes from Banning's face. But he was cool and impassive.

"You're absolutely correct, Jamie, it isn't my decision. I can only make recommendations. Vera would have to agree before any change is made, as would the judge.

Unfortunately you do not have a vote in the proceedings if they occur before your thirty-fifth birthday." Banning calmly laced his fingers together and rested his hands on the table. "I would never do anything to jeopardize the value of the estate."

I already knew this to be true, but that didn't mean I liked it. But as I sat there, I realized there was an avenue I hadn't explored yet. The judge was still a mystery to me. Shaking my head to clear my thoughts, my gaze landed on Vera.

"Don't sell anything. Not yet. I still have questions that need answering." With that I pushed back from the table, snagged the portfolio, and stormed out of the room.

****

A heavy hand pounded on the outer door, demanding attention. Blowing out a disgusted breath, I marched over and pulled it open. Bert took one look at me, snorted a laugh, and drew me close for a hug. He was alone. I pulled him inside and kicked the studio door shut.

"One of these days, that redheaded temper of yours is going to get you into something you can't get out of."

"How did you find me?"

"It wasn't hard. You're upset about losing the connection to Peter again. You'd want to be around his art, soaking it all in. Where else would you go?"

"He was pissing me off."

Bert choked back another laugh. "Yeah, I got that impression. So are you feeling any better now that you've had a little time?"

"Yeah, I just needed to cool off. But there are a few things I can do."

He slid his arm around my shoulders and we slowly walked through the studio and the storeroom. I wasn't in a talkative mood. How rare is that? Bert stopped when we were in the back corner, standing in front of "Fleeing

Beauty."

"Do you think we should sell anything?" I asked quietly.

He squeezed me against him. "That's not my decision."

"Come on, Bert. Give me your opinion."

He gave it a few minutes before answering. "No, I don't think you should. There is plenty of money in the trust. Vera certainly doesn't need it and you seem to be doing just fine on your own. I can't picture these treasures losing any value in the near future. So, no, I wouldn't sell anything."

"Why didn't you speak up at the meeting?"

"It's not my place, Jamie. This is between you and Vera and the attorney. I'm just along for the ride."

I tried to poke him in the ribs with my elbow but it was like jamming it into a stone wall. "I don't want to hear about your sexcapades with Vera."

"That's not what I meant."

"I know. But I still value your opinion and your advice."

We gazed at the statue for a minute without speaking. In a room filled with so many examples of his talent, this was without a doubt my favorite piece. There was no way I could imagine it being in some stuffy billionaire's collection, gathering dust or being used as a coat hook.

"Maybe you and Vera need to figure out the best course of action," Bert said.

"You're probably right. Is she still at Banning's office?"

He shook his head. "No, Banning had another meeting out near her hotel, so he was going to drop her off. She's worried about you."

"Not worried enough to come here herself?"

"Vera's always had trouble dealing with stubborn redheads. So I offered to track you down and make sure you're okay." He turned me around until we were face to face. "Are you okay, Daughter?"

I stepped into his arms for another hug. "Yeah, I'm

okay, Bert. Just angry and confused and maybe a little crazy."

"So in other words, you're back to your old self."

Everyone's a smartass.

****

Back at home I shed my summer business suit and pulled on shorts and a tank top. It was the last week before Labor Day. The kids were already grumbling about going back to school. Ian's summer of baseball was over. There were a few pickup games here and there, but not the regular flurry of activity. Tomorrow Malone was off work, so we were taking Ian and Caitlin to a water park. Brittany was also going, as was Linda. Malone said he had to go or Ian would be suffocated under a tidal wave of estrogen. We were planning to make a day of it, with a big picnic lunch, sort of a farewell to summer. It was exactly what I needed to get my mind off the studio.

On the computer, I reviewed all my notes about Meredith Bell. There had to be a clue in here somewhere. But if there was, it was too elusive for me. I scrolled through the files and the photos of the statue. It was possible she had posed for other works Peter had done on commission or sold before his death. But there was nothing that gave me any hint as to where she was or even if she was still alive. Frustrated, I put my heels on the desk and rocked back, replaying today's meeting.

Recalling Banning's statement about the estate made me think of the third member of the trust. The judge was another part of the puzzle I'd never considered. I did a quick search on the Internet.

Dante Barolo had been a judge in Oakland County for over twenty years. Prior to ascending to the bench, he worked in the prosecutor's office, specializing in criminal cases. He was extremely successful, trying many of the biggest, headline grabbing cases. His track record made it easy when he ran for a spot on the bench. I found a listing for the courthouse and left a voicemail message with his assistant, asking for a meeting on Thursday. With the long holiday weekend on the horizon, I hoped to catch him before the break. I'd never met him, but he must have known Peter well to be named as a monitor for the estate. My eyes grew weary with the research. Malone was due soon. I shut down the computer. For a moment I thought about calling Vera at the hotel, to see what she could tell me about Judge Barolo. The image of interrupting her and Bert in the middle of some nocturnal activity made me smile.

I stretched and wandered into the living room where one light was on low. The house was quiet. The windows were all open and a cool breeze fluttered the curtains. The ceiling fan slowly spun the air. I felt the Jewish Aunt call to me. Last week Brittany and Ian were tangled up on it, the sofa working its magic of pushing the occupants together. Brittany could not stop giggling. Apparently the girl was very ticklish. I flopped onto the sofa and sank into its comfort.

So many things had been discovered this summer. The treasures at the studio. A first love for Ian. A stronger relationship between Ian and Malone. And a growing relationship for me and Ian. Malone was still with me. There were few quiet moments with the kids around, but it didn't seem to bother him in the least. It wasn't difficult to picture Malone with kids of his own. I'd never really thought that much about having children, but it seemed like I had developed an honorary part-time family.

The click of the back door brought me out of my reverie. Malone appeared in the archway from the kitchen.

"Hey, Jamie."

"Hello, Octavio."

Shaking his head he came over to the sofa. Malone snagged my ankles with one hand and lifted them high enough so he could settle onto the cushions, then lowered my legs into his lap.

"Do you hear that?"

I hesitated and listened closely. "I don't hear anything."

"That's exactly what I mean. Silence. Peace and quiet. No boisterous teenagers making weird noises, just the gentle sound of your breathing."

"Want to make me breathe louder?"

He stroked my legs softly, sliding his hands up the calves to the knees, then dipping his fingers around to lightly graze the tender flesh behind the knee. Shivers danced up my spine.

"Maybe later. Right now I'll settle for the quiet."

I told him about the meeting with the attorneys and my reaction to Banning's recommendation. Malone's fingers hesitated in their efforts to caress my legs when I mentioned how much the collection was worth.

"Ten million dollars is a great deal of money, Jamie."

I shrugged, wiggling my ass into the sofa cushions. His attention was getting me very aroused. "That's in addition to the other assets already in the estate."

"So it appears I've fallen for a rich broad."

I brought my head up off the pillow. "Broad? Seriously, Malone is there any part of my body that is broad?"

"It's just an expression, Jamie."

"I always thought I was more narrow than broad."

Malone lifted my ankles high and yanked me closer so that my ass was now on his lap. He loomed over me, releasing my legs, and grabbed me around the waist. In a blink I was now straddling him, my hair hanging down into my eyes as he drew me close for a kiss. "Jamie, I think you're wearing far too much clothing."

Flashing back to a similar interlude earlier this summer, I was only wearing what was visible—the shorts and the tank top. Even in the dim light of the living room, I sensed Malone already knew this. I expected him to quickly peel off my clothes. But Malone had other plans.

With one arm around my waist, he held me close. I felt

his other hand cup the back of my head as he held me still, driving me crazy with a long, slow, wet kiss. I was squirming on his lap with excitement now. And he knew exactly what he was doing to me.

He released my head, drawing his hand slowly down to my breast. I tipped my head back. He was licking and kissing my throat. Electricity was running wild through my core. And then just as suddenly, Malone was standing, holding me in his arms. This was no easy trick, getting out of the clutches of the 'aunt'. Without a word, he eased me down until my feet touched the hardwood floor.

"Malone?"

"Hush, Jamie. I want you to do exactly what I say."

He stepped over and switched off the light. For an instant I was nervous, until I saw the mischievous sparkle in his eyes. He turned me around so that I was facing one arm of the sofa. Malone guided me back to the cushions, only now I was kneeling with my back to him. I could feel the stubble of his beard lightly scratching my shoulders. He turned his head enough to inhale the perfume I'd splashed on when changing. It wasn't strong, but it lingered. I felt a tingling sensation race down my arms as Malone's hot breath warmed my shoulder blades. He tugged the tank top. Now his lips were slowly moving down the ladder of my spine. I couldn't move. Even if I wanted to.

A solitary fingertip lightly slid down the back of my arm. He was barely touching me, but oh, baby, where he was touching and how he was touching was setting me on fire. He shifted lower. I felt the bottom of the tank top move up, exposing my stomach, the small of my back and my ribs. I cried out in surprise when Malone nipped me with his teeth, lightly grazing the spot on my back where my kidneys were. The fingertip continued to graze my arm.

I felt his lips move back to my spine. Now his tongue flicked out and danced the rest of the way down, pausing at the waistband of my shorts. His fingertip was gone now, darting quickly in front to undo my shorts. Somehow he shoved my shorts down until they were bunched up by my knees. Then his fingernails were lightly scratching my legs from the hips to the thighs while he continued to kiss the bottom of my spine. I was shaking. A solitary fingertip glided across the back of my knee.

"Take me, Malone. I can't stand it."

"Soon, Jamie. Soon."

"Now, Malone, please!"

I felt his palm squeeze my left calf. My orgasm was building so intensely, I was afraid I was going to implode. His lips danced across the cheeks of my ass. He nipped me again.

"Malone! You're killing me!"

He pulled back for a heartbeat. Somehow he managed to free himself from his jeans. I felt him press against me. I was so wet, so aroused, I screamed when he entered me. My body was quivering, delightful spasms causing my whole being to quake. Never before had I experienced something so intense, so overpowering. And still he held me, driving me forward, urging me on for more. I screamed again as he exploded inside me.

At last he relaxed his grip on me. Gasping for air, hoping my heart would stop galloping in my chest soon, I slumped forward over the arm of the sofa. He was still pressed against me, his body molded to mine. Eventually I was able to gather enough oxygen to speak.

"Welcome home, Octavio."

"It's good to be home, Jamie."

I smiled as he brushed the hair away from my face. "What brought that on, Malone? Not that I'm complaining. I'm just curious."

"Thought I'd better change up my technique. Since you're a rich broad now, I need to keep you interested."

I managed to turn around and face him. "Somehow, you're going to pay for calling me a rich broad."

"There was no doubt in my mind."

CHAPTER SEVENTEEN

Late Thursday morning I was sitting in the outer office of Judge Dante Barolo's chambers. While at the waterpark yesterday, the judge's assistant called and informed me that his honor could squeeze me in at lunch time. Not sure what to expect, I'd opted for a summer shift with some sandals and a simple gold necklace. The shift was a nice cool turquoise color that went well with my hair and eyes. The assistant was busy, typing away at some reports. She was an older woman, probably late fifties, who wore reading glasses down at the end of her nose. I had to restrain myself from reaching over and poking them back up toward her eyes.

Just before noon her phone buzzed. She shot me a quick look and lifted the receiver. There was a short conversation before she racked the phone and raised her eyes to me.

"Judge Barolo is in his chambers. You'll be joining him there for lunch. We're ordering from the deli downstairs. What would you like?"

I hesitated, considering the jittery condition of my stomach. "I'm really not hungry."

"The judge detests dining alone. I'd suggest you order

something otherwise he might get cranky." She inclined her head toward the door and lowered her voice. "Trust me, you don't want that."

"What's the judge having?"

"He ordered the northern Michigan salad. Fresh greens, dried cherries, apples, bleu cheese and a trace of bacon, with a vinaigrette dressing. It's his favorite."

"I'll have the same."

She nodded and picked up the phone. "Go on in. Lunch will be up shortly."

I took a deep breath and walked to the doorway beside her. I rapped my knuckles twice on the wood and heard a deep voice beckon me in. Here goes nothing.

Judge Dante Barolo was getting to his feet behind his desk. I didn't know what to expect, but the wide smile and brilliant white teeth were a pleasant surprise. He had a full head of thick black hair swept back from his forehead. There was a streak of gray at his temples. Barolo had a goatee, neatly trimmed that was almost jet black. He wore a navy blue suit with a starched white shirt and a gold tie. The judge was my height, with a solid build. Dark eyes sparkled as he came away from the desk and gestured me toward a pair of comfortable chairs, pausing just long enough to shake my hand in a firm, dry grasp.

"Jamie, it is indeed my pleasure to see you again."

"I didn't realize we'd met before."

His smile flashed again. "It was a long time ago. I've often wondered what you've been up to all these years. But I'm sure you're not here to listen to an old man wax nostalgic."

"Actually, if that nostalgic waxing concerns my father, I'm all ears. I was hoping for a little bit of a history lesson. Particularly your relationship with Peter."

Dante hunched forward in his chair. "Your father was a very talented man. He had such a gift, an ability to take a glimmer of an idea and bring it to life in marble and stone and steel. But surely your mother has told you about our relationship."

"Vera has not been very forthcoming about that time of her life. It was only recently that I learned about the trust and your involvement."

He rocked back in his chair and let out a deep, booming laugh. "That sounds like her. She was always one to live in the moment. How is she?"

"Vera is well. She travels a lot and seems to enjoy her life."

"I'm sure she's not without her suitors." He paused and gave me a cool, blank stare that must have had witnesses and attorneys cringing. "Lincoln Banning has kept me apprised of the situation with the studio and the sculptures. While I haven't had the pleasure of viewing the findings, he's assured me that these are some of Peter's greatest works. But why does that bring you to my chambers?"

I took a deep breath and calmly spelled it out. There were so many gaps in my knowledge of my father that I wanted to fill them in. For years, he'd been a distant memory, a ghostly presence that appeared occasionally in my early childhood. Vera's insistence on moving forward blocked my awareness of him. Now I was hungry for information.

The clerk interrupted briefly and brought our salads. Judge Barolo waved me toward the food and cast a brief scowl in my direction until I tasted the salad. It was excellent, with a light cherry vinaigrette dressing. It came with a little buttery croissant. I nibbled the edge and gave him my very best innocent look. Barolo caught it and laughed again as the clerk quickly left the room.

"Nice try, but I've got a wife and two daughters. I'm immune to that look. Well, most of the time I am."

"Tell me how you knew Peter."

Slowly the tale came out. Barolo had been a rising star in the Oakland County Prosecutor's office. His conviction rate in the courtroom was impressive. He was single, handsome, and incredibly successful just two years out of law school. It didn't take long before his presence was requested at many of the biggest social events in the area. Whether it was a black tie affair at the auto show, benefits for cancer research and the heart association, or any number of political causes, his handlers guided him. There were obviously great things on the horizon for Barolo.

The judge paused in his tale for a sip of water. "I had to listen to my rabbi and do what he said. Some of these events weren't open for debate."

I paused with a forkful of salad in midair. "You're Jewish? I thought Barolo was Italian."

"Oh, I am Italian and I'm not Jewish." He chuckled and picked at his salad. "In politics and in some other areas, a rabbi is a form of counselor, a wise man who will guide you and hopefully, help you avoid problems and pitfalls that can ruin your career. My rabbi was an Irish Catholic attorney who was also one of my professors at law school."

Barolo resumed the story. It was during one of those society events that he met Peter for the first time. Both men had been dragged to this particular soiree with every intention of making a brief appearance and disappearing as soon as the rubber chicken was served. They were introduced and wound up at a table outnumbered by single females, the daughters of various political movers and shakers. Barolo recognized Peter's discomfort in the surroundings and realized they mirrored his own. So the quick thinking attorney came up with a plan. He'd caught a passing waiter's attention and had a brief conversation with him. As the waiter left, he turned to Peter.

"You're an artist, right?"

"I am."

"I need your help. There's a case I've been working on that just broke. But I need someone who can create a sketch from a couple of witnesses. My regular guy is out of town. If I don't get the details quickly, I'll lose the chance.

Can you break away for a while?"

"Well, if it's really important, I think it's my duty to help you." Peter stood quickly and made his apologies to the ladies.

Barolo did the same, quickly downing his drink and grabbing Peter by the arm. Together they hustled out of the room.

"There was no case, was there?" I asked.

The judge seemed taken aback by the question. "Of course there was. It was a case of single malt Scotch that my father kept in the basement. He'd been saving it for a very special occasion."

"And the sketch?"

"Peter drew an excellent rendition of the bottle and some very distinctive glasses. We became good friends that night."

"Did you use that excuse often?"

He nodded. "Occasionally. The challenge was to know when we had to suffer through an entire evening and when we could make a quick escape. Your father's benefactors wanted to showcase him as well as his talents at every opportunity. They wanted him to be in demand as much as his work."

"So you knew him before he married Vera?"

"Yes. I was at the wedding. It was a small affair, but very tasteful. After they married, the pressure was off when Peter attended social functions. He didn't go as often as I did. We would get together as friends frequently. He was an amazing man."

I knew he had to get back to court soon. "Can I ask about the estate?"

"Of course. But I would assume Lincoln can provide you with every detail."

"Did you help him set it up?"

He smiled widely, his eyes alight with the memory. "Yes, I advised Peter. He wanted to diversify his holdings. He was a superstitious old soul. Peter believed that the old building he'd discovered for a studio had the spirits of other artists, their energy, all of their creative influences. Once he became successful, he wanted to make sure the building would always be his studio. And that it would be available to other artists. It was a haven."

"What about the other investments?"

Barolo's eyes flicked to an antique clock on the wall. "Almost time to get back to work. I did make some suggestions on stocks and was pleased to see Peter consider them. My father was a stockbroker. He was very adept at the market. A diversified portfolio was one of his trademarks. I got advice from him for both of us."

"Sounds like you did pretty well."

"We both did. Now it's my turn to ask a question."

"Of course."

"You have Peter's inquisitive nature. Why has it taken you so long to learn more about your father?"

His directness rocked me. "I was only seven when he died. Over the years, I thought I knew everything about him. But Vera was never one to talk about Peter. She didn't exactly bring me around to see his old friends. I've always been curious, but just didn't realize it." I gave my head a shake. "Pretty sorrowful excuse for a loving daughter, isn't it?"

"Not at all." He pushed the remains of his salad to the center of the table and stood up. "As I said, I know Vera too. There was a period of mourning, about a year. Lincoln and I saw her several times. Once she was assured that Peter had taken care of the financial worries, she began to get on with her life. On several occasions she commented that there was no sense in looking back. It was time to move on. Vera is many things, but I doubt she is one to while away a day reminiscing."

"Not her style." I stood and extended a hand. "Thank you, your honor."

"Jamie, in the privacy of my chambers, or anywhere outside the courtroom, you can call me Dante."

"Thank you, Dante. Would you mind if I came back sometime? I'd love to hear more about your friendship with Peter."

"I'd really like that," he said, flashing me another smile.

With that I leaned forward and planted a kiss on his cheek. He chuckled. I pulled back and realized he was now adorned with a bright red lip print. Embarrassed, I pointed at the tissues on the corner of his desk.

He chuckled again. "Better not let my wife see you do that. She's the jealous type."

"She's a smart woman."

****

Walking out of the courthouse, I paused to enjoy the late August sunshine. There was a small grassy area between the building and the parking lot, with a couple of wrought iron benches. I stepped over to one and sat down. I closed my eyes and tilted my head back. I thought about Dante Barolo and the stories he'd told. Every step brought me a little closer to my late father. Too many years had gone by. It felt strange to miss him.

"May I join you on this beautiful afternoon?" a deep cultured voice asked.

My eyes snapped open. I recognized that voice.

"It's been a long time, Mr. Mundy." I gestured at the bench.

He settled beside me, taking a moment to pluck at the crease of his trousers. "You look well, Jamie. I thought we agreed to dispense with formalities."

"Sorry, Harry. It slipped my mind over the last couple of months."

"No reason to apologize."

"So how did you know I'd be here? I'm not a believer in coincidence."

The hint of a smile tugged at the corner of his mouth. "Neither am I. But I thought it was prudent that we meet.

I have given your situation a great deal of consideration."

"So you figured out how someone stole part of the collection?"

Harrison Mundy was sitting erect on the bench, his hands resting on his knees. He raised the index finger of his right hand and swept it back and forth like a metronome.

"As I said, a great deal of consideration. I sense that something will occur soon."

"But you're not prepared to tell me who, or how, or when, are you?"

He turned to me and flashed another dazzling smile. He and Barolo could do billboards for a dentist. "I am disinclined to acquiesce to your request."

"So all you're willing to say is something may happen soon."

"Precisely."

"Did anyone ever tell you that you're a frustrating man to talk with, Harry?"

"Frequently."

Effortlessly he rose from the bench. As I scrambled to my feet, he lightly took my hand and raised it, brushing his lips across my knuckles. The gesture was so unexpected I didn't know what to say. Then he winked at me and turned away. A dark green Jaguar sedan pulled up beside to the curb. His exotic companion, Jocelyn, was behind the wheel. Harrison Mundy reached the passenger door and turned back.

"Please give my regards to Miss Davis."

"Of course, Harry."

And as quickly as he'd appeared, he vanished.

What the hell was that all about?

Soon.

What the hell kind of help was that?

****

Linda left for her dinner date. Ian had persuaded her to leave Logan with him, so he had an excuse to spend more time with Brittany and her dog. Like the kid needed an excuse! But that was how they'd met earlier this summer, walking the dogs. It was cute to see them together. We'd split a pizza earlier. Now I was at my desk, staring at the computer. Something Linda said before she left was bouncing around in my brain.

"If you were a thief, Jay Kay, how would you do it?"

That was an excellent question. I went to the Internet and pulled up the website for Odon Krippendore. In addition to some of his works, there was a calendar of events. Krip was going to be at a big arts festival up near Rochester. With it being a holiday weekend, there were a lot of events to herald the end of the summer. I could think of three different ones, mixing food, music, and artists that were taking over various downtown areas. On a hunch, I called Krip at the studio. His voice boomed across the phone when I identified myself.

"Jamie, I was just reminiscing about your father."

"Good things I hope."

"Of course. Peter was always a class act. So, what's on your mind?"

"I see you're doing a show up in Oakland County for the holidays. Is it a big deal?"

"Yes indeed. There will be over a hundred different artists with displays. This is a juried event, so it's always important to have a good showing. You should come by."

"I was thinking about it. Maybe I'll bring Ian so he can check it out."

"Jamie, that's a wonderful idea. The event begins on Saturday and runs through the holiday. But Saturday and Sunday are the better days."

"Will most of the other artists from the studio be there?"

Krippendore took a moment to consider it. "Seems to me the majority of them will be gone. I know the pottery folk will be out near Ann Arbor at a show and there's another festival out near Brighton. Of course, the one downtown will draw a few as well. It's our last hurrah for the summer, so everyone will be out, flaunting their wares."

"Thanks, Krip. We'll try to get out there this weekend."

"I look forward to it. Ciao, Jamie."

Another piece of the puzzle clicked into place. Too bad I didn't realize it.

****

I was restless when Malone came home. He found me in the office, sitting in the dark, staring at the computer. I'd pulled up the image of "Spring Dance" and couldn't take my eyes off it. I needed to figure out who'd stolen it and how they had gotten away with it. I told him as much when he pulled me from the chair and kissed me.

"Let it be, Jay. It's late. Staring at it all night won't help."

"That's easy for you to say, Randolph."

His eyes twinkled as he shook his head. "Randolph? Jay, that's almost tame for you."

"Sorry, I guess I'm preoccupied."

Malone sat in my desk chair and pulled me onto his lap. With one hand, he was able to shut down my computer. His other hand somehow slipped under my tank top. I felt his fingernails lightly scratching their way up my spine, sending shivers throughout my body. Malone is very good at distracting me. My body wasted no time reacting to his attention. As the computer powered off he turned his full attention to me. With the light from the monitor gone, I was forced to use my other senses. Malone turned me slightly. As he kissed me I could feel both hands beneath my top now, one sliding across my ribs, reaching for my breasts. The other was still pressed against my spine, supporting me. He had me trembling.

"Jamie," he whispered in my ear.

My voice was nothing more than a gasp. "Yes?"

"Do you realize we've never done it in here?" His lips were on my ear now.

I could feel his breath, his tongue darting out lightly, pulling the lobe with his lips. I squirmed. Malone was turning me into a wanton female. Right now, what I wanted was him. When I'd changed clothes, I must have been subconsciously thinking of Malone, for I'd shed my lingerie and was only wearing the shorts and the tank. Malone quickly figured this out.

"We can't do it here," I gasped. "The kid is right next door."

"No screaming."

I turned to face him. Malone's lips found mine and silenced any other comments. With an uncanny display of dexterity, he managed to lift me enough to yank the shorts off my hips. Dripping with desire, my hands fumbled with his belt and zipper. When he was free, Malone spun me around so my back was pressed against his chest. Eagerly I guided him inside. He brought one hand up and clamped it over my mouth. Somehow, some way, we found a rhythm without squeaking the chair or knocking the computer off the desk. I opened my mouth and nipped his palm as I hit my peak. Malone nuzzled the hair out of the way and pressed his mouth to my neck. I felt him suck on it like a vampire as he exploded inside me.

It was a moment before either one of us could speak. Slowly his hand slid from my mouth, stroking my cheek. I rolled my head to the side to look back at him.

"Randolph, will you always be this passionate?"

"Only one way to find out, Jay."

I managed to get to my feet and walk to the door wearing nothing but the tank top. I gave him my best over-the-shoulder-come-hither look, but wasn't sure he could see it in the dark. It didn't matter. He'd know where to find me. I padded as quietly as possible across the hall to our room. Malone arrived moments later, my shorts dangling from his fingertips. He quickly stripped and joined me between the sheets.

"That was a lovely distraction, Malone. But I still need to figure it out. "

"Let it be, Jamie."

"You know I can't. It's like asking me to stop breathing."

"But you still have the rest of the collection. We know everything is secure."

I took a moment to put my thoughts in order. "But that's part of the collection. The first piece we opened. It's a part of Peter. A part of the history we shared. And until I figure out who took it and where it is, it's like I'm missing a part of me. Can you understand, Malone?"

He nodded and drew me to him. "Yeah, and something tells me no matter how much I encourage you to let the police handle it, that you're not going to leave it alone."

"That's part of me too, Malone. Guess you know that by now."

"I do. But be careful, Jay. Don't do anything impulsive."

"I can't guarantee anything, Malone. But I'll do my best."

He chuckled just before we fell asleep. "That's about what I expected. You are one stubborn redhead. Beautiful, but oh so stubborn."

CHAPTER EIGHTEEN

I couldn't stand it. Late Friday afternoon found me staring at a blank page on the computer and it was driving me crazy. I was in the middle of some notes for a new story when I realized I couldn't concentrate. My mind kept wandering back to the stolen sculpture. I thought of my conversation with Harrison Mundy. Then I focused again on the last words Linda had said before she'd left last night. "How would you do it?"

I started doodling on a note pad. One thought triggered another. It was a scattershot approach, not linear in any form, just random ideas related to the topic. After twenty minutes, I leaned forward and snagged a red pen from the ceramic holder next to the monitor. A circle here. Another one. Then a third and a forth. Two more. I numbered them and sat back.

"What the hell?"

I made one call to confirm something. Then I dashed out of the house, grabbing my keys and my bag on the way.

****

The receptionist gave me a quizzical look. I wasn't really dressed for a business meeting. This morning had been overcast and cool. I was wearing tan jeans and a black summer top with sandals. I hadn't taken the time to change or make an appointment. What I wanted to ask wouldn't take long. And with it being the last day before the holiday weekend, I didn't want to risk a benevolent boss closing the office early.

The door to the conference room clicked open and Helen Gaines stepped out.

"Jamie, I didn't realize you'd be joining us."

"Joining who?"

"Your mother. She's meeting with Mr. Banning right now." Helen inclined her head toward the conference room. "There were a few things she wanted to discuss while she's still in town."

I barged into the room. Banning and Vera sat at one end of the table, a file folder spread out before them. They both looked up in surprise at my entrance.

"What are you doing, Vera?"

"Jamie! What on earth brings you here?"

I could feel my temper rising. "Answer my question first. What's going on?

"We're merely reviewing the financial status of the estate," Banning said. "Without taking into consideration the collection, everything is in excellent shape."

I turned to Vera. "Is that true?"

"Of course, Jamie. I'm headed to San Francisco to spend some time with friends at a vineyard. I don't know when I might be back, so I asked Lincoln to review the finances with me. It's a matter of course we try to do on an annual basis."

"So you're not discussing selling off any part of the collection?"

Banning sat back and crossed his arms over his chest. I noticed Helen Gaines come into the room and shut the door. She stood against it, shifting her weight from one foot to the other. Maybe her knee was bothering her. The silence in the room was weighing heavily on everyone. Vera cleared her throat.

"We will not be selling anything. I have asked Lincoln for his recommendations on loaning a few pieces to a museum, perhaps in Manhattan or Los Angeles. But nothing is going to be sold."

"Really?"

Banning nodded. "Vera has asked that I research those options. She instructed me to gauge the reactions and to work with you on identifying the best pieces for a display. We also talked about insurance and security precautions. I expect to have the details shortly after the holiday concludes."

I saw Banning glance at the ornate clock on the wall. It was already after five. Quitting time. I'd been so certain something was going on here. Something crooked. Banning shifted his gaze to Vera and then back to me. If he had weekend plans, he was being cool about it.

"I don't think Mr. Banning has any intention of placing Peter's sculptures with a museum for a showing," I said. His eyes were on mine as I moved to stand beside Vera's chair with the windows at my back.

"Really, Jamie, what are you getting at?" Vera asked.

Banning cleared his throat. "Jamie, I have always managed the assets of this trust with the family's best interest in mind."

"Maybe so. But that was before we discovered the storeroom. Now you can't stand the idea of it just sitting there. All that money and you can't get your grubby little hands on it."

"Jamie! Apologize to Lincoln right now!"

Banning calmly raised a hand toward Vera. "It's quite alright. I can understand Jamie's concerns. But I must assure you that I would never to do anything to jeopardize the trust of your family. Peter was a true friend. Yet I wonder why you think I would do something so egregious, stealing from you."

I leaned forward and planted both palms on the conference table. "Because you're the only one who could have stolen the sculpture. You're the only one who saw it, the only one who had keys. Because I sent you the damn video files, every time, like the trusting fool that I was. Because deep down you're nothing more than a thieving rat bastard!"

Vera gasped beside me and started to struggle out of her chair. I pushed her back. My eyes were still locked on Banning's. His face flushed red. I couldn't tell if it was shame at being called out or anger. Maybe he didn't expect a stupid woman to figure it out.

Slowly he pointed a narrow finger at me. He shook it back and forth without uttering a word. Then he regained control and lowered his hand to the table.

"You are mistaken, Ms. Richmond. I did not enter that building during the time in question. I was out of town that weekend, sailing with a few friends up to Port Huron. The police have already verified my alibi. Your theory about my involvement is nothing more than vapor."

I banged a fist on the table. "You engineered it. I'm surprised you didn't take more. After all, you had already seen the video. You had to know what was there. The piece was portable. You just couldn't let it sit there. You just had to get your hands on it, didn't you, Banning?"

"As I just explained…"

"Shut up!" I pushed off the table and turned my back on him. Vera's hand reached out and clenched mine. I could feel her shaking. Or maybe it was just me. Movement caught the edge of my peripheral vision. I glanced away from the windows and saw Helen Gaines staring at me with wide eyes. Realization hit me like a kick to the stomach.

There was a double tap at the conference room door. Helen drew a deep breath and pushed away. She swung the door open. Two burly men in jeans, boots, and work shirts marched into the room. One held a shotgun with a pistol grip, the barrel dangling alongside his leg. The other held a small revolver is his right hand, pointed directly at Lincoln Banning. Behind them marched a slender man with an olive complexion and a neatly trimmed mustache. He was wearing a business suit with a white shirt, the collar undone. He paused alongside Helen. Quickly he reached over and cupped her head, drawing her close for a rough kiss. She seemed to melt at his touch.

"You have done well."

Banning started to rise. Revolver guy stepped up and whipped him across the face with the gun. Banning crumpled into his chair, his hands clutching his nose. Blood oozed out between his fingers. Vera was up, moving beside him. Revolver guy extended his arm and cocked the gun.

"No!"

The command came from three voices. Me, Helen, and the olive skinned guy. I don't know which one had the greatest impact, but revolver guy eased the hammer back and lowered the gun to his side. Vera pulled a hanky from Banning's coat and began trying to treat his wounds. I realized shotgun man was standing beside me. There was no expression on his face. The olive skinned man reached down and caught Helen's wrist and pulled her close.

"I was hoping to avoid any confrontations," he said.

"Who are you and want do you want?" I asked.

His eyes flicked to Vera and Banning for a moment. He dismissed them and turned to face me. With a two-fingered wave, the shotgun man took a step back.

"I am Anton Tancredi."

The name meant nothing to me. My face must have told him as much.

"But that is not important. I'm afraid you've disrupted my plans." He turned and pulled Helen close. I could see her trembling in fear as he wrapped an arm around her waist. "You did right, calling me."

"Does it ruin everything?" she asked quietly.

He smiled and stroked her hair. "Hardly. We'll just have to adjust the timetable."

"So we're okay?"

"Yes, my darling, we are very okay."

Helen shuddered as he released her. Tancredi dipped a hand into his jacket pocket and handed her a small pill. Helen's eyes grew wide as she popped it into her mouth and jerked her head back to swallow it.

"What are we going to do, Tanc?" the guy with the shotgun asked.

"We speed up the timetable."

A thousand questions raced through my mind, but I was too numb to sort them. I took a tentative step toward Vera. Banning's face wasn't bleeding badly. Apparently the pressure on the bridge of his nose was helping. I took another step. No one tried to stop me. I bent down next to Vera.

"Are you okay?"

She nodded. "I'm scared, Jamie. What is all this about?"

"I don't know."

"Oh, but I think you do know," Tancredi said. He tapped revolver guy on the shoulder. "Put that away. Go to the shop and get the truck."

The guy nervously tucked the gun in his pocket. "Tanc, you can't be serious! You said we were gonna wait until after midnight."

"Paulie, there are always contingency plans. Besides, it will be less suspicious if we're out in broad daylight. So many people will be celebrating the weekend, a stray truck here or there will hardly be noticed. George and I will be just fine. Have Skeech come with you. We'll meet you at the loading doors in an hour."

Paulie hesitated for a moment. He shrugged and went out the conference room door.

"See if you can find something to clean up Mr.

Banning," Tancredi said to Helen. "We want him looking respectable when we go out. No reason to raise any suspicions. Perhaps someone will think he walked into a door."

"You should have thought of that before your monkey attacked him," I said, resting a hand on Banning's shoulder.

Tancredi smiled at me. "I've heard about you. The quick tempered redhead. You've certainly been a complication to my plans. But I enjoy a challenge."

Helen reappeared with a thick towel. She offered it to Tancredi. He gave her a brief smile and threw it across the table to me. "Clean him up."

Using a pitcher of water from the conference table, I soaked one end. Vera moved aside. Tenderly I wiped traces of blood off Banning's cheeks. The gash across the bridge of his nose was starting to clot. His eyes burned into mine. With the dry end of the towel, I patted his skin. He looked better, but still a long way from good.

"I'm sorry, Linc. Guess I had it all wrong."

"No, Jamie. It would appear that you had the right office, just the wrong player."

"So what do we do now?" Vera asked.

We all looked at Anton Tancredi. He gave us a wry smile and a shrug. "We wait."

****

Forty-five minutes later, Tancredi motioned for us to get up. Vera and I each took one of Banning's arms to steady him. While he seemed to be okay, he had a little trouble walking. Helen ran ahead to call the elevator. Before we'd left the conference room, she'd taken my cell phone and switched it off. She did the same with Vera's and Banning's. All three phones were dumped in the center of the big table. George walked in front of us, the barrel of the shotgun held tightly against his leg. Tancredi chose a spot right behind me. He inclined his head slightly. I could feel his breath on my ear. Goose bumps covered my arms. Not the pleasant kind that Malone triggers.

"Don't do anything foolish. There's no reason for anyone else to be hurt. All I need is a little bit of time. Do you understand, or do I have to use your mother as an example?" His voice was low and tight.

I turned my head enough so he could see my face. "I understand."

"No heroes. Buy me some time and we'll all live to see the sunrise."

We rode the elevator to the lobby in silence. Outside I could see a large SUV parked right at the curb. George moved quickly around the hood and slid in behind the wheel. Helen somehow scrambled over the seats and moved all the way to the rear. Tancredi opened the passenger door.

"Put the old lady up front."

I expected a snappy retort from Vera at being called old, but she silently climbed into the cab. Without being told I opened the rear door and helped Lincoln Banning inside. He was holding a torn piece of the towel over his face, keeping pressure on his nose. I glanced at Tancredi. He nodded. I followed Banning inside, taking the middle spot. Tancredi climbed in and closed the door.

"Let's roll."

George eased the heavy vehicle away from the curb. I noticed there was little traffic in the downtown area. A few miles away the festival was underway, but in this stretch of office buildings, the week had already ended. People had evacuated early to start the holiday celebrations.

Tancredi bumped me with his leg. "Figure it out yet?"

"I'm working on it."

"And Helen kept telling me how smart you are! It's really not that difficult."

I could see Vera tensing up in front of me. Was this really happening? My options were limited. There was no way I could risk doing something that would put her in danger, or anyone else. Tancredi had placed me right in the dead center of the vehicle. Helen Gaines was perched on the rear seat directly behind me. I knew she was athletic, but I didn't know how strong she was. If I tried to attack George to cause an accident, Helen might be fast enough to stop me. Or Tancredi could. Although he hadn't brandished a weapon, that didn't mean he wasn't carrying one. And what if he decided to make Vera or Banning pay for my efforts? I pushed those thoughts aside.

"I'll tell you what I know," I said.

"We could all use a little entertainment," Tancredi said.

"When the storeroom was discovered, it made the news, big time. There was a lot of attention at first. Then when no scandal or details came out, they moved on to other stories. That's normal. We began opening the crates and I sent Lincoln Banning the video files each night. That was supposed to be for his eyes only. But he mistakenly trusted Helen with that information, not knowing she's a junkie."

A fist knotted in my hair and viciously yanked me backward. "I am not a junkie!"

Tancredi made soothing sounds and pried her fingers out of my scalp. "She's spinning a tale, my darling. There's no reason to think otherwise." He shifted sideways in the seat, pressing his back against the door so he could watch us more closely. "Continue."

"Helen either copied the videos or forwarded them to you. She was able to swipe Banning's keys for the studio building. She took you there to see the art work. And your first big mistake was to swipe 'Spring Dance'. That really tipped your hand."

"It's such a lovely piece. I couldn't resist it."

"I know what you mean," I muttered.

"Tell me more. What else did you figure out? What brought you storming into the law offices this afternoon?"

"At first I thought Banning was behind it. Maybe he

was tired of the life. Maybe he was frustrated that all of this priceless art was just beyond his reach. Maybe it irked him that he could never hope to own even the smallest piece in the collection. But the theft had to stem from his office. No one else knew about the works we'd unpacked or had the keys to the building. It had to be him." I leaned forward slightly, hoping my hair was out of her reach. "Or it had to be someone within his office. That left Helen."

Tancredi seemed to be enjoying this. "Surely there could have been another associate?"

"It's a small firm. Helen was almost always with Banning. I remember how she acted when they brought Vera to the studio to check our progress. She was mystified. But she was acting funny, the way she stayed apart from the others. I think she was taking video with her phone too. That was your second big mistake. She should have just kept sending you the video files. Whatever she filmed wouldn't be very helpful."

"You're very perceptive."

I shook my head in disgust. "Yeah, right. If I was so perceptive, I would have figured this out weeks ago. It was an inside job. I'm just surprised you tipped your hand the way you did."

"Jamie, what are you talking about?" Vera asked.

I turned to face Tancredi. "We're on our way to the studio so they can rob us."

In the front seat, Vera began to cry. Tancredi smiled widely and slowly began to clap his hands. "Well done. So tell me, are there any other mistakes I've made?"

"Why come to the law offices? You could have waited until we were gone, then had Helen swipe the keys again and emptied out the building over the weekend. Why the confrontation today?"

"Actually, that's your fault."

I was stunned. No one knew I was going downtown. The only call I'd made was to make sure Banning's office was still open. I hadn't even identified myself.

"What are you getting at?"

Tancredi extended his left arm over the seat. He cupped Helen's cheek tenderly. Then with a lightning quick move, he slapped her. I could see her head snap back in my peripheral vision. She whimpered, but made no move to slide out of his reach. He kept his hand there until she obediently moved back where he could caress her once again.

"We were waiting for Helen just down the street. I knew the anticipation was getting to her. She was wired. So as soon as she left work, we were going to pick her up. Darling Helen knows how important this is. When you arrived so unexpectedly, she called me. Helen dismissed the receptionist, who was the last person in the office besides you three. She waited until we came in, then joined you in the conference room. So really, this is all your fault."

Before I could think of a retort, George pulled the vehicle up to a stop. "We're here."

****

A large moving truck was backed up to the loading dock of the studio building. Helen pulled a big ring of keys from her purse and unlocked the door. George encouraged us forward, gesturing with the shotgun. Tancredi was humming a tune as he strolled down the hall. He paused outside of Peter's studio and waited. Helen fumbled with keys. I could see the imprint of his palm and fingers on her cheek. As she opened the door, Tancredi made a grand sweeping motion with his arm. Silently we walked into the studio. Tancredi hooked his thumb at the back of the building. Helen and George went to unlock the dock doors.

"Open the storeroom," he said to me.

I guided Vera and Banning to one of the worktables near the desk. Then I walked to the wall and triggered the hidden switch. There was enough daylight coming in from the northern windows that we didn't need to turn on the lights. Tancredi walked into the archway between the studio and the storeroom. He put his hands on his hips and let out a low whistle.

"This is so much more impressive than the videos. Your father must have been a very talented man."

I wanted to snap off a sarcastic response, but nothing jumped from my tongue. My brain was busy, trying to formulate a plan out of this. Footsteps sounded down the hall. I could hear the low murmur of voices. I glanced at Vera. She was ghostly pale, clutching Banning's hand. Through the doorway stomped Helen Gaines, Paulie, and another man. This one was scrawny, wearing baggy jeans and a torn T-shirt. Tattoos ran down both arms, daggers and chains and swirls. He pushed a two-wheeled hand truck in front of him. I noticed Paulie was carrying a big three ring binder. George appeared in the doorway, pushing a cart loaded with blankets.

"Where do we start, Tanc?" Paulie asked.

"Let's see the book."

When he opened the binder I realized it was a copy of the portfolio we'd provided the experts with a few weeks ago. The pieces were still arranged in the same displays. Tancredi checked the book and pointed at one of the sculptures just inside the door.

"Start with that one."

I watched the three men move to the sculpture and lift it off the display. George wrapped it in a thick, quilted blanket, the type used by furniture movers. He secured it with some heavy strapping tape. Then Paulie moved the hand truck into position and he and the other man rolled it out of the room. George huddled with Tancredi for a moment at the binder. With a nod, he left the room as well. Tancredi whispered something in Helen's ear. She brightened like a child on Christmas morning. He handed her the binder. As she turned away he swatted her on the ass, hard. Helen squealed and looked over her shoulder at him, beaming a smile. She walked over to the display and passed two sculptures before putting a tag on one. I watched her move on, skipping another one before selecting another sculpture. What was going on?

"You won't get away with this," Banning said. His voice was muffled by his blocked nasal passages, but he managed to speak with some authority.

"And what will you do, counselor? No one will find you until after the weekend. We will be so far away, you'd need a miracle to track us down."

The attorney kept trying to challenge Tancredi. Ignoring them, I watched Helen Gaines. She was practically skipping around the room, finding specific sculptures indicated in the binder. It was as if she had a shopping list. What was it about the pieces she'd tagged? I tried to figure out what they had in common. Some were bronze. Others were steel. She hesitated at one and flipped back and forth through the book. She giggled and stuck a tag on it. In the doorway Paulie and the other guy appeared. Together they moved the loaded hand truck into the room. Paulie pulled a large knife from his pocket and cut the tape. They pulled the blanket off. It was the same sculpture they'd taken away. Why were they bringing it back?

Watching them lift it into position on the display, I felt eyes on me. Tancredi remained by the worktable. But his eyes locked on mine. Helen drifted over and whispered in his ear. He nodded. She turned to walk toward the storeroom. Tancredi reached down and pinched her on the ass. Helen squealed again and rushed into the other room.

"Figure it out yet?" he asked me.

"Why do you treat her like that?"

He shrugged. "Helen likes it rough. She was a tomboy with three brothers."

"I think you like hurting her."

Another shrug. "It serves the purpose. Figure it out

yet?"

"You're not here to steal the entire collection. You're swapping out certain ones that you've somehow been able to make copies of."

"Very good."

"You're picking the less complicated ones. Those must have been easier to replicate. You had the video files, along with copies of the notes regarding what elements were used to create each sculpture and its dimensions. What is this, paint by numbers?"

He nodded several times and gave me what could have been a smile of admiration. "Not quite. But I do have a few starving artists in my employ who are good enough to recreate something. Since the collection was already authenticated by your group of experts, no one will ever doubt the pieces I'm substituting as anything but the genuine article."

"So you replace the real ones with your fakes. But what makes you think we won't tell the world about the theft."

Tancredi raised his palms in a simple gesture. Vera voiced what I refused to admit.

"Because we won't be alive to tell anyone."

CHAPTER NINETEEN

I was too numb to do anything. We were outnumbered. I had no weapon or cell phone. George and Paulie were definitely armed. I had to assume both Tancredi and the other guy would be too. It was hopeless. I slumped against the rolltop desk. Vera and Banning sat on stools, holding hands. I watched the trio of men fall into a rhythm. They would take a piece that Helen tagged, wrap it up and haul it away, only to bring a replacement back a few minutes later.

Time dragged on. Tancredi walked into the storeroom. From my perch I could see Helen. She had taken off her jacket and draped it around a sculpture. Now her shoes were dangling from another piece. Apparently she had found a new way to tag the collection. I was wondering how far she would go. Tancredi watched her pull off her blouse and hang it from the outstretched arms of "Fleeing Beauty".

"Not that one," he said, snagging the garment and throwing it at her.

"But I like that one!"

"So do I. But we stick to the plan."

Helen walked to another piece and threw the blouse

over it. He nodded and leaned against a crate, watching her. Helen checked the binder. She began to sway back and forth, twisting and turning. She spun in front of him and bent at the waist, shaking her ass at him. As Tancredi reached for her, she stepped away. Looking over her shoulder, her hands went behind her back and undid the zipper on her slacks. Still swaying, she began to wiggle the fabric down her legs. She stepped out of the slacks and spun to face him. Tancredi motioned with two fingers. She scooped up the slacks and threw them at the base of another sculpture.

"I could have modeled for him," she said. Helen continued to sway, wearing nothing but her bra and panties.

"Yes, you could have. But this is not the time for fun."

"I want to," she pleaded. "I want them to watch us." She jerked her head in our direction. "I've put up with his pompous shit long enough. He always acts so superior. I want to show him who's in charge now."

Tancredi grabbed her roughly and yanked her to him. "Make no mistake. I am in charge."

She squirmed against him. "Anton, please. We're in this together."

"I am in charge. You're just along for the ride." He pushed her away with a disgusted look on his face. Perhaps the honeymoon was over.

"But Anton…"

He slapped her again. "Stop it. Get dressed. We're not done yet."

"But Anton…"

I don't remember pushing off the desk or marching into the storeroom. But before he could strike her again I found myself between them. Helen was quivering with fear. There was a look in his eyes, a combination of disgust and rage barely being contained. I took her by the arm and moved her out of his reach.

"Get dressed. You don't want to make him any angrier

than he already is."

She turned her back to him. Leaning against a crate, she began to step back into her slacks. This close I could see the nasty surgical scar on her knee. There were others as well, long jagged ones on her thighs and small puckered ones on her abdomen and back. Helen caught me staring at them.

"Cigarette burns. My brothers used me as an ashtray." Her voice was devoid of emotion. "Until I hit puberty. Then they used me for other things."

"That must have been awful."

She gave a little shrug. I held her blouse open and helped her slip it on. As she was buttoning it up I retrieved her jacket and shoes. While she was dressing I kept shifting my eyes back to Tancredi. Deep down I knew what he was planning. My mother was right. There was no way he'd leave witnesses behind. Vera, Banning, and I had become dispensable as soon as he entered the conference room. I wondered if that part of the plan was an improvisation, triggered by my late arrival. But that didn't make any sense. If only Tancredi had waited a few more hours, there would have been no witnesses to deal with. It would have been the perfect crime.

Either way, I had to stall him. I put an arm around Helen and steered her back to the studio. Perhaps whatever drug he'd given her earlier was wearing off.

"Aren't you the protective mother hen?" Tancredi said. "Even willing to help the one who sold you out?"

"She didn't come up with this scheme and go out on the street looking for thieves. So how did you find her anyway?"

He pouted at me. "Poor little Helen has a bit of a dependency problem. She got hooked on Percocet, even before her knee surgery. It's stronger than the things she's used in the past. Of course, once her prescriptions ran out, she was desperate to find another source."

I settled Helen in a chair by the desk and walked over

to the wall between the studio and the storeroom. Tancredi followed. "So you're not just a thief, you're a drug dealer too?"

"I like to think of myself as an enterprising businessman. I prefer to have interests in many areas. You never know when an opportunity may present itself."

"It's a little hard to believe that this lady lawyer just happened to end up on your doorstep, looking for painkillers."

Tancredi gave me a thin smile. "She was making the circuit of a few nightclubs. Word filtered to me that she was something different. I arranged to meet her. She offered money, but that was just the tip of the iceberg. When I learned more about Helen's position, I knew it was only a matter of time before one of those estates would bear some viable fruit. Imagine my delight when this little gold mine was discovered. By then I had her hooked. She could get through the day as little Miss Law Degree. But by night, she was my puppet. I gave her what she needed. In more ways than one."

I lowered my voice. "So are you leaving her behind or does she have some other duties she can fulfill for you?

"Don't you worry, I have many things in mind for Helen."

At some point Tancredi switched on the lights in both rooms. Darkness had fallen a while ago. I wondered how many more pieces they were prepared to switch. There were at least four more sculptures that Helen had tagged earlier with her clothing. I watched George, Paulie, and the guy they called Skeech trudge out of the storeroom. Moving those sculptures was hard work. They were running out of steam. I wondered if that meant we were almost out of time.

George drifted over to the worktable to flip through the binder. Paulie and Skeech moved slowly down the hallway toward the loading dock.

"Getting down to the wire, Tanc," George said.

"I count six more pieces."

"Sounds about right."

Tancredi turned to me. "It looks like your evening is about to end."

My mind was racing, trying to think of any options. George was about to push away from the table when the sound of gunfire ripped through the night. Tancredi stared at me in disbelief. His arm, quick as a snake, went around my waist and yanked me to him. An automatic pistol appeared in his free hand, pointed at the doorway. George rushed across the room and scooped up the pistol grip shotgun from where he'd propped it against a light stand earlier. I watched as he racked the slide, pumping a shell into the chamber. George pivoted and aimed the shotgun at Banning, Vera, and Helen who were clustered together.

A burly figure stepped into the doorway. His face was in shadow, but I'd know that silhouette anywhere. He took another step into the room and moved to the right. In his hand dangled a large automatic weapon.

"Party's over, boys. Drop your weapons before someone else gets hurt."

"I'm in charge here!" Tancredi snarled. "Who the hell are you?"

He took another step into the room and the overhead light shined down on him. Even at this late hour, he was dressed in a charcoal business suit, complete with a starched white shirt and a crimson striped tie. Despite the circumstances, I couldn't help but smile.

"Hello, Jamie."

"Hey, Bert."

"Looks like you brought your mother along for the ride this time." His eyes flicked from me to the group by the desk. "Are you all right, Vera?"

"I'm doing better now."

"What is going on?" Tancredi snarled again.

Before anyone could answer another figure stepped through the doorway and moved to the left. My heart had been beating pretty rapidly before, but now it jumped a couple of times. As he stepped into the light, Malone extended his right arm. He was still in uniform. His weapon was pointed at Tancredi. The thief yanked me in front of him as a shield.

"That's my lady, you piece of shit. Do the smart thing and let her go."

Tancredi tightened his grip around my waist. "You can kiss my narrow Sicilian ass."

"Not a chance. Let her go or I'll kill you."

"You won't shoot. You might hit her."

"You really want to take that chance?"

"Michigan State Police have the building surrounded. The two men loading the truck made the poor choice of trying to shoot it out," Bert said calmly. "Those two are in custody, what's left of them anyway. There's no reason for any further bloodshed. Drop your guns."

"Fuck you, old man."

Bert swung his weapon up and pointed it at George's head. "From this distance, I can't miss. And I know the sergeant is an even better shot than I am."

Tancredi twisted his wrist. Now his gun was pressed against my temple. I was staring at Malone. His eyes went cold. I couldn't breathe.

"Don't hurt her," Vera shouted, "Please, don't hurt her!"

"I'm walking out," Tancredi said.

"Anton, what about me?" Helen said. "You can't leave me here."

"I'll be back for you, my darling."

"Last chance," Malone said. I'd never seen his eyes so cold and hard.

"You won't shoot me," Tancredi said with a snarl, "you don't have the—"

Those were his last words.

My eyes had been locked on Malone's face. When he inclined his head a fraction of an inch, I knew it was time.

I held perfectly still. Malone fired. His shot tore through Anton Tancredi's right eye and entered his brain. I went slack and fell to the floor. I don't think I fainted.

Well, maybe I did.

Malone was on top of him in an instant, pulling the gun out of the dead man's hand. Bert closed the distance on George. The big man lowered the shotgun to the floor and put his hands up. Bert spun him around and slammed him against the wall. Three uniformed cops raced into the room. Two of them rushed to help put the handcuffs on George.

Helen stumbled her way across the room. Tears were streaming down her face as she slumped to the floor and cradled what was left of Anton Tancredi's head in her lap. Strong hands gripped my arms and pulled me to my feet.

"Hey, Jay."

"Malone. I am so glad you're a good shot." I wrapped my arms around him and buried my face in his chest.

"I don't miss, Jay. Sorry it came to that. I couldn't risk him hurting you."

I didn't realize until that moment that I was shaking violently. I must have been hyperventilating. Malone held me close. I looked across the room. George had been searched and was being led outside. Two paramedics came in and went to check on Lincoln Banning. Vera was stoically sitting on the stool, her arms looped around one of Bert's massive biceps. Bert looked over her head at me and nodded. There were so many questions. Who was going to give me the answers?

****

It took some time before things settled down. After the paramedics had taken care of Banning, they attended to Vera. Helen Gaines was arrested, but they strapped her to a gurney and were taking her to the hospital for observation. I expected that she'd enter into a detox program somewhere along the line. A good lawyer would probably get her a reduced sentence for her involvement in the robbery, due to her addiction problems. One of the paramedics had done a quick examination on me as well. I was still a little shaky. Now the place was swarming with cops and a forensic crime scene team. Bert was obviously in charge. He remained next to Vera, a protective arm wrapped around her shoulders.

"Sergeant, I think these folks have had enough excitement for one day. Let's get them out of here," Bert said.

"Sure thing, Captain."

Malone waved over one of the troopers and instructed him to take Lincoln Banning home. My car was parked at the office building's garage. Although it was close by, I didn't think I could handle driving tonight. Malone sensed this.

"Let's go home, Jay. We can drop Vera off at the hotel."

Vera stirred and looked a question at Bert. He ducked his head and whispered something in her ear. I watched her draw a deep breath and steady herself. Then with a great display of courage, she shrugged off Bert's arm and got to her feet.

"I could use a good stiff drink and a very hot bath. Let's go, Malone."

Bert walked us outside. As we reached the car, I turned to him. Automatically his arms wrapped me up in a comforting bear hug.

"Jamie, I'm beginning to think mischief follows wherever you go."

"Thanks for finding us, Bert."

"Don't thank me. It was Malone's magic that found you."

I tilted my head back to look at him. Most of his face was hidden in the shadows of the parking lot. "How did you guys find us?"

"I'll let Malone tell you. But do me a favor. Stay with your mother until I get there. I'll be out of here within an hour. I don't want her to be alone tonight."

"Vera's pretty tough."

"She's not as tough as she pretends to be here. And neither are you. Stay with her?"

"Sure."

Vera was in the backseat of an unmarked police car. There was no safety cage or bullet proof glass between the front and back seats, but there was no mistaking it for a cop's car. Malone gave me a wink as I opened the other rear door, slid in beside Vera, and took her hand. He nodded, got the car running, and whisked us out to Novi to her hotel.

She was silent on the drive out, her eyes closed and her head tilted back. There were traces of Banning's blood on the shoulder of her dress. I doubted it would come out. I knew she wouldn't care. Vera tried to shoo us away when we got to the hotel, but neither one of us would consider it. We walked into her suite and Malone and I went for the little sofa by the window.

"I'm going to run a very hot bath and disappear into the mist," Vera said.

As she ducked into the bathroom, I scooped up the ice bucket next to the little refrigerator and handed it to Malone. He nodded and walked down the hall. I could hear the roar of water in the bath, filling the tub. When he returned I dropped three big ice cubes into a cut crystal glass and grabbed two small bottles of scotch from the mini-bar. Knocking lightly, I heard a muffled response and entered the bathroom.

The lights were on a dimmer switch and Vera had dialed it down low. She was in the tub, submerged under a cloud of fragrant bubbles. Only her face was visible. A small smile touched her lips when she saw what I was carrying.

"You're a good daughter, Jamie."

I poured one of the bottles over the ice and handed her the glass. She took a healthy sip and settled back.

"Are you going to be okay, Vera?"

"I'll be fine, dear. It may take a few days, but I'll be fine."

I sat on the edge of the tub and tried to relax. Wet fingers reached up and clutched my wrist. I turned and looked at my mother in the dim light.

"My greatest fear tonight was losing you," she whispered.

"I'm still here."

"Yes, you are. I've not always made the smartest decisions in my life, Jamie. But I'm certainly proud about choosing Bert."

"He is a very good man, Mom."

There was silence for a moment while she sipped her drink.

"I can't remember the last time you called me that."

"Sorry. I guess after everything that happened tonight, it just seemed natural."

She gave my wrist another squeeze. "I don't mind, Jamie. As long as it's only in private, darling. Only in private."

****

When Bert arrived he was driving one of the marked patrol vehicles. Malone and I took it back to the post. Malone ran inside long enough to get his clothes from the locker room and the keys to Jeep. Then we drove home. I was too wired to sleep. It was four in the morning. Malone took one look at me and led me into the shower. I realized that since the shooting, I'd maintained physical contact with him almost every minute. While the shower was warming up, he slowly undressed me. I spun around and roughly tugged at his clothes. Soon his uniform joined the pile on the floor. We stepped into the shower and let the steam pound us.

I thought I was okay. Malone squirted shampoo into his hands and churned up a thick lather. Then he turned my back to him and began to wash my hair. I could feel the tremors still shaking my body. He turned me around to rinse. I started shaking harder. He stepped into the spray, drawing me closer.

"I'm right here, Jamie."

"I was so scared, Malone. I thought we were all going to die."

I clung to him as the tears overtook me. The events in the studio kept replaying in my mind. There was so much that I would have missed if Bert and Malone hadn't shown up. A montage of scenes like some bizarre art film rushed through my mind. Linda and Vince, sunrises, Bert, Malone, sunsets, Ian, and Vera. Places I wanted to visit mixed with ones I've been to. Sobbing, I collapsed against him. After a while Malone pulled the soap from the rack and began to scrub my skin. We stayed in until the water ran cold.

Malone refused to let me go. He wrapped me in my terrycloth robe and rubbed my hair dry with a towel. I was still shaking, but not nearly as bad. He pulled on a pair of jeans. I couldn't figure out what he was doing.

"C'mon, Jamie."

Numbly I followed him, clinging to his hand. We went into the kitchen. Malone scooped me up as if I were a child and perched me on the counter beside the stove.

"Two things we need, Jamie. Food and sleep." He dug a skillet from the cupboard and began pulling food out of the refrigerator.

"I can't eat, Malone."

He leaned over and kissed me. "Hush. Just stay with me."

I leaned against the cupboard and watched him. Soon veggies were sizzling in the pan. Red peppers, mushrooms, and onions were joined by thick chunks of ham. Malone cracked four eggs into a mixing bowl, added a dash of milk, and whipped it into a foam. He dumped this on top of the veggies and put the lid on. While the eggs were cooking, he washed out the bowl. I watched him dice some Colby cheese. When the omelet was ready, he added the cheese, folded it in half, and covered it for another minute. He poured two glasses of orange juice and set them on the table. The eggs went onto one plate. When everything was ready, he lifted me from the counter. Malone sat at the table and pulled me onto his lap. I remembered the first time he'd done that, the morning after we'd become lovers. How long ago had that been?

We sat there quietly and ate. He was right. I did need food. After the first few bites my stomach awoke and wanted more. I ate more than my share.

"Jamie, you know I would never let anything bad happen to you."

"But how did you find us, Malone?"

"It's very late, Jay. Maybe we should get some sleep."

"We need to let our meal settle. You don't want me to have nightmares, do you?"

He gave me one of those low voltage smiles, where just the corners of his mouth twitched and a little merriment touched his eyes.

"No, we don't want that. C'mon, let's go watch the sunrise."

I hadn't noticed the sky turning lighter. We went out to the backyard and sat at the picnic table. The only thing I had on was my robe. Malone was bare-chested, just wearing his jeans. The dew tickled our feet as we walked across the grass. I sat close to him, relishing the feeling of his arm across my back.

"You'd better tell me, Malone. How did you find us?"

He turned his head to watch me. "It was late in my shift. I tried calling you but the phone went right to voicemail. That was odd. I called Linda. She was with Vince and they hadn't seen you. Then I got a strange phone call. A guy wouldn't give me his name, but said I should take a look at the studio. So I called Wyatt Donohue to see if there was any activity on the security system."

The cameras must have caught all the activity from the moment Anton Tancredi forced us into the room. Helen Gaines had unlocked the studio with the keys taken from Banning's office. We'd never given the attorney a remote device.

"It took me a while to track down Wyatt. Once he dialed up the footage, he knew what was going on. I called Bert and we scrambled downtown. Bert didn't bother notifying the Detroit Police until we were on the scene. He called four guys from SWAT and four uniforms. We got there, observed what was going on and took action."

"What happened to Paulie and Skeech?"

"Who?"

"The two guys loading the truck."

"We had them surrounded. One of them tried to shoot it out. A guy from SWAT shot him in the leg. He'll survive. The other one surrendered."

"What about all the artwork?"

"The truck was still at the dock. Everything was seized, including the duplicates. Bert ordered two guys to guard the place until further notice. It's a crime scene. We'll have to go through everything and figure out what's authentic and what's fake."

We sat quietly, watching the sky. All around us, birds began chirping and squirrels were chattering. Everyone was waking up. I was exhausted. All I wanted to do was go to bed.

"The originals all have Peter's trademark on the bases. Tancredi didn't know about it. And since the stamp is on my bookcase, he'd never be able to use it on the fakes. Sooner or later, someone would have tripped to it."

"It's over, Jamie."

"Almost, Malone."

His eyes had been on the sky. Now he shifted and

looked at me. "Almost?"

"I'm too tired for talk, Malone. Let's go to bed."

"Good idea."

CHAPTER TWENTY

It was afternoon when I awoke. Malone had closed the blinds in the bedroom and even draped a blanket over the window to help keep the room dark. I could hear the soft murmur of voices from the other room. Crawling into the bathroom, I splashed water on my face and ran a brush through my hair. I pulled my robe on and went looking for Malone. He and Bert were in the kitchen, mugs of coffee on the table before them.

"Hey, guys," I mumbled.

"Hello, Daughter."

"Where's Vera?" I dropped into a chair between them. Malone poured a mug of coffee and set it in front of me.

"Still at the hotel. She took a sleeping pill before I left."

I nodded and gulped the coffee. "So what happens now?"

"We're going to need statements from you, Vera and Lincoln Banning," Bert said. "Helen Gaines and the others are being interrogated today. The building has been secured."

"What about the artwork?"

Malone slid his chair close and put an arm around me. Subconsciously I'd been reaching for him since coming into the kitchen. I saw a glimmer of a smile cross Bert's lips, but he quickly hid it behind his coffee mug.

"All of the originals have been returned to the studio. The duplicates will be placed in a police evidence locker. The guys we arrested last night gave us the location of the warehouse they were using and the names of three forgers. Two of them were picked up earlier today. There will be an armed security team on the building throughout the weekend. Wyatt Donohue will be installing a new system for the whole building next week."

"Are you sure the originals were all returned?"

Malone nodded. "Odon Krippendore came in early this morning. He knew about Peter's trademark. He checked each piece as it was being unloaded. That was done before noon."

I realized it was about the time Malone would be going to work. Part of me trembled at the thought of being alone. Bert seemed to know what I was thinking.

"Malone's on administrative leave because of the shooting, Jamie. It's routine."

"He saved my life, Bert."

"And I owe him a great debt. But it's just a routine matter. Besides, I'd rather he stay with you today. I'd like you to stop at the post and give a formal statement."

I realized Bert was wearing a different suit than last night. "Did you get any sleep, Bert? You look fresh as a daisy."

"I feel more like a black-eyed Susan. But I did grab a couple of hours earlier. I'm going to see Lincoln Banning and take his statement. He's meeting me at his office."

"My car is still down there. We should go get it."

Bert and Malone shared a silent conversation.

"Go get dressed, Jamie. We'll all ride down together."

****

Lincoln Banning was dressed in khakis and a black golf

shirt with red piping along the sleeves. There was a bandage across his nose. Otherwise he looked as if nothing had happened the day before. On his desk were my cell phone and the one Vera had been carrying. I noticed Bert slide that one quickly into his pocket. Banning sat on the corner of his desk.

"I'll never be able to repay you both for your efforts last night," Banning said after shaking hands with Bert and Malone.

"Glad we got there in time," Malone said.

"I'm still having difficulty understanding how Helen got involved with those men. She was a good attorney. A bit troubled at times, but she had potential."

"Sometimes we never really know what drives a person," Bert said.

"That's so very true."

I cleared my throat to find my voice. "I owe you a very big apology, Mr. Banning. Everything I thought and said about you was wrong. Can you ever forgive me?"

"Jamie, the way I see it, you saved my life. And your observations were accurate. The problem stemmed from my office. You were very close in your analysis of the situation."

"But I accused you."

He waved my protests away. "Nonsense. It was perfectly logical. I'm responsible for hundreds of millions of dollars in estates and investments, not just for your family but many others. It's not unreasonable to think that I may have been jealous about your father's success and fame. But he did give me two things I consider priceless."

"What's that?"

"His friendship and his trust." Banning took a moment to look at each of us. "Peter trusted me to take care of his family, to make sure their financial means would always be sufficient. He knew that I would always look out for them. And he knew that I would never let him down."

"Why do you think I saved your life yesterday?"

"Face it, Jamie. No one came looking for me. I was just fortunate enough to be along for the ride."

Bert waved a female trooper inside. Behind her were the two Detroit Police Detectives, Rayburn and Suarez, who had come to investigate the original theft from the studio. Because of the complexity of the case, Bert had arranged to have all parties present while Banning gave his statement. Malone took that as his cue and steered me out of the office. He didn't say anything until we were back in my car, heading for home.

"Are you going to tell me the rest now?"

"The rest of what?"

Malone reached over and took my hand. "Let's start with that phone call I got last night. The trooper who caught the call said he asked for me by name. And his message left no room for discussion."

I turned a little so I could see his face while he drove. "What did he say, Malone?"

"He said, 'Jamie's at the studio and she's in trouble'."

I wondered if Harrison Mundy would have stepped in himself somehow if Malone and Bert hadn't arrived when they did.

"It's a long story, Malone."

"Suddenly, Jamie, I have a lot of free time."

"I'll tell you when we get home."

He considered it for a moment and nodded. "Fair enough. But this time, you tell me everything?"

"I will, Malone. But I need to ask you something first."

"You can ask me anything."

"Does it bother you that you had to kill Tancredi?"

Malone was quiet for a bit. I tightened my grip on his hand. "It does. But it's part of my job, Jamie. I don't like to do it and I've been in situations in the past, both in the military and on the job, where I've had to shoot someone."

I don't know why but I was surprised by this. "You never told me that before."

"You never asked, Jay. It's not something I like to

spend a lot of time thinking about. But there was no way I could avoid it last night. I couldn't let him hurt you."

"I'm very glad you stopped him, Malone."

He raised my hand and kissed it. "Me too."

When we got home, it was too hot and bright for this conversation to take place outside. I steered him to the 'aunt', switched on the ceiling fan, and collapsed beside him. The sofa worked its magic and soon I was entwined in Malone's strong arms. It took a while, but I told him everything about my feeble efforts to unravel the mystery of the theft. I told him about how Linda and I went to meet Harrison Mundy and even my discussion the other day with Judge Barolo and Mundy's sudden appearance outside the courthouse. Malone never interrupted. He just let me ramble until I ran out of words. Malone shifted until he was supine on the sofa, pulling me on top of him. He was slowly running his fingers through my hair. I could feel the steady thump of his heart as I pressed my cheek to his chest.

"So how did Mundy know where to find you?"

"I have no idea, Malone."

"If he was able to track your phone that would explain the courthouse. But your phone wasn't at the studio."

"I'm stumped. I'm not complaining, but it does make me curious."

Malone chuckled softly. "I'm not sure I can handle a curious redhead right now."

"How about a very quiet redhead?"

"That I can handle."

"I just want to stay right here for an hour or two. Maybe take a nap. Did you sleep at all last night, Malone?"

"Not much. A nap sounds like a very good idea."

I realized we'd both been yawning. A minute or two later, safe and secure in his arms, I fell asleep.

****

My stomach was to blame. It was growling loud enough to wake both of us. We were debating about going out for something to eat when my phone rang. Vera's voice floated in my ear.

"Jamie, darling. Why don't you come for dinner at the hotel? Bert will be here keeping me company. Let's make it an hour."

"We'll be there."

"Excellent. I've invited Vince and Linda as well."

Linda must have been going crazy. Malone told me earlier that she'd called this morning, anxious and worried. He'd reassured her that I was fine. I didn't have the energy to call her then. Malone came out of the kitchen with half an apple and a wedge of cheddar cheese in each hand. The appetizer would quiet our stomachs until we got some real food.

"Do we have time for a shower?" Malone asked.

"Is that a polite way to say I smell bad?"

He grinned and pulled me off the sofa. "No, it's just an excuse to get you naked."

I batted my lashes at him. Apparently the nap had done us both good. "Will you wash my hair, Malone?"

"Eventually."

We shed our clothes in the bedroom. Malone hesitated in front of the sink while I got the shower started. I realized he hadn't shaved earlier. He was reaching for his razor when I pulled him to me.

"Leave it, Malone. A man with a little stubble can be very sexy."

"Why, Jamie, what did you have in mind?"

"It's easier if I show you."

Under the pulsing spray of hot water, I dragged him closer. He'd grabbed the soap and did an admirable job lathering both of us up. My attention was focused on him and one particular spot. Malone's slippery hands slid down my back and cupped my ass. As he lifted me up, I found something hard to hold onto. He angled his shoulders back until the wall supported him. I squirmed up and guided him inside me.

Nothing else mattered. Nothing else existed outside the confines of the shower stall. It was just the two of us, the hot, pounding water, the scent of the soap, the feel of our bodies entwined, the clutching, the thrusting, the groans and moans of anticipation and delight. We had no words, nothing more than primal grunts. I threw my head back as a scream burst from my lungs as a climax shot from my core. Malone followed a nanosecond later, exploding inside me. His fingers dug into my ass, squeezing me tighter. We clung to each other, gasping for breath. My legs, which had been wrapped around him, untangled and slid down his body, reaching for the floor.

Laughing, Malone relaxed his grip on me. I slumped against him. It was a moment before either one of us was steady. He found the shampoo and turned me around, building a lather in my hair. It's one of the sexiest things any man has ever done, washing my hair for me. If he did it every day for a decade, it would still send tingles through my body. Somehow I was able to stand without support and rinse my hair. I watched him wash up and quickly traded places before we ran out of hot water.

"We're going to be late, Jamie."

"Are you complaining?"

He leaned down and locked his lips on mine. I'll take that answer any time.

Vince and Linda were waiting in the lobby when we arrived. Linda was on her feet as we came through the door. She hugged me so tightly I think she cracked one of my ribs. She was still holding me when Vera and Bert appeared. Vera looked as calm as ever. She greeted Vince with a kiss on the cheek. I watched her move to Malone. She pulled him down to kiss his cheek as well and whisper something in his ear. He smiled and nodded once. She linked his arm and guided us into the dining room. Linda moved to Vince's side and followed. Bert stood before me.

"You look better, Jamie."

"We talked a bit and grabbed a nap."

"You're going to be okay, Daughter."

I smiled and hugged him. "I like it when you call me that."

We went to join the others. Vera was already holding court, ordering a few appetizers and a round of drinks. Somehow she'd commandeered a quiet corner of the restaurant, away from any other patrons.

Dinner was an easy, relaxed meal. Without going into specifics, Vera told Vince and Linda about the events of yesterday. She didn't include the details of the shooting, but accurately described the kidnapping and the attempted theft. As things were winding down, Linda caught my eye. We went to freshen our makeup. Alone in the restroom she gave me another fierce hug.

"You scared the crap out of me, Jay Kay."

"I was pretty scared myself."

We clung to each other for another moment, then took care of our makeup. As we were walking back to the table she stopped me.

"Are we still going to the art festival tomorrow? I know Ian and Brittany are looking forward to it."

"I'd forgotten all about that."

"If you're not up to it, Vince and I can take them."

I flashed back to our conversation on Wednesday, when we'd gone to the water park. The idea of going to the festival where Krippendore would have his works on display had been an instant hit. Ian confessed that he wanted to wander around and see what other artists created. Back then it sounded like a relaxing way to spend the afternoon. I couldn't disappoint him.

"I want to get back to normal. Let's meet at Krip's booth at noon."

"Jay Kay, I'm beginning to think we have two very different definitions of normal."

I had no comment for that.

****

Our little crowd descended on the festival. Malone and I brought Brittany, since she lived so close. Ian had come with Terri and Caitlin. Linda and Vince were there, looking as if they'd just stepped out of the pages of a fashion magazine. Krippendore was delighted to see us. He had some of his best work on display inside the large booth. He was perched at the entrance in a director's chair, a steaming cup of coffee balanced on the arm.

"How has business been?"

"Very good, Jamie. The weather has been perfect and that's led to an excellent turnout. I've sold quite a few paintings and had to run down to the studio last night to pick up a few more. Fortunately the security men allowed me in."

"Did they rough you up?"

He chuckled. "Actually, one of them helped me bring down a few canvases. He'd been on duty yesterday morning when I was helping out."

I heard a shriek from inside the booth. Krip flashed me a grin and jerked his head toward the rear. I went to investigate.

The others were grouped around the back wall. There in a simple wooden frame was Ian's sketch of Brittany. This was one of the early drawings he'd done in pencil. Apparently Krippendore lifted the drawing without Ian's knowledge. Attached to the bottom of the frame was a small blue card that read SOLD. Everyone was talking at once as Krip came in behind me.

"Let me explain," he said softly. The room went silent. "First, I should apologize to Ian. I borrowed that sketch when he was at the studio. I thought it would be interesting to put it on display and see what kind of reactions it got at the festival." He turned to face Ian. "In case you didn't want to believe the ravings of this old man,

I thought you might find the comments from other artists and the general public encouraging. And I have to tell you, I could have sold that sketch fifty times this weekend."

"But you sold it!" Ian said in disbelief. "I told you I could never sell that."

Krip raised a hand. "I didn't sell it, lad. I merely stuck a tag on it so people would give up trying to buy it. My intention was to see what reactions it drew and then give it back to you."

Brittany hugged Ian. "You could sell it."

"No way."

"Way. And then you could draw another one."

"No. I might sell others, but not this one."

A puzzled look crossed her face. "Why not?"

"Ask Mr. Krippendore. Maybe he can explain it."

She turned to face the old painter. "Tell me."

"A true artist can never part with his muse. You're his inspiration. Selling his drawings of you would be like selling a piece of his soul."

Everyone was quiet. Vince cleared his throat and reached for Linda's hand. When they were together, they were rarely apart.

"I think it's time to explore some of the other artists. Anyone care to wander?"

Terri and Caitlin went with them. Terri said something to Malone, who gave her an agreeable nod. Krip pulled a map of the festival exhibits from his pocket and handed it to Ian.

"The booths that are circled belong to other artists I've known for years. These are talented people whose opinions I respect. They've been in to see your sketch. Introduce yourself to them. They all want to meet you."

The kid nodded. Malone guided them toward the entrance. He looked back over his shoulder at me. "Are you going to join us, Jay?"

"In a minute."

When they were gone I put my hands on Krip's

shoulders. "You're really serious about his talent aren't you?"

"Jamie, with some training, Ian can be a star. I wasn't kidding before about interest in that sketch. I could have sold that a dozen times or more."

"What kind of training are we talking about?"

Krip shrugged. "He's young and raw. After high school, a good art school could help him develop his techniques. Deepen his understanding of light and shadows, the mix of colors, contrasts and so much more."

"You really think he's talented, don't you?"

"I may joke about many things, but not about this."

I leaned up and kissed him on the cheek, which was surprisingly smooth. Over his shoulder I saw two women enter his booth.

"Go charm the ladies and sell some paintings."

Krip comically wiggled his eyebrows. "It's a dirty job, but somebody's got to do it."

CHAPTER TWENTY-ONE

There were butterflies the size of footballs dancing in my stomach. I couldn't remember the last time I'd felt this nervous or excited. It took all my willpower not to squirm in discomfort. Just when I thought no one would notice, Malone slipped an arm around my waist and drew me close.

"Relax, Jamie. Everything is going to be fine."

"I am relaxed."

He chuckled and grazed my cheek with a kiss. "And you're a terrible liar, Jay. Take a deep breath. You look absolutely gorgeous."

I did as he instructed. "You're not just saying that?"

"No. And if you have any doubt that it's true, wait until the doors open and the people start streaming in. Every guy in the joint will be checking you out."

That got me to laugh. "Sure, as long as Linda is standing beside me."

"They would only be looking at Linda because they know you're with me."

Across the way I saw Vera enter the gallery. She looked like she'd just stepped out of a fairytale, in an ivory evening gown. She made a beeline to where two guys were patiently awaiting her arrival. The sight of Bert wearing a tuxedo was enough to make me smile. He caught my eye, threw me a wink and a broad smile. Beside him Lincoln Banning was greeting Vera.

"Let's go say hello," Malone said.

"Stay close to me. I might fall out of these heels."

This whole thing had been Vera's idea. It was late September and we were in the gallery at the Center for Creative Studies. On display were sixteen of Peter's sculptures. This was a mixture of his work over the years. A week after the failed robbery, Vera and I met with Banning and drew up the plan. Tonight was opening night. For the next two weeks, his work would be on display for the general public. After that, this part of the collection would begin a cross-country tour, with stops in most of the major cities. Banning had hired a curator and a security team that would oversee every step along the way. Vera was looking forward to being wined and dined by the high society folks at each visit. She would fly ahead to each city to mingle with old friends and create new relationships. Tonight was a black tie fundraiser, with proceeds going to create scholarships for young artists. Deep down, I think Peter would have been proud.

"Jamie, you look beautiful," Vera gushed.

"Thank you. It must be hereditary. You look great."

She did the air kiss thing. "I hate to admit it, but it's taking me longer to get ready for these things than it used to."

"That's time well spent," Bert said. "That's some dress, Daughter."

I twirled, letting the skirt on the turquoise evening dress float. It had little spaghetti straps on the shoulders, with a tight bodice and full skirt that had a daring slit along the left side, showing off my legs. There were also a few areas that were almost transparent with strategic segments of lace. Linda had talked me into this dress.

"Everything is in order," Banning said with a smile.

"Are you ready to open the doors?"

"What the hell. Let's get this party started," I said.

We formed a receiving line to greet the guests. The two-hundred tickets were quickly snatched up when the event was publicized. Malone tried to edge away and melt into the background, but I latched onto his arm. If I had to stand there pressing the flesh, so did he.

A steady flow of patrons entered, all anxious to get the first look at Peter's work. There were local dignitaries, political movers and shakers, a few art critics, and many of society's elite. After a while they all became a blur. Linda and Vince were among the crowd and they brought with them two bright-eyed and unexpected guests. I couldn't hold back the grin as Ian and Brittany came through the line.

"Hey, Jamie," Ian said, giving me a quick hug.

"Not so fast, kid. I expect kisses from handsome young men in tuxedos."

His face flushed in embarrassment. I turned my head and tapped one finger on my cheek. I think he sighed with relief as he leaned in and granted my wish. In her little black dress, Brittany was a radiant glimpse of what she'd look like when her teens were behind her.

"I'm a bit surprised to see you two tonight."

"Malone didn't tell you?" Ian asked. "It was his idea."

"Shut up, kid," Malone muttered.

"They're with us," Vince said, planting a kiss on my cheek.

"Yes, Cinderella and Prince Charming are in our care," Linda said with a laugh. She gave me a squeeze and moved over to Malone for a kiss.

"Go have fun. We'll catch up later."

After the initial group passed, we broke the line and mingled. Malone had just left my side to get some tonic water when I sensed someone move up beside me. A cultured voice reached my ear. "Good evening, Jamie." I didn't even have to turn around to know who it was.

"Hello, Mr. Mundy. I was hoping you'd be here."

He took my hand and did the knuckle kiss thing. Beside him was Jocelyn, the exotic beauty with the raven hair. She was wearing a very tight red dress that accentuated her curvaceous figure. Jocelyn offered me a demure smile and nod.

I took his arm and guided him around the gallery. Jocelyn followed. Mundy made appreciative remarks after the first couple of pieces. My impatience took over.

"I don't know whether to be pissed or pleased by your actions, Harry."

"Perhaps some common ground between the two would be appropriate."

My Irish temper flared. "You are one crafty son of a bitch."

"I will deign to take that as a compliment."

This was not the place to make a scene, so I kept my voice low as I moved him along. "You tagged my phone with some kind of high-tech global positioning device." I saw him about to speak and waved it away. "Of course, you yourself didn't do it. Your darling daughter here did."

Jocelyn leaned forward. "I told you not to underestimate her," she said in a sing-song voice. In my peripheral vision, I saw her smile and wink at me.

Harrison was unflustered. "That is quite an engaging tale. Please continue."

"There was only one way you could have gotten into the studio and viewed the collection in advance. You posed as Oliver Guthrie, one of the art experts."

"You really are quite resourceful, Jamie."

"Cut the crap, Harry. I'd like the truth. I think you owe me that much."

"As you wish. Jocelyn is in fact my daughter. She is also my associate, helping to resolve crimes related to art. Considering your relationships with the local police, I am certain you can understand how confidential this information is."

"Who would I ever tell? And better yet, who the hell would ever believe me?"

"Points taken. I frequently consult with the Federal Bureau of Investigation. As such, they have created several aliases for me, including Oliver Guthrie. With the assistance of a makeup expert, I am able to change my appearance significantly. That allowed me the opportunity to view the collection and to make some very fortuitous preparations."

"No shit, Sherlock. You tagged the artwork you were supposed to be evaluating." His prim and proper manner was bringing out my vulgar side, but I really didn't care.

Mundy twitched a little smile. "How did you discover my involvement?"

"After it was over, I kept thinking back to our conversations. There was no way you could have followed me to the courthouse, so I took my phone to a tech guru I trust. He found that fancy bug. I left it in place. Then I went to the studio and looked at the sculptures. I found similar bugs on certain pieces. They are so tiny, no one would notice them."

"Unless they knew what to look for," Jocelyn said.

"Exactly. You only tagged the pieces that would be easy to replicate."

Mundy gave me a sage nod. "I was operating under the assumption that the thieves would only have a limited amount of time and talent. There was no reason to take the entire collection. Taking only a few pieces would allow them time to properly duplicate the more challenging sculptures."

We were silent for a moment as a small group passed. I looked around the room. Malone and Bert were chatting, but they were both looking in my direction. Vera and Banning were still greeting late arrivals. Linda, Vince, Brittany, and Ian were in what looked like a serious discussion in the far corner.

"You called Malone when it all came down."

"I am but one old man, Jamie, with a young daughter as my companion. My days of dashing to the rescue in the nick of time are far behind me."

"You knew I was at the studio."

"It was a logical assumption. Your phone was immobile, yet there was movement of the sculptures at the studio. Those devices were also designed to detect motion."

"I have a question," Jocelyn said as we came to the end of our tour. "How did you know I was his daughter?"

It was my turn to twitch a little smile. "I didn't know for certain until Harry confirmed it. But all the research I did on the Mundy family indicated that they were always very close knit when it came to the tricks of the trade. I couldn't see Harry taking someone under his wing, no matter how beautiful you may be, unless he knew there was a bond that couldn't be broken. And there were a few society photos I found of him with a very exotic looking woman who could have been your mother."

"What were you saying about underestimating her?" Harry asked.

I turned them around so they were in front of the last sculpture on display. Jocelyn took a step closer and spun around to face me.

"You can't be serious?"

"I am. After everything you two did on my behalf, it's the least I can do."

A wide smile crossed Harry's face. "I would say that is payment enough."

The last sculpture was "Spring Dance". Following the shooting at the studio, the police had searched the home of Anton Tancredi. The sculpture was recovered and returned. Now it sat proudly on a pedestal, perfectly lit by a spotlight shining down from above. On a placard in front of the pedestal was a card that read, "Generously on loan from the private collection of the Harrison Mundy family." Vera and Lincoln Banning didn't know the whole story but didn't complain when I made the request.

"I hope you don't mind if this piece is included as part of the traveling collection."

"I would not have it any other way. We are only in town for a short while," Mundy said. He took my hand and did the knuckle kiss thing again.

He stepped back and Jocelyn surprised me with a hug.

"Off to thwart another dastardly crime?"

"It may become a working vacation in Italy." He linked Jocelyn's arm in his.

I pointed in the general direction of Linda. "You'd better say hello to her, or I'll never hear the end of it."

With a nod and a sly smile, they walked away. I watched Linda greet them and introduce them to the others. Malone appeared at my side.

"So that was Harrison Mundy."

"Yes, with his daughter."

"Were they pleased with your generosity?"

I turned and gave him a kiss. "Whatever are you talking about?"

"Jay, you are a terrible liar."

"I'm not lying, Malone, I just prefer not to talk about it."

We did a turn around the room. The reception tables with appetizers and wine were well attended. Malone found a small table where we could enjoy some shrimp and puff pastry. I watched Odon Krippendore, escorting a lovely woman, stop to chat with Ian and Brittany. At the entrance a familiar figure caught my eye as he paused and looked around the room. When he saw me he headed in our direction.

"Trouble?" Malone asked.

"Hardly."

He slowed before us, flashing that dazzling smile of bright white teeth. As he took the last step, he smoothed out his goatee with his left hand and extended his right to me.

"What a wonderful event, Jamie."

"Thank you, Dante. I'm glad you could join us."

"I wouldn't have missed this for the world." He turned to Malone. "I'm Dante Barolo."

"Would that be Judge Barolo?" Malone asked.

Barolo hesitated for a moment, and then roared a laugh. "I was about to say guilty but thought better of it."

"I understand you were good friends with Peter Richmond," Malone said.

"Yes, he was an excellent friend. If I live to be a hundred, I'll never be able to repay his generosity and his kindness."

I was confused. "Peter loaned you money?"

Barolo shook his head. "No, Jamie. Peter gave me something priceless. Something only a great and honorable friend can give."

"Would you like a tour?" I asked.

"I'd be delighted."

We walked along, chatting about Peter. I thought Malone would be bored, but he was right there beside me, asking the occasional questions to keep the conversation flowing. At each sculpture, Barolo would pause, reading the descriptive passage from the program and study the piece. Then he would draw in a deep breath and move on.

"Did you see Vera?" I asked.

"She was occupied when I arrived. A few of high society's social butterflies were trying to draw her into a cocoon." He laughed again. "I thought it would be safer to wait until the crowd thins."

In the center of the room, as if this was the sun and all the other sculptures were planets revolving around it, was my favorite piece. It had taken hours of deliberation before I agreed to let them include it. Now we moved to it, as if drawn by a magnetic pulse. Dante was in the middle of a comment when he stopped dead in his tracks and stared at "Fleeing Beauty".

"Sort of takes your breath away, doesn't it?" Malone

said.

"You have no idea," Dante replied.

Malone was lightly holding my hand. We were at a ninety-degree angle to the judge, watching him take it all in. Slowly he moved around the statue, his eyes riveted. Malone and I waited until he came back around.

"This is incredible," Dante said. There was a look of dazed wonder on his face.

"I know what you mean. I could spend hours just staring at it."

"There you are!" A throaty feminine voice floated toward us. Dante's face relaxed and he extended both arms. Striding toward him was a lovely dark blonde woman almost as tall as me. Her evening gown was the color of champagne. Her green eyes sparkled as she took his hands and leaned forward for a kiss.

"There goes another pair of stockings! Why is it I can't walk more than twenty feet in nylons before they snag?" She turned to me and smiled. "Does that ever happen to you?"

I nodded. "All too often. I'm ready to give up on them."

She sighed. "I would too. But for reasons that escape me, men find it incredibly sexy when a woman is wearing stockings."

"On behalf of men everywhere, I hope you never stop wearing them," Malone said.

"A man after my own heart." Dante gave his head a shake. "Where are my manners? Darling, this is Jamie Richmond, Peter's daughter. And this is Malone. This is my lovely wife, Milo."

There was something familiar about her. Her smile was full of mischief. I tried not to stare while we were chatting, but she must have sensed it. She turned her full attention to me while the guys went for drinks.

"Is there something wrong?"

"Not at all. Have we met before?"

Her eyes dazzled as she shook her head. "I don't think so."

"Milo is a very unusual name."

"That's Dante's pet name for me. He's called me that forever."

I liked that idea. It reminded me of the pet names Linda and I have for each other. Milo turned her attention to the sculpture behind her. Her eyes went wide. For a moment I thought she was going to clap a hand over her mouth in surprise, but she just stood there, slowly shaking her head. I was about to say something when she raised her left hand to silence me. I watched as she walked closer to the statue and gradually circled it. When she was back beside me there were tears in her eyes.

"It's beautiful," she said.

Realization hit me like a hammer. "You never saw it finished."

"No, I never did." Her voice was barely more than a whisper.

"You're Meredith Bell."

She gave me a timid shrug. "Not anymore. I've been Meredith Barolo for twenty-seven years now. I never knew what Peter did with all his drawings and pictures. He would only tell me that it was going to be a masterpiece."

"He was right." I reached over and took her hands. "Can you tell me about him?"

She laughed, a sultry tone that was similar to Linda's. "We met at a cocktail party. My aunt and uncle were hosting. I was going to college, taking some nursing classes and working as a secretary. He charmed me from the very first moment. Persuaded me to pose for him. It was so exciting. Everyone was all atwitter about this young artist, this genius. I half expected him to seduce me. But he never did. Peter was a perfect gentleman. He kept sketching me. Then he got me to pose for his camera. He promised to show me the piece when it was done. After all these years, I assumed he never finished it." She gave me a weak smile.

"The memory of it all faded with time."

"So what happened?"

"My aunt was hosting another party. I didn't want to go but Peter convinced me to attend. He promised me that I would enjoy myself. I thought he was going to try something, maybe make some kind of announcement or sweep me off my feet in front of the crowd." She gave her head a little shake at the memory, causing the dark blonde hair to sway. "That was the night I met Dante. Peter orchestrated the whole thing. He was playing Cupid. I took one look at Dante and forgot all about every other man. I felt like something out of a fairytale. I was infatuated with Peter, but Dante took my breath away. I was crazy about him from the first moment." She smiled sweetly. "I'm still crazy about him."

"He knows you posed. That's why he calls you Milo."

She brushed the tears from her eyes with the back of her hand. "Yes, that's his little joke. Venus de Milo. Dante never mentioned it was completed."

"I don't think he knew until tonight."

"He didn't know what?" Dante asked. We hadn't noticed the guys had returned.

"That you didn't know about "Fleeing Beauty" being finished." I said.

"You're right. This is the first time I've ever seen it."

Malone slid an arm around my waist. "Peter did a wonderful job capturing you, Mrs. Barolo. I can see the same spark in your expression as on the statue."

I gaped at him. "How could you possibly have made that connection so fast?"

"I'm a cop, Jamie. I've been trained to be observant."

"And he watched my reaction before Milo joined us. I'd be willing to bet Malone figured it out then," Dante said.

"We need to mingle," Milo said to her husband.

"Would you mind if we got together sometime to talk about the past? I'd like to learn more about Peter."

"I'd like that," Milo said.

"Call my office, Jamie and we'll set something up. For all four of us."

I watched them blend into the crowd. This was turning into quite an evening.

****

We were home. The house was quiet, with a faint breeze fluttering the curtains on the bay window. After all the excitement of the evening, I needed to slow down. Even the drive from downtown hadn't helped. My mind was still spinning. Malone sensed this and was silent on the way, lightly running his fingers through my hair as I stared out the window. That connection kept me grounded, kept me alive. Now I leaned my back against him as he wrapped his arms around me.

"It's been a long day, Jamie."

"But a very good one."

"That's true. Have you unraveled all of the mysteries now?" He tilted his head and gently kissed my neck. A shiver ran along my spine.

"Most of them, but not all."

"So what's left?"

I turned to face him and pressed my lips to his. Malone drew me closer, if that was possible, and I felt two fingers slide the zipper down on my dress. I broke the kiss and looked up at him.

"You look pretty dashing in that tuxedo, Malone. I feel like I'm being seduced by James Bond."

His smile flashed in the dark. "At your service, m'lady."

I expected him to peel me out of my clothes in a flash, but Malone took his time. My heels had been kicked off in the car. Slowly he inched the straps off my shoulders and down my arms. Anticipation was getting the better of me. As he started kissing me I managed to undo his tie and several buttons on his shirt. Malone held me at arm's length and inched the gown down my body. He dropped to a knee and gently raised one of my feet and then the other, pulling the gown free. Amazed at his self-control, I watched him lay it gently on sofa. Satisfied that it was safe, he returned to me.

"Malone, I can't believe you're making me wait."

"The pleasure can be intensified by anticipation."

Even in the dim ambient light, I could see the devilish look on his face. Underneath my gown had been a lacy black strapless bra. Originally there was a pair of matching panties, a pair of black thigh high stockings and a black garter belt. Before leaving the exhibit, I'd ducked into the ladies room and removed the panties. I could tell Malone liked my surprise. He drew me close for another kiss and deftly unhooked my bra. I struggled valiantly with the last of his shirt buttons. I hadn't noticed earlier, but he'd managed to leave the tuxedo jacket on the sofa as well.

With my arms around his neck, Malone grabbed my hips and lifted me off the floor. I was about to wrap my legs around his waist, but he had other ideas. Somehow he turned me, with one strong arm behind my back and the other beneath my knees. Still kissing me, he navigated the short hallway to our bedroom. He eased me onto the bed. I watched him kick off his shoes and remove his clothes. His eyes were on me the whole time. When I ran a hand down my side to unhook the garter belt, Malone's eyes stopped me. I was trembling with desire as he climbed on top of me. He took my hands in his and held them up above my head. Another kiss followed—long, slow and so incredibly hot, I almost forgot to breathe.

"What are the other mysteries, Jay?"

"What?" It was all I could gasp out.

"What are the other mysteries you haven't solved?"

He couldn't be serious! Malone was poised just above me. I tried to urge him to me, coaxing him inside, but he was showing incredible will power. Or maybe it was won't power.

"I haven't been able to open the puzzle box," I stammered.

"We could break it."

"No! It's from my father. Even if I never figure it out, just the fact that it's from him from all those years ago is enough."

"That makes sense." His body remained frozen just beyond my reach. I squirmed and rocked my hips to no avail. "What else?"

"Malone, you're driving me crazy!"

He dipped his head down and rewarded me with another kiss that left me breathless. "What other mysteries, Jamie?"

My whole body was flushed with desire. How could he do this to me? But he looked capable of maintaining this pose and withholding from me until I answered.

"The name. I haven't solved it yet. I still don't know your first name."

"You've stopped guessing, Jay."

I managed to nod. "After the shooting, it just didn't matter anymore. I don't care what it is. All I care about is that you're with me. If you only use Malone, I can deal with it."

"It's not like you to give up."

"It was silliness, Malone. You killed a man to save my life. It's time for me to grow up."

That earned me another kiss. Yet still he hovered. I thrust upward with my hips enough to briefly make contact. If he didn't take me soon, I was going to faint.

"My name is…"

"No!"

"Why not?" There was a curious expression in his eyes.

I managed to shake my head. "Someday, I may want to try and solve it. But after all this time, Malone, if you just told me, it would be like I gave up."

"And you're too stubborn to give up."

"Exactly. And who says we can't have a few mysteries

of our own."

"Good point. Any other mysteries you haven't solved?"

I managed to give my head a negative shake. "Malone."

"Yes, Jay?"

"If you don't take me right this instant, I'm not going to be responsible for my actions."

"If you insist." And with that, we were finally connected.

The End

ACKNOWLEDGEMENTS

A special note of thanks to Joanna Huestis who for reasons that escape me enjoys reading the early drafts of these stories and helps me make some sense of it all.

ABOUT THE AUTHOR

Mark Love (yes, that's really his name) lived for many years in the metropolitan Detroit area, where crime and corruption are always prevalent. A former freelance reporter, Love is drawn to mysteries and the twists and turns that mirror real life. He is the author of "Why 319?" and three books in the Jamie Richmond Series "Devious" "Vanishing Act" and "Fleeing Beauty" and several short stories.

Love resides in west Michigan with his wife, Kim. He enjoys a wide variety of music, reading and writing fiction, cooking, travel, most sports and the great outdoors. You can find his blog at the link below and on Goodreads, Facebook, and Amazon.

http://marklove024.blogspot.com/
https://www.goodreads.com/author/dashboard
https://www.facebook.com/MarkLoveAuthor
http://www.amazon.com/-/e/B009P7HVZQ

D EVIOUS

A JAMIE RICHMOND MYSTERY

Curiosity and stubbornness can
be a dangerous mix.

MARK LOVE

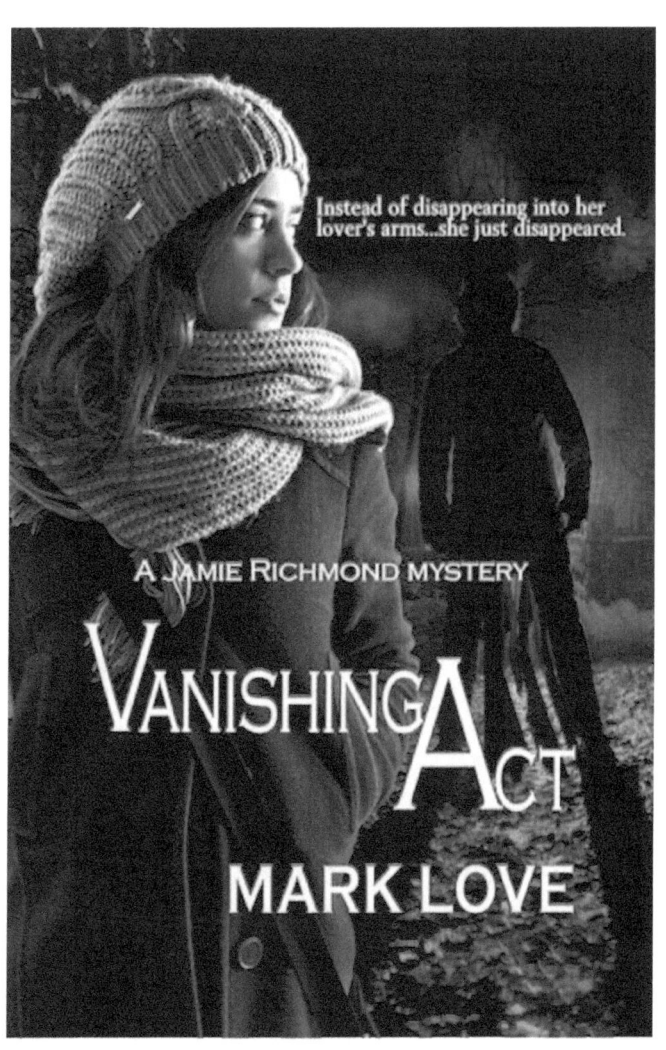

Instead of disappearing into her
lover's arms...she just disappeared.

A JAMIE RICHMOND MYSTERY

VANISHING ACT

MARK LOVE

www.ingramcontent.com/pod-product-compliance
Lightning Source LLC
Chambersburg PA
CBHW020303200626
46814CB00006BA/2058